# TERMINATOR 2®
## HOUR OF THE WOLF

# ALSO AVAILABLE

TERMINATOR 2:
<u>THE NEW JOHN CONNOR CHRONICLES</u>
by Russell Blackford

Book 1: *Dark Futures*
Book 2: *An Evil Hour*
Book 3: *Times of Trouble*

# ABOUT THE AUTHOR

**Mark W. Tiedemann**'s love for science fiction and writing started at an early age, although it was momentarily sidetracked—for over twenty years—by his career as a professional photographer. With the publication of "Targets" in the December 1990 issue of *Asimov's Science Fiction Magazine*, he began selling short stories to various markets; his work has since appeared in *Magazine of Fantasy & Science Fiction*, *Science Fiction Age*, *Tomorrow SF*, and a number of anthologies. His novel *Compass Reach* was nominated for the 2001 Philip K. Dick Memorial Award. Tiedemann lives in St. Louis, Missouri, with his companion, Donna.

# TERMINATOR 2®
## HOUR OF THE WOLF

MARK W. TIEDEMANN

BASED ON THE WORLD CREATED
IN THE MOTION PICTURE WRITTEN BY
JAMES CAMERON AND WILLIAM WISHER

**ibooks**
new york
www.ibooks.net

DISTRIBUTED BY SIMON & SCHUSTER, INC.

An Original Publication of ibooks, inc.

Based on the world created
in the motion picture written
by James Cameron and William Wisher

Distributed by Simon & Schuster, Inc.
1230 Avenue of the Americas, New York, NY 10020

ibooks, inc.
24 West 25th Street
New York, NY 10010

The ibooks World Wide Web Site Address is:
http://www.ibooks.net

ISBN 0-7434-9308-7
First ibooks, inc. printing July 2004
10 9 8 7 6 5 4 3 2 1

Printed in the U.S.A.

# ONE

The old man opened his eyes to an unfamiliar landscape. Litter shifted under him as he rolled over. The air smelled of rotting food, cooling asphalt and the fading odor of hot plastic and ozone. The walls between which he stood up showed signs of neglect—stains, old graffiti, windows broken or boarded up. The light came from a nearly full moon just visible at the edge of the left-hand roof. A chill breeze flowed over him.

Standing, he felt the tension in his arms and legs, the pressure in his lungs, the bruising in his stomach that came from—

From what?

He blinked at the night sky above and stood very still, listening. Wherever he was, he was alone. He heard nothing. Good. If the transfer had gone wrong, if he had landed in the wrong place, the wrong time, he would not be alone. He walked toward the end of the gangway and stepped into the open, to stand on broken pavement. Bare feet. He glanced down; he was naked. Curiously, that seemed normal.

No lights came from any of the buildings, none of the street lamps glowed. Only the moon gave any illumination by which he could see details of his surroundings. Nothing to compete with the display overhead. The sky was filled with stars. He could not remember seeing so many—ever. The sky rarely cleared enough to let even a few show. From

1

where he had traveled, the normal atmospheric condition was a dense, low-lying layer of dirty cloud: particulates thrown up long ago—

Long ago.

*This was—is—long ago,* he thought. *I'm not where or when I come from...*

He lowered his gaze, suddenly very aware that he did not know who he was.

His attention sharpened. The buildings lining the street. The deserted street—cracked, long unused. No lights anywhere. No sounds...no, not quite. Wind, not much, and...voices?

He increased his audio acuity. Yes, voices. Hushed, intimate...*that* direction.

He started walking, taking long strides, his feet coming down on shards of glass and gravel without pain, and the weariness seemed to radiate out of him. Strength suffused his limbs, his breathing deepened. He felt powerful. His mind cleared as well. He recognized the nature of his surroundings. Barracks. Abandoned.

He crossed the road, pausing to sift out echoes. That way still. Not far.

He turned down the gangway between two barracks and stopped at the far end. Another row of the utilitarian structures lined the far side of the next roadway. A pale glow filled a window of the third one to his right. He listened to the voices, counting.

"—out back o' the Shoprite, found a couple cases—"

"—don't care where you found it—"

"—fine vintage, that, reminds me of my time in New York—"

"—your ass, time in New York, I swear I hear that again—"

Three of them, all males. The old man felt a distant twinge of sympathy, though he could not say why. He moved up to the lit window, crouching, silent, and waited, listening.

"Benton ain't comin'."

"Why not? Wha'd you hear?"

"Busted."

"Again? Don't he learn? Ever?"

"Ain't always his fault—"

"Bullshit! My daddy use to say, 'wolves in season oughta dress like sheep!'"

"You know, your daddy musta been one sorry mother—"

"Shh!"

"What?"

"I heard somethin'. Did you—?"

The old man stopped his breathing and checked the last several seconds for background noise. Nothing.

"Nobody's out there, for—"

"You keep your mouth shut about my daddy. He was a righteous smart man in his day."

"I'm sayin' though, this ain't his day."

Laughter—dry, ragged, contained. The old man heard despair in that sound, deferred but always present. He started breathing again, and drew back toward the rear of the barrack.

Then he heard it. A vehicle, the tires crackling thinly on the desiccated pavement, coming closer. The engine was nearly silent—electric, maybe a hybrid. He rounded the corner of the barrack and moved to the next building, then the next, until he saw the ivory glow of a searchlight at the far end of a gangway. He focused on the street and waited till the vehicle passed by. In his mind, he froze the image and enhanced it: United States Air Force, Military Police.

No doubt a routine patrol, he thought, and his best option would be to stay where he was, react only if discovery was imminent. But his curiosity overrode reason.

He sprinted back to the occupied barrack, mounted the three steel steps to the rear entrance, and tried the doorknob. It gave easily, the tongue sliding back with a barely discernible rasping. He pushed inward. The hinges remained silent for about seven inches, then grime or rust or age grabbed one of them and it began to squeak. He stopped, waiting, listening.

The three men suddenly stopped talking. Their silence

extended several seconds, then one of them moved, quickly. Something fell—glass, from its sharp sound—and the other two reacted.

Then the front door burst open.

"Police! Stay where you are!"

"Shit!"

"Down! Down! Hands in the open!"

The old man pushed the door open wide enough to slip inside.

A narrow hallway ran several feet past doors on either side. He walked past each and peered in, vision amped to the max, rendering everything in pale greenish-gray and black. Shower, lavatory, storage closet, office space.

Ahead, flashlights stabbed the darkness where two uniformed men stood over three men in shabbier clothes, now lying face down, hands behind their backs. Both uniforms held handguns. As the old man watched, one of them holstered his weapon and deftly ensnared each man's wrists with a thin plastic tie. The old man stood a couple feet back from the doorway into the main room.

"You boys have been warned about this," the MP still holding his weapon said. "This is federal property, off-limits. You're trespassing, in violation of national security code—"

"We was all military!" one of the prisoners shouted. "I was Marine Corps!"

"But you're not now." The MP sounded bored. This was a familiar scenario for him, evidently. His partner straightened. "Now we're gonna do this one more time. Next time we catch you squatting, you're up on charges. That ought to make you feel real military, just like the old days. Ninety days in the stockade."

"Food would be better," one of them said.

"No," the other MP said. '"No food anymore. Budget cuts. Prisoners get to live on air and water and occasionally each other."

"Asshole."

"Enough," the first MP said. He holstered his pistol and

4

leaned down. "Come on. Let's go for a ride." He began to help one of the indigents to his feet.

The last one got to his feet—and looked directly at the old man. "Someone's back there!"

The MP holding him jerked him roughly. "Don't give me—"

The old man took three quick steps backward and pivoted through the door into the office. The glare of a flashlight swept the floor of the hallway where he'd been standing.

"Are you playing with me, Lee?" asked the first MP.

"No, I—"

"Shit, you know Lee sees in the dark!" one of the indigents barked. "He says someone is back there—"

"We've spent enough time on you for one night. We're leaving now, gentlemen. Come on."

The old man listened to the sounds of the three indigents being shuffled out the door, then into the patrol vehicle. Doors slammed shut. The vehicle hummed to life and rolled away.

He examined the office in the blue-white moonglow coming through the single, high window, a steel desk shoved against the wall below it. Paper littered the floor. A closet door stood slightly open; he pulled it wide to find hangers, and a pile of rags in the corner. He opened the drawers on the desk—loose papers, paperclips, one old pencil. He took out some of the papers and shuffled through them. A letterhead caught his attention.

Cannon Air Force Base.

It sounded familiar, but...

The letter itself concerned the base closing under the BRAC guidelines. The Base Re-Alignment and Closure Commission recommended...pursuant to...base to be closed down in 2005...bids to be opened by 2007 for local redevelopment...in cooperation with the Clovis Chamber of Commerce...

He went through the rest of the papers quickly, but nothing clarified his situation.

*Why can't I remember my name?*

He closed the drawer quietly. An old map hung crookedly on the wall. It showed the state—New Mexico—and an inset displayed the base and the nearest city. Clovis.

Clovis, New Mexico.

On the floor beneath the map lay a sheaf of papers. He picked it up. A calendar. 2006.

He amped his vision a bit more and the walls came into stark relief. He moved from room to room.

Near the front door he returned to the area where the three men had been. Blankets lay scattered around a battered portable heater, they had wired into a large, nickel-iron battery. It was off now, but he still registered the heat in infrared. Bottles littered the perimeter of the small area, most of them empty—gin, scotch, vodka—and a few paper bags and Styrofoam containers holding the remnants of food.

He rifled through the blankets and sorted out cloth-ing—pants, a T-shirt, a torn jacket. No shoes. The pants did not fit. The jacket was too large. He found boxes further back from the space heater, most of them shabby, held together by duct tape and string. Ragged black scrawls occluded each other, like palimpsests, but the old man could sort some of it out: names, lists of contents, places—MY STUFF appeared in red marker on the largest box. When he opened it he found it filled with bric-a-brac: curios, souvenirs, sheaves of greeting cards, letters, a stack of photographs. The addresses were to Lee Portis.

Portis. That felt familiar. He closed his eyes, concentrating on the name. Portis. Not quite right. Port...something. He opened the top envelope and pulled out the pages, sat on a pile of blankets, and started reading.

The letters came from all over the country—New York, South Carolina, Illinois, California—from a variety of people, most of whom seemed to be ex-military. A few were from relatives. One in particular came from Denice Portis-Lury—his sister from the phrasing—who lived in Hawaii. Because her husband had recently lost his job, she could send no more money for a while, until things "settled down a bit." She apologized several times. She hoped his brother Danny was still sending him something, she would call him to see. She wished he would get a regular residence so he had a phone or at least Internet access. Writing was difficult with her carpal tunnel...

Some of the other letter writers also apologized for no longer being able to send Lee any money. They all hoped he would manage, certain someone else was still helping him. The old man remembered every line. He cross-referenced all the well-wishes and terminations of aid, and a picture emerged of a man who had, one by one, lost all his support. The last few had come general delivery to the Good Hope Shelter, Clovis, New Mexico. The most recent date was February 2007.

February. Not February, but April. Something about April 2007.

He needed to know the date.

He set the letters aside reluctantly. The story he derived from them moved him.

He took out a cigar box, within which he found three long jewelry cases. Each held a medal of some kind. At the bottom, more envelopes. Discharge papers from the Marines, dated 2004. Letters from the Veterans' Administration, first promising to consider his claim, finally rejecting it. Another set of letters from a psychiatric clinic supporting Lee Portis's assertion that he suffered PTSD—Post Traumatic Stress Disorder—stemming from duty in Iraq. The VA had likewise gone over his claims but regrets to inform...

"Typical," the old man muttered. He paused. "Of what?"

*Typical of the period,* he thought. Not his own voice. He remembered it from a class or something.

More papers, rubber-banded together, covered the bottom of the larger box. Old driver's licenses, various IDs, discount cards, ATM cards, ads and circulars, several issues of the Good Hope Shelter newsletter. One of the licenses had Lee Portis's social security number. He pocketed that one.

In the corner of the box he found a sewing kit.

He closed Lee's box, keeping the kit, one newsletter, the

last communication he had received from the VA, and the driver's license. He searched through the other boxes, but found nothing else useful.

He went to the front door and studied the empty street. The MPs were long gone. He kicked up his hearing as far as he could—a flood of insect noises, the rush of the faint breezes, and the sharp yowl of a coyote in the distance—and, satisfied that he was now alone in the abandoned base, went back to the blankets.

He opened the sewing kit. Not nearly enough thread. He studied the material around him and found remnants containing stitching. He grasped the stitch puller and began teasing out the thread. He needed pants that fit. He spared only a small part of his attention for surveillance, then turned all the rest on the task of making clothes.

By morning he had made a pair of serviceable pants, patched the jacket, and scrounged a tanktop that, though filthy, fit.

No shoes. Still no memory.

He needed to get to California, though. He knew that. Not like a memory, just as an imperative. He needed money, transportation, familiarity with his surroundings. First, though, he needed an identity.

Even if he remembered his name, he knew he could not use it here.

He made a bindle out of one of the blankets and a leg from one of the old bunks, stuffed Lee Portis's box into it, then stepped into the morning sun. He stared at the cloudless blue sky for a long time.

He walked north, bindle over his left shoulder.

In the clarity of day he recognized the mothballed negligence of the buildings, the lack of maintenance, cracks, crevices, scoured paint flakes clinging to weathering wood. The steel roofs glinted in the sun, the shadows promised to deepen as time passed. He reached an intersection and knew to turn west. Another hundred yards brought him to a large complex of buildings he recognized as base command center.

The windows were all boarded up and a padlock secured the main set of double doors. He set the bindle down on the long, sand-blown front porch and circled the entire structure. None of the windows or doors had been opened in some time. He retrieved the bindle and went to a rear entrance. The knob resisted turning for a few seconds, then the mechanism cracked under his pressure. The door swung in. The old man entered an empty room.

He spotted motion sensors along the ceiling line, but none of them appeared active. As he walked from room to room, he checked constantly for alarms, any sign of active electrical outlets, signs of recent use. Nothing. The structure had been emptied of anything important, sealed up, and forgotten.

He found several offices still containing desks and a few chairs on castors. In the largest room, an area map hung on one wall. The old man studied it. Highway 60 connected the base to Clovis. Six miles.

He checked for more clothes, found none, then went through all the desk drawers. Paperclips, useless pens, odd scraps of paper. He went back to the map. Portales was south of Clovis. Just south of Cannon AFB lay Eastern New Mexico University.

He closed his eyes. The map expanded in his mind. West-Southwest was Roswell. Further, Alamogordo. North, up by Santa Fe, was Los Alamos.

*This is the eastern boundary of the new Cauchy Horizon...*

That explained—was *an* explanation—why he had appeared here. The western edge of the horizon would be in or near Los Angeles, perhaps further out, in the Pacific. The northern edge would be north of Denver. The south—

The southern rim did not matter. The key points, he knew, were all connected to Skynet activity, especially high-energy fusion experiments. The Cyberdyne installation outside Denver was critical, but the old man understood that he had to get to Los Angeles instead.

He staggered back from the map. All this information flooded his consciousness, not as memories would, but like an imprint, an instruction table. There were files. When he closed his eyes now he saw them, access nodes, available at command. Frightened and fascinated, he traced the connection tree.

*What am I?*

A file unwrapped itself. He saw the hardware implanted throughout his body—augments, carbonile bone grafts, oxygenation amplifiers, blood scours, mesh casings enclosing vital organs, lists of accessory components both increasing efficiency in organic cells and others simply replacing tissue with hybrid tech—and in his brain. A catalogue told him he contained over two hundred thousand files on various topics.

*Who am I?*

Nothing. The search protocol stopped. He waited, but nothing happened.

*What am I doing here?*

In an instant, a new file opened. FIND JEREMIAH PORTER, PRIMARY MISSION. JOHN CONNER AND SARAH CONNER, SECONDARY MISSION AND RESOURCE. CURRENT DISPOSITION OF PRIMARY: UNKNOWN. CURRENT DISPOSITION OF SECONDARY/RESOURCE: LOS ANGELES, CALIFORNIA. BIO OF PRINCIPLES FOLLOWS—

Jeremiah Porter. That name was very familiar. Very.

The particulars continued unveiling within his mind, but he found that he could let it load into a standard memory format without paying direct attention. Porter, whoever he was, had something to do with string theory and time travel. The old man could become better acquainted with the details later. After he established himself.

He opened his eyes. Clovis was as good a place as any to start.

# TWO

Normality returns," John Connor said, surveying the dingy room. He grunted. "At least as much as can be expected."

Ivory light pushed through the dirty windows, picking out paper scraps and dustballs across the dark hardwood floors. The walls might have been white at one time. He started counting electric sockets and phone jacks—eight of the first, five of the second. They would need to upgrade substantially. The next room was larger than the first, but contained fewer outlets of both kinds. If they avoided arrest long enough, though, the place could be made very useful, very now-tech. The ceilings did not show any evidence of leaks, and none of the windows were broken.

John inspected the two bathrooms, the closets, and the alleyway behind the building. Typical L.A. The steel door opened onto pale concrete, opposite the graffiti-emblazoned brick wall of a large warehouse. Industrial trash dumpsters squatted, large and blue, to the far end of the alley. A car rolled past the nearer end, overpowered speakers thumping out a hip-hop beat.

Back inside, he found his mother, Sarah, and the leasing agent in the first room.

"—your ad says 'will upgrade to suit client needs,' " she was saying. She waved the folded-up paper in her left hand.

"So what does that mean, exactly? Fresh coat of paint and spare plywood boards for future broken windows?"

"You haven't specified yet what upgrades you're asking for," the agent said. He cast a worried look at John. "We can't sign off on some open-ended deal that lets you upgrade forever. We need to know what you need."

Sarah cocked her eyebrows at John, shrugged, and walked away.

"Dedicated wireless," John said. "More power outlets, circuit breakers for eight hundred amp service—"

"What do you plan on running here?" the agent laughed nervously. "A high-energy physics lab?"

John held up his hands. "You never know. Seems like this neighborhood could do with a bit of high-end money-draw. What do you think, Sis, a physics lab be something that might attract the high rent crowd? Across the street you could open a pricey watering hole for the PhDs and undergrads, down the street a yuppiemobile dealership—"

"He's kidding, right?" the agent asked Sarah.

"Just so long as the air conditioner works," Sarah said. "Everything else is Sean's concern."

"The inspection certificates are current," the agent said. "You can have your own inspector, obviously."

"Till then," John continued, "we'll want steel-reinforced doors and frames and a security system integrated into the space. We'll pay for that, don't worry, but we want the permits for installation."

The expression on the agent's puffy face might have been relief, but John could not be sure. They had run him all over the city for the past three weeks till they found this place. It was still a bit small for what they wanted, but it was close enough and—unlike most of the other places he had shown them—affordable.

John had the feeling that Sarah wanted this neighborhood to begin with, regardless. They were three blocks from Pico, in an area that had slipped a bit in the last few years.

The agent sighed. "We can do that. I might have to make an adjustment—"

Sarah whirled around. "You weren't even going to tell us about this place. How come? I found this ad and what do you know, it turns out to be offered through you."

"Look, we go to some trouble to fit the client to the property, okay? And before you think that's a load of crap, let me assure you, it's pure self-interest. These upgrades you're asking for suggest to me that you're bringing in a lot of expensive hardware. Fine, you move in here, install all that equipment, and get cleaned out by the local free market entrepreneurs—we don't want to be held responsible. I didn't show you this place because I think the neighborhood is wrong for you. But hey, it's your money, your time. Make me a list of the upgrades you want and let me see what I can do. I suggest you take out a big theft policy, though."

"So what were you thinking of putting in here?" John asked.

"A bodega or something. There's some federal seed money for the right client."

John caught Sarah's eyes. A bodega already stood at the nearby intersection.

"No takers?" John asked.

The agent shrugged. "It's been on the market for six months. We just added the upgrade offer this past week to see if anyone would move on it."

Sarah smiled. "Then you can afford to be very accommodating on the upgrades."

"But—"

"But what? Anybody lined up behind us?"

The neighborhood had been very upscale not three years ago. The building was on Calder, near Pico, along which nightclubs, restaurants, shops, and expensive loft apartments had stretched for miles. Most of Pico still boasted trendy boutiques and clubs, was still vital, but this end had experienced a decline.

The agent scowled briefly, then nodded. "Get me a list, I'll see what we can do when. But I think we'll want six months down."

13

Sarah looked ready to explode. John extended a hand. "Sounds reasonable. Let's see what can be done, then. Thanks for taking all this time with us."

"Um...sure, no problem. Let's say we meet in my office tomorrow afternoon?"

"Fine," John said, shaking the agent's hand.

On the street, he bade them have a nice day and strode quickly to his car. The alarm chirped twice and the engine started when he touched the door. John and Sarah watched him drive off, a little too fast.

"He'll be thrilled by tomorrow," John said.

"Half a year down?" Sarah said. "You don't think we gave him too harsh a deal, do you?"

"A little sweet'n'low can work wonders sometimes. Besides, we're going to end up buying the place from him anyway—what difference does it make?"

She shook her head, though in wonder or disgust John could not tell. She studied the facade of the storefront. The exterior of the building was plain in the extreme—white-washed stucco around a large ground-floor store window, now boarded up, and the second floor apartment window. John had given the apartment a quick look—nothing special, one bedroom, a shower, kitchen with stove and refrigerator—and found a direct access to the ground floor that opened from a door in the utility room. For a start-up, it would do.

"So other than the fine ambience of the neighborhood," he asked, "is there a reason we're taking this one?"

"Several. Mainly, it's large enough and priced right. Hell, I thought Santa Fe was bad. I had no idea property values in L.A. had gone so high. This neighborhood fits our needs. It's not nearly as bad as he thinks it is."

John agreed. "Decline" was a relative term.

They had discussed it thoroughly before making the move from New Mexico to California. Chief among them was to attract as little attention as possible. Too much cash to throw around was still the surest way to draw scrutiny.

They could afford to take a place in Bel Air, but that was the wrong kind of camouflage.

John still was unsure why they had to come back to L.A. at all. Sarah wanted to. Maybe she was homesick, but he doubted it. Sarah rarely made decisions based on sentiment. Business had been good in Santa Fe and Albuquerque—good enough that they had opened a small office in Colorado Springs and another in Denver—but Sarah insisted they return here. An expansion, not a relocation. L.A. would be another new branch. After a few arguments, John stopped fighting and started doing the logistics. They were leaving the company offices open in New Mexico and Colorado. The company was incorporated under a shell identity, easily severed from themselves, but now employed eighteen people. Security investigations and consultations just kept gaining importance among people whose wealth had come from less than legitimate sources, who had taken shortcuts in building their businesses, and now wanted to be as legit as possible—and the money flowed like desperation. John assuaged his doubts knowing there was someplace to which they could run if things went awry.

All the hardware with pertinent material on it had come with them to L.A.—pertinent to their ongoing investigations of Cyberdyne and Skynet. They had kept that distanced from the rest of the business, on entirely separate machines, in isolated files, away from everyone else. The Cyberdyne file was their project. The skills developed over years of researching the company and its government affiliations and its major project, Skynet—all without being traced—proved lucrative when they turned them to private security, identity prophylaxis, and related corporate matters. They could hide things, change them, unbury the past, reinvent entire histories for people—or do the exact opposite for law enforcement. They had developed a not unfriendly working relationship with local authorities in New Mexico, and with a little care they hoped they could duplicate that here.

Of course, here there might still be people who knew them.

*After all this time, how many?* he wondered.

The truth was, Sarah picked this place out of nostalgia. John rarely knew her to be sentimental, but she had lived here, twenty-three or so years ago. She had shared an apartment with a close friend, a friend who had died in her place when the future paid a visit and changed her life. They had been unable to get the same building, which was gone, but if John had it right, this one was only a couple of blocks away. In a bizarre sense, she wanted to return to the beginning. If anyone understood that time did not work that way, they did. But once in a while Sarah surprised him. Symbolism occasionally meant something to her.

He was curious to see how well their current identities would hold up under scrutiny—test to destruction, in a way. Better to know sooner than later, perhaps. But they had passed all the examinations in New Mexico, even the federal ones, without raising a red flag anywhere. What could the L.A.P.D. do that the feds could not—beyond possibly having a witness who could place them on the scene of a great deal of destruction, years earlier.

*Back on* terra cognita *now,* he thought wryly. *Step cautiously, for here there be demons.*

Since fleeing California in 1994, there had been a number of names—Lawes, Cannerly, Soquoro, Smith—but all of them had been practice. With the work John had done since returning to the United States, it was highly unlikely anyone would make the connection between Sean and Julia Philicos and the Connors who had caused so much destruction thirteen years ago.

Thirteen years. So long. So much time. Time in vast quantities. But never enough.

Sarah wandered north, toward the intersection, arms folded matter-of-factly. She walked with an almost military bearing. Nearly forty-five now, she could still take down all but the best trained men. Squared shoulders, long legs, slim waist—the dark blue silk blouse and cream pants covered solid muscle—and a multitude of scars. Her hair was dyed black now, pulled back today in a ponytail that touched her back between the shoulder blades.

Not a lot happening, though it was already past ten in the morning. The bodega was open; two men sat under the awning, drinking from bottles. Music played, muffled and distant, indistinct. A couple of old cars, lovingly restored, cruised by, chrome glinting electrically in the crisp sunshine. Long shadows. Spring. Warm, but not oppressive, not yet. L.A. summer was weeks off.

*Every morning with a clear sky is a blessing,* John thought.

Sarah headed for the bodega. John started to follow, but his cell phone chirped.

He checked the incoming number—the main office in Santa Fe—and pressed TALK. "Talk to me."

"Boss, it's Jenny." Juanita Salceda, who ran things while John and Sarah traveled.

"What's the word, Jenny?"

"Got a client call you might want to check personally."

"We won't be back for a week at least—"

"This one is L.A. local. Besides, he *asked* for you personally."

"Jenny—"

"He asked for John Connor."

John stopped, momentarily stunned. "Uh-huh. Was this a referral or something?"

"Maybe. He was kind of vague about that. But I checked the company, and it's all legit. Might be a good piece of change in it. Besides..."

She let that hang. Besides, it would be worth finding out who knew his real name and that it was connected with PPS Security Investigations.

"All right, feed me the file, I'll check it out." He switched his phone to data transfer and watched the screen while the information Jenny sent loaded. It flashed RECEIVED, and he switched back to voice only. "See what else you can find out about this guy. Do a personal search—"

"What do you pay me for? Already on it."

"Good. Let me know if—"

"—if I find anything important. Right. I just love this spy stuff. What about your search? Find anything yet?"

"Yeah, we've got a place. Just need to rebuild it a little, sign all the papers, and start moving in. I'll let you know when the lease is signed."

"How does it feel to be back in L.A.?"

"Not eerie enough—which is freaky."

"Freaky but not eerie."

"Not eerie enough."

"You'll have to explain the difference to me some time."

"My pleasure. Later, though."

"Right. Stay in touch, boss."

He closed the phone and slipped it back into its belt pouch.

Sarah was coming toward him. She frowned. "What is it?"

John frowned. "We may have a problem."

Destry-McMillin Research occupied a twenty-five-acre campus a mile north of Caltech. John stopped at the main gate and handed his ID to the guard.

"You're expected in Building H, Mr. Philicos." The guard handed back the card.

John pocketed his ID and drove through. The voice on the phone had been polite, almost cheerful, but completely uninformative. McMillin wanted to meet John face to face before anything important was discussed. He had not pressed the point, but surely he had known John could not refuse.

McMillin had agreed to a meeting two days later. John wanted to be present when the leases were signed and the construction team showed up to begin installing them in the new building. Ken Lash and his people had been standing by—one call, and the truck appeared a few hours later. When John was satisfied that Sarah could handle anything that might come up, he headed for the meeting, more than a little apprehensive.

Tall trees lined the curving road through the campus. He glimpsed low, steel-and-glass buildings through breaks in expensively landscaped woodland. His brief research into the firm painted a picture of a high tech R & D company doing contract work through Caltech and other university affiliates, and a certain amount of government work. High-energy plasma physics and superconducting superfluids came up as their chief areas of expertise.

He pulled into the parking lot around Building H, which turned out to be a five-floor, amoeba-shaped structure—the showpiece of the complex, the public face of the facility. John suppressed a shudder at how much it reminded him of the Cyberdyne building he and his mother had destroyed.

He followed the sidewalk encircling the undulating floor plan to the main entrance, where another guard checked his ID, then led him to an elevator. He rode up—alone—to the top floor and stepped into a front office of rich scarlets and turquoise. The air itself seemed custom-fabricated; all his senses felt heightened. A receptionist came smartly around her oversized glass desk, professional smile and hand ambiguously extended, either to shake his or take his elbow or return to her side, whatever his body language might tell her to do.

He shook her hand.

"Mr. Philicos, welcome to Destry-McMillin. Mr. McMillin is expecting you. This way, please."

He entered a much larger office, floor-to-ceiling windows curving around almost 120°, giving a spectacular view of the company campus. To the southwest, a huge block of a structure rose up out of the surrounding trees, off-white and windowless.

A large, gray-haired man stood in front of the immense black desk, his back to the view. A white beard framed a squarish face that featured wide-set, small eyes, and a broad nose that had been broken once or twice.

"Mr. Connor to see you, sir," the receptionist announced, then retreated from the office.

"Mr. McMillin, I presume?" John said, stopping a few feet from him.

"And you are *the* John Connor," the man said. "I may be the only one in the state who knows that." He grinned. "So please, don't demolish my life's work."

"I didn't bring a single explosive device with me—except, perhaps, my temper."

McMillin's laugh burst out, loud and full of surprise. He gestured to a set of comfortable armchairs around a low coffee table. "Sit, sit."

"There's an explanation, of course?"

"Of course. But first..." He leaned over his desk and pushed a button. "Tess, could you see some refreshments are brought in? My usual, and—" He looked at John. "Coffee? Something stronger?"

"Coffee's fine."

"Coffee, two cups. Thanks, Tess." He waved at the chairs. "Please."

As he sat down, John saw a man past an athletic prime, who might once have been physically formidable. Football, perhaps, or even rugby. He retained much of the aura of the powerful body, but he was in his fifties now. According to the information Jenny had managed to gather on such short notice, most of McMillin's work had been in research and, in the last ten years, building a company.

"First off," McMillin said, "I want you to know, I *do* require your services. I've got a small problem that needs tending and I can't do it internally. I'm familiar with your company, your work, and I'm impressed. I know your rates. There's a bonus in this at the end of a successful commission. So I have not gotten you here on false pretenses."

"But there must be a dozen first-rate firms like PPS right here in L.A."

The door opened, and a porter rolled in a tray. He set a coffee service on the table, placed a cup before each man, then set a tall glass filled with light brown, creamy liquid in front of McMillin. He placed a last tray filled with cheeses, crackers, and cookies, then left.

"There are," McMillin said as the door closed. "But I want you."

"For reasons other than our expertise?"

McMillin poured John's coffee, then filled his own cup. "After I investigated you, I find that it is precisely how good you are that recommends you most. Not in the security business—as you say, there are a dozen firms here as good, if not better—but in your own abilities to...work the system?"

John stared silently at him for a few moments, then decided he'd been polite enough. "How do you know who I am?"

McMillin took a long drink from his glass, then leaned back. "Philicos. Interesting name. You've chosen less symbolic ones in the past, but maybe you're tired of being Bill Smith. Philicos means, loosely, 'wolf lover.' The Gaelic root of Connor is *Conchobhar*, which means 'lover of wolves.' Sean is one of the more common derivations of John, of which most people are blithely unaware. So you've come back to America wearing your own name for no one to recognize. I admire that."

"My cover's been broken by etymology—imagine that. But unless you do this sort of thing as a hobby, I doubt you would have simply stumbled on it."

"Correct. I was told to look for you."

"By whom?"

McMillin's eyebrows rose. "Why, by you."

# THREE

Deirdre dropped her backpack on the couch and rolled her head around to work the soreness out of her neck. Across the apartment, Bobby Porter sat at the kitchen table, legs pulled up with his heels on the edge of the chair, legal pad in his lap; the Macintosh sat on the table, screen glowing into his face. Evening sun teased through the drawn blinds behind him.

"Your eyes will melt," Deirdre said, and stepped out of her sandals.

"Someday, maybe," Bobby said. He frowned at the legal pad, then at the screen, and made a sudden series of notes on the pad. He touched the mouse and studied the screen for a time, still frowning.

Deirdre sat down on the sofa, sighing loudly. The mail was laid out neatly on the coffee table. She picked through it until she found an envelope addressed to ROBERT PORTER, CALIFORNIA INSTITUTE OF TECHNOLOGY, PHYSICS DEPT. C/O PROF. MICHAEL COJENSIS from Cyberdyne Technologies.

"What's this?" she asked, sliding out the folded sheet.

"What's what?" Bobby asked.

"You know what. What else would I ask about?"

He glanced over at her. "Do you have no sense of my privacy?"

"Of course I do—it's mine. This is not private. This is sig-nificant." She opened the letter.

"Did you have a good workout?" he asked.

"Don't change the subject. Yes, I did." She skimmed the opening, then came to the body of the letter. "They want to interview you."

"They do."

"Did you send them an application or something?"

"I didn't."

"Then how—?"

"I wondered the same thing, considering."

"Did you ask Cojensis?"

"Not yet."

"You're not going to the interview, then?"

"Why shouldn't I?"

Deirdre looked at him. He closed down his computer and rubbed his eyes.

"Is that a real question?" she asked.

Bobby stood, stretched, then went to the coffeepot. He swirled what was left pooled at the bottom, scowled, and took the urn to the sink. He rinsed it out, then began to make a new pot.

"Cyberdyne does government work," Deirdre said. "Translate that as military."

"Your dad does government work."

"Not military."

Bobby gave her a skeptical look, then continued preparing the coffee.

"Maybe peripherally," she said, "but so what? That doesn't mean I'd approve of you working for *him,* either."

"I never said I intended to accept a job from Cyberdyne."

"Then why go to the interview?"

"I want to see if I can *get* the job." He flipped the BREW switch, then came over to the sofa. "It's a test. I could use the ego boost."

"Why? You're the best student Cojensis has."

"I don't know that."

"Why else would he steal from you?" When Bobby's face went rigid, Deirdre felt guilty. "Look, this doesn't sound

23

like something you should even play with. I mean, what if there's a security check?"

Now Bobby looked embarrassed. "Well, maybe they already did that. Maybe they think they can get me for Cyberdyne because I've got a problem. In any case, if I *don't* show up, they might blow the whistle out of spite."

"And if you turn them down, why wouldn't they blow the whistle then? Out of spite, as you put it."

"But then I know it won't matter. I'll know I can land *something.*"

"Without your degree? What good—"

"Look, I'm going, okay? I feel I need to do this, okay?"

Deirdre's ears warmed. Bobby almost never raised his voice, not to her. She dropped the letter back on the coffee table and headed for the refrigerator. For nearly a minute, the tension pressed around her. She found a bottle of water and twisted the cap off. Leaning against the sink, she guzzled half of it down. She sighed explosively, glaring at the back of his head, and the dark, nearly black hair that curled delicately at his collar. She could tell by the set of his shoulders that he felt the bad air between them, and was looking silently for a way to alter it, bring it back to their normal condition.

*Normal condition*—whatever *that* might be. Deirdre ran through it again. Lower middle class boy from a blue-collar neighborhood with a natural aptitude for theoretical math, living with a rich girl off-campus—at her expense—while usurping a relative's scholarship; a relative whose whereabouts no one knew. The real Robert Porter might be dead, might be in the Far East, might have joined some borderline psychotic religious group; no one knew. As far as Deirdre knew, no one had ever called the police. She imagined they had, but Bobby—this Bobby, this near stranger she could not keep away from—had never said. He also had never said he resented her money, her class, her ease with all the rest of campus life. Never said it, but sometimes it surfaced when least expected, like now. He needed to feel, to know, he could do something substantial without cheating or relying on her status to get him through.

But he never had relied on her status, that was the thing. He treated her like an equal, a person he liked—loved—being around. She had never received that kind of consideration from any of her peers before. Sometimes he seemed embarrassed on her behalf, that she had to exist with the burden of family wealth along with all the other things she carried—and carried well, she thought.

Ninety-five percent of the time, they shared a common space with each other free of all possible obstacles. It was good. Really good. Now and then, though, something snapped, and he became defensive and irascible. She thought she understood. Maybe she did, slightly, but she had never lived any part of his life. Empathy went only so far.

Just as she opened her mouth to apologize, he said, "I'm sorry." The tension went out of his shoulders, his head slumped a little forward, and Deirdre felt the good space embrace her again. She set the bottle down and went to him. Her fingers dug into his shoulders, worked at his neck. She looked at the monitor on the table.

"What were you working on?" she asked.

"Visser transforms," Bobby said. "Seems to me there's a conservation-of-mass violation in my last set of equations. I'm trying to see if it's compensated for through $\underline{n}$-space folding."

Deirdre hesitated, working through the language. If there was any resentment on her part in this relationship, it was over the seemingly effortless way he slipped in and out of this level of theory. "Wouldn't it be just a relativistic shift? Frame of reference?"

"Maybe. But we're actually removing mass from one frame and inserting it into another that has no other con- nection than that it exists along the same timeline. In order to do that, I treat time as just another frame, but I'm not sure if I *can* do that. I'm removing a frame from the other three to which it was originally connected. Look." He got up and went to the table. Deirdre followed.

"Happens at the subatomic level all the time," she said.

"We assume it does." Bobby straightened in the chair and pointed at the screen. "It may be that what we're describing there is just a convenient way to make the numbers come out. We don't *really* know if there's any temporal flux going on."

"Didn't you say once that in order for the universe to move through time, there had to be a wavefront? Something to precede the universe to sort of open the door?"

He waved a hand impatiently. "Play. I was tossing around ideas to see where they landed."

"And the wavefront," Deirdre went on in mock lecture voice, returning to the sink and her water bottle, "is what we see with the appearance and disappearance of element-ary particles in empty space—'quantum fizz,' I believe you called it. Suppressing that fizz in a small volume of vacuum will give rise to stable though small quantities of exotic matter with which we could prop open a wormhole of suf-ficient size to conduct limited time travel experiments. The fizz itself is the net distribution of time traveling—or 'tun-neling,' I think you preferred—particles over sufficient volume to prevent, through some sort of conservation of energy function, the spontaneous formation of stable wormholes."

Bobby laughed. "Very good, Ms. McMillin—you get a passing mark on your defense. You may go straight to Fermilab for a tenured position if you can explain to me how to suppress that fizz, and how to determine direction through the wormhole. And what exactly the wormhole leads to."

"Got me there, Professor. Ain't got a clue."

"Me, either." He switched off the monitor and stood. "And I can't risk taking this to Cojensis for help."

Deirdre grunted. "This is so off-the-wall theoretical, I doubt he'd risk stealing it."

"If he helped me, he'd see it has potential." He rolled his

eyes. "Hell, who'm I kidding? If I don't find a way around him, I'm screwed."

"Change mentors."

"And get found out?"

"By now, do you really think they'd throw you out? You've been doing great work. I think they might make an exception—"

"I don't *want* them to make an exception! I want—"

"You want the universe to be fair."

"Well...yeah."

They both burst out laughing simultaneously. Bobby stepped up to her and touched her hair. "God, you are so..."

She eased up against him and leaned her head back to let him kiss her neck.

"Salty," he said, and licked her throat.

"Mmm, ready to cook."

Later, unable to stay asleep, Deirdre opened the letter from Cyberdyne again. She was tempted to call her stepdad anyway. She knew he would take her advice about Bobby and offer him a position. He might even be able to intercede on his behalf with the university. But she knew that such an act would be the beginning of the end for them.

Still, a little information might be useful. She studied the name at the bottom of the invitation: Franklin Casse, Special Projects, Vice President. Maybe it would be a good idea to know who Mr. Franklin Casse was.

She returned the letter to its envelope and replaced it among the others. She sorted through the rest—bills, ads, requests for donations—but left them unopened. She picked up the television remote, then dropped it on the couch, unactivated. She ran her hands down her stomach and along her hips. Good workout today. Two good workouts...

From the picture window she had a clear view of the parking lot. Few cars remained at this time of day. One she now noticed she had never seen before—midnight blue, large, and backed into a slot just across from their apartment. Someone sat behind the wheel, but the late afternoon sun glinted off the glass. Deirdre felt briefly like stepping back, but their windows were all polarized so no one could see in. She noted the license plate anyway, a habit she had carried with her since childhood. She used to turn them into puzzles to be solved—at first word games, then later number problems.

She picked up the phone and poised a finger over the speed-dial button for her stepfather's office.

*No,* she decided, returning the phone to its cradle. *He needs to do this. I need to let him.*

Still, the Cyberdyne logo troubled her. It had been a long time since they had been in the news with all the destruction at two of their facilities, the one in L.A. an almost total loss, the one in Colorado Springs compromised but...No public statement had ever been released concerning what had been lost at Colorado Springs, or even what they had been doing there. Secrecy and weapons, the dogs accompanying modern-day Mars on his way to war. And Cyberdyne was one of the kennels.

"He said he wouldn't take the job," she murmured. "Trust him."

She did trust him. What he said he would do she could count on. She worried, though, that he could get hurt.

She checked the address where he was supposed to meet Mr. Casse, early next week.

*He never told me to stay home that day...*

His dreams unfolded with shapes he could describe in numbers. He had always done this, he had always recognized these landscapes. When he discovered mathematics, through his cousin Bobby, as a child—not yet twelve and playing games with differential equations—he knew he had found, if not his voice, his true language. The lattice-like way in which all his dreams seemed to order themselves began to make sense as matrices. He could not be sure which came first—the obsession with numbers or the mathematical nature of his dreams—but it no longer mattered.

Now he watched a string unfold itself from a tight coil of bright matter. Along the length of the string, planes attached. Through the planes, porous to the intrusions of certain colors, glowing threads coiled, following the main trunk, almost becoming helices, but never quite crossing over each other, encountering new planes and changing direction or ending. A few, in ways he could not quite make out, seemed to penetrate one plane only to emerge from one "below," as if it had crossed to a before-place. He tried to go around the ever-complicating construct, to look at the specific planes where this happened, but the entire structure turned with him, locked to his frame—or he locked to its frame. There was something about the shape of those particular planes that made no sense, but he could not quite see how. They sprang from the main string, but curved away, as if dragged downward by gravity. They ought to have dimpled, and recovered their original level, but it did not appear to be the case. If only he could move around to the other side...

He saw then that he stood on one of the planes, and that was the problem. His reference was set, established on this level. The entire assembly drifted upward as he looked, coiling gracefully along the spine to which his plane attached. If he could leave this plane, step off it and follow the threads that shot around him, interpenetrating the planes above and below him, he could get a good perspective on how the warp and woof of the still-recomplicating structure related to itself, in all its parts.

But that, of course, was the difficulty: he carried his plane with him. Breaking free was impossible because he and the plane existed solely in relation to each other. In order to get a better perspective, he needed to take it with him. If he could roll it up and detach it from the main string, or even let it flow freely along the length of the string, riding with it...

How to fold it up, though.

Folding it up, it would disappear.

No, it became a point.

Folding it up, riding with the condensing volume of space-time (when had it become a volume instead of a plane?) he watched the string grow thicker, become the overwhelming fact of his perception, expanding to absorb his four dimensions into a point just inside the infinitely thin body of the string. A singularity within a singularity.

Was that allowed? Could two singularities exist at the same point? Two particles could not occupy the same space at the same time, but a particle was not a singularity—nor was it separate from a frame.

He saw...one vast color, a variation of sameness...All frame of reference was gone.

The dream faded, blended with memories of other things, and he lost the thread.

Bobby opened his eyes in fading afternoon light. The blinds cast angled shadows across a painting Deirdre had bought from a recent art bazaar: an abstract, supposedly depicting music, all in rich tones of azure and violet and emerald, with splashes of gold and scarlet. He had doubted her claim that she had paid very little for it; in fact, the more he looked at it, the more he believed that she had paid a lot for it. But he loved it. There was an organizing element to it that helped him, upon waking, cope with the divergence between his dreams and the so-called real world. Only a few seconds, that was all it took, but gazing at the fluid lines set against subtle rhythmic patterns grounded him.

He sat up in bed. *Could two singularities occupy the same point?*

*Funny, the things you think of after sex,* he thought, smiling. *Actually, maybe that one isn't so strange...two singularities, same point...*

He stood, stretched, and went into the bathroom. He pulled on a pair of shorts before going into the living room, looking for Deirdre.

He found her lounging naked on the sofa, talking on her cell phone. She waggled her fingers at him, smiling, and

continued talking. Bobby stood still for a few seconds, admiring her body. She worked hard at it, and the effort paid off in defined muscle, sleek skin over power-at-rest. Some of it was bought—the tan, the overall effect of massages, the trainers—but it also showed her discipline. Others, her friends, often disdained the work involved, but Deirdre paid no attention to their subtle—and occasionally unsubtle—teasing.

Not often, but occasionally, Bobby wondered what she saw in him, why she stayed with him. Early on there had been arguments about it, but it had been his own insecurity, sometimes bordering on paranoia. He mostly got over it. Without her, he felt, his university career would have been very short. He loved the math, the physics, but she had tutored him through the rest, most of which failed to attract his interest.

Bobby continued into the dining room, sat down, and booted the Mac up again. The equations lay on the screen, inscrutable and clear at the same time. They reminded him of something else. He wanted to model a wormhole as a description of a temporal loop. Spatial dimensions gave nicely balanced equations, everything eventually equaling everything else, net zero. But these just left him with an open-ended...something.

Maxwell. Bobby blinked, recognizing the pattern. Maxwell's equations describing electromagnetism. The electrical charge side of them balanced, plus and minus giving symmetry, but while the same equations described magnetism—as related phenomena, one would expect they would—there were no discreet poles in magnetic fields. They came as a set, always linked, north and south. Loops. Hence, symmetry broke down. They described what they described perfectly well—at least, usably—but that failure of symmetry had been irritating physicists for decades.

Bobby's wormhole models displayed the same asymmetry when applied to time.

"What was it they wanted to find...?" he mused, tapping his lips with a forefinger. "Magnetic monopoles...yeah..."

In theory, magnetic monopoles ought to exist. Just as particles came with positive and negative charges, magnetic charges ought to come with north and south components—separate, discreet components—but none had ever been found. What do you get when you cut a magnet down into two parts? Two magnets. One hypothesis suggested that all magnetic fields existed as coiled loops, folded in on themselves. They could express both poles only when undivided. The actual "thing" that might be the opposite charge was *inside* the coil, hidden like a snail in its shell.

He studied the equations on the screen. So time came folded up *inside* space? Its effects could be expressed, but not separated out...

In string theory, there were more than simply four dimensions. The others had long since diminished to relative insignificance, or curled up inside the four dominant dimensions that represented the universe in which everything existed.

Or was that too simplistic? An easy answer to describe something entirely different?

Time possessed an arrow, but unlike space, one could not travel back and forth on that arrow at will. Why not? Einstein had described how time and space came as a package, inseparable, even though entirely dependent on the observer's frame of reference for its specific effect. What if—

"You are the *only* man I know who does science after good sex." Hands slid down his chest from behind.

"Yes, but I also do sex after good science."

Bobby let his head fall back against Deirdre's belly. He gazed up at her face, smiling down at him.

"I promise I won't take the job," he said.

"All right."

"Who were you talking to?"

"Daddy."

Bobby felt himself tighten. "About what?"

"I just wanted to know who this Mr. Casse is. Just information."

Bobby sighed. "Dee, you know how I feel—"

"Yes, I do. But frankly, in this, I understand just a little bit more than you do. Cyberdyne does military R & D. Twice in the last thirteen years someone has blown up their facilities. Both times, the government pumped more money into them, and the only explanation they offered the public was a wild story about two crackpots who thought Cyberdyne was building a doomsday machine."

"And you believed that?"

"No. What I believe is that they're doing something that makes them a target for some seriously unpleasant fanatics. Their history of funding from the Pentagon makes me think those fanatics know more than we do."

"I told you, I just need to find out if I can *get* the damn job!"

"That's fine. But when you deal with snakes, it's best to know which end has the fangs."

He really could not argue with her. Between them, they shared a powerful belief in being informed. She simply had resources he lacked. She could ask questions of someone who could get them answers about certain things they could find no other way. And it would be good to know as much as possible about these people—for instance, how this Mr. Casse had found him. Scholarship was open, certainly, it could have been nothing more than someone noticing his academic achievements. But his experience with Cojensis made him suspicious of simple explanations. How had Cojensis been involved? This was the first time Bobby had been approached this way; it scared him a little. Deirdre was only helping by contacting her stepfather—Dennis McMillin was privy to a great deal of information—and Bobby appreciated it on a certain level.

33

On another level, he felt coddled.

"Okay," he said not wanting to ruin the mood any further.

"So," she said, leaning over his shoulder, peering at the screen, "you want to explain this to me again?"

# FOUR

Sarah resisted the impulse to micro-manage. Ken Lash knew his job; this was, after all, the fifth time he had done an install like this for them. His crew worked efficiently, installing the new security hardware in the building. Arrangements for the new doors had been made at the signing of the lease agreement, and the permits were being fast-tracked. Everything was well in hand, and she should leave Lash alone—her meddling would only slow him down. She made herself ascend the rear stairs to the second floor apartment, newspapers tucked under her left arm.

Her boot heels cracked sharply on the hardwood floors as she walked to the living room. The place contained little furniture. Sarah did not care so much, but John preferred things to be comfortable. For now, two armchairs, a coffee table, sofa, and a television, all newly arrived, gave her more than enough comfort. More importantly, a computer squatted on the kitchen table—her link to the world.

She dropped the stack of papers beside it: *Los Angeles Times, USA Today,* and the *Wall Street Journal.* The bodega down the street carried the first two normally. During her first visit, she'd asked them if they could get the *Journal,* and they said yes. They had had it tucked aside for her, no other copies in sight.

She booted up the computer. While she waited, she unfolded the *L.A. Times. Knowledge is power,* she thought.

*That's what John says. Of course, I taught that to him, even though he thinks it's all his idea now...*

She went directly to the business section and scanned the copy for anything about Cyberdyne. Then she opened *USA Today* and did the same. The screen on the computer informed her that the system was ready. She tapped instructions, linking to the Internet. Once connected, she started her robot programs tracking down information about Cyberdyne. Several new articles popped up quickly. She skimmed them, ignoring the ones that were clearly spin generated by the company itself. A few came from disarmament groups, and a few more from independent newshounds trying to uncover anything that looked like government black projects. Cyberdyne had been remarkably resilient at fending off bad press, at least any that might seriously impact them. Sarah had watched them deploy harassment lawsuits to shut down some inquiries, buy off reporters, get federal agencies to investigate others. All the rest they somehow buried with charm. Cyberdyne possessed one of the finest public relations machines in business. Even while she hated them she conceded a grudging respect at their adaptability. It was only fitting that Skynet should emerge from such a company.

*Will emerge,* she corrected herself. As yet there was no Skynet—not here, not in this timeline. Sarah still balked at the ramifications of time travel and its related branches. She had been through it—them—and still had only the most basic understanding. *Doesn't matter. What I do understand is that so far we've stopped Skynet from happening several times.*

Of course, that was no guarantee Skynet would remain unbuilt, in this timeline or any other. Skynet had appeared—many times—and Armageddon had happened —many times—and still there was the possibility of undoing it, somewhere, in some reality.

When they had finished their time-hopping and found themselves in a reality where Skynet did not exist, they had decided to stay and try to make sure Armageddon never happened in *this* one. It was unlikely, but Sarah, at least, needed a bit more stability. One time, one reality.

*"It doesn't work that way."* She could hear Rosanna Monk's complaint.

"And where are you now, Rosanna?" Sarah murmured as she turned her attention back to the *Times*.

She worked her way through to the obituaries. John had used them when assembling their new identities. Helping him, Sarah had developed the habit of skimming them. Once in a while she saw a name from the distant past—from before 1984, when the first Terminator and Kyle Reese entered her life—usually a friend now dead with whom she had lost all contact after leaving Los Angeles for the desert and the life she had led since. Morbid, John called it. Maybe, but she did it automatically now, and when she did see a name she knew it gave her an odd sense of connectivity to something almost normal.

At the top of the page a banner piece announced the death of a professor of mathematics at the Massachusetts Institute of Technology: Dr. J. Hewit Porter died in a car crash; police investigating reports of another vehicle involved.

Sarah scanned down to the columns of deaths, a few with small pictures. She paused, catching something familiar. Another Porter: J. Porter, found dead in his apartment, natural causes...

She finished the obituaries, refolded the paper, glanced at the computer. Still searching. While her electronic trolls prowled the web for Cyberdyne data, she opened a new window and began a search for "Connor, Sarah," just to see if anything came up. The contemporary listings were about other Sarah Connors. A few older articles appeared about the 1994 Cyberdyne incident and the 2001 incident, but nothing more recent.

She opened the *New York Times* site, heading immediately to the business section. She had become adept at interpreting the stock listings for signs of movement in the specific tech industries that had connections to Cyberdyne.

Destry-McMillin...

John was there now. She closed the *Times*, opened a search engine, and requested a profile, and sat back to read. John had already gone over most of this. He might have missed something, though, with all he had to do—setting up a new office in a city distant from where they had successfully made a home, and the complications of trying to find out if anyone else knew about them. That had entailed a call to Jack Reed, something they tried to keep to a minimum; but in this case, it seemed necessary. Jack told them not to panic, he would check and get back to them. That did not exactly mollify Sarah—she disliked relying on people so removed from them, from their experiences—but Jack had been good to his word since their return. She just needed to learn to trust him.

*After all, it's Jack's people downstairs once more installing our on-site security...We'd better be able to trust him...*

She opened Destry-McMillin's website. The lab had been founded in the mid-Eighties by partners Ian Destry and Dennis McMillin, both PhDs in physics. The lab had begun small, then leaped ahead by taking advantage of the digital boom. Because they had invested as much (if not more) in the actual hardware end of the physical sciences, they survived the dot-com crash at the turn of the century.

The list of research areas was impressive: astronomy and astrophysics, atmospheric science, robotics, computing, energy research, environmental science, lasers and optics, materials science, microtechnology, physics, sensors and instrumentation. She clicked on some of the links to specific areas of research. Ultrawideband communications, multicell proteomics, ultrasonic nondestructive evaluation of multilayered structures, multifluidic systems for solution array-based bioassays, carbon-nanotube permeable membranes—

She paused at that one. Nanotubes. Nanoprocessing.

There was a link called "Working With Destry-McMillin"

that brought up a list of partnering programs with other labs. Cyberdyne was one of a dozen.

"Partnering in what?" she hissed, hitting the link.

It took some time to find the project, and when she did it made little sense to her.

"'Exchange coupling in magnetic nanoparticles, combined with a study of covalent attachment of metallic nanorods to nanocrystals.' What the hell does *that* mean...?"

She bounced around on the site for a time, trying to locate anything that might explain what any of this was, but all she found were more lists. The term "nano" appeared far too often for her comfort.

She did not want to run an open inquiry right now on Cyberdyne, although she doubted she would be traced and identified if she kept to their main website. She would wait until Lash and his people finished their work downstairs. For now...

She flipped open her cell phone and punched John's code; on the second ring, he answered. "John, it's me. Where are you now?"

"In Mr. McMillin's office. What's up?"

"A question for him. Destry-McMillin did a project in partnership with Cyberdyne, involving nanoparticles."

There was a pause. "I'll ask."

"Is everything all right?"

"Everything is...weird. I'll fill you in later."

"Be careful."

"Always. Thanks for the call."

The connection broke. Sarah sat back, staring at the screen, wishing she had paid more attention to the talks between John, the Specialists, and Rosanna Monk when they had discussed the science. Even John admitted that he understood very little.

She went back to the search engine. Sounds of construction came from beneath her. In a few days, Lash would have the office intrusion-hardened, connected to well-shielded phone, satellite, and Internet connections, and equipped with state-of-the-art equipment top to bottom, all courtesy of Jack Reed and his federal off-the-books discretionary funds. She still felt anxious about their connection to Reed—there would be a price down the line, she knew that—but for now it was the only way they could operate in this country, and Reed at least was on their side.

*For now,* she thought grimly.

Not knowing what else to check at the moment, she typed in "J. Hewitt Porter" to see what came up. Below the primary entries—his university profile, a website dedicated to mathematical considerations run under his name, a couple of links to published papers—were other obituaries.

A string of "Porter, Jerry, Jeremiah, Jerard, etc.", many of them deceased—recently, within the last ten months. Sarah began opening each link.


John folded his phone and slipped it back into his jacket pocket. McMillin watched him with a faint smile, waiting, a study in patience.

"You've worked with Cyberdyne," John said.

McMillin grinned. "I wondered how long it might take you to bring that up."

"Were you going to mention it?"

"Eventually. When we began discussing my security problem."

"How about discussing that relationship with Cyberdyne, instead?"

"Why is that?" McMillin said, waving a hand for emphasis. "Concerned that at any moment a—what did you call them?—a 'Terminator' might come out of my closet and try to kill you?"

"Or worse. What would you expect me to do?"

"Oh, I don't know—something dramatic, I suppose. Take me hostage, start shooting up my staff."

"You would've taken precautions against that."

"Of course."

"You might expect that I'd know that."

"I did. I *hoped* you'd act accordingly. People are often irrational when they feel threatened."

40

"My rationality is on a short leash right now. Let's assume I could rise to extremes at any moment unless I'm given a good reason not to."

McMillin laughed. "I can see why Cruz hates you."

"Oscar Cruz? Former Cyberdyne executive?"

"Is there another who might hate you? Yes, Oscar."

"He's in prison."

"Was. Three months ago he was released. I understand some people in Washington are quite upset about it."

John heard the contempt in McMillin's voice, subdued but clear. There should have been no way for Cruz to be released. Several other minor players from Cyberdyne who had also gone to jail after the 2001 debacle that effectively closed down the company's Colorado Springs operation had been paroled, but the primary actors—Cruz, a few lab people, a number of federal employees and military people—had been buried under layers of charges and red tape, most of them in solitary confinement.

Oscar Cruz, out of prison. How had that happened?

"My late partner and myself early on established a principle that we would do no weapons research," McMillin continued. "Nothing directly for any Pentagon or Department of Defense program. Of course, it's virtually impossible to be in this business without government contracts of some kind, so we had to find ways to skirt our own ethical standards. Sounds perverse, doesn't it?"

"Sounds like life in our times. Not many people would admit to it."

"More than you might think. Honesty as a salve to a bothersome conscience." McMillin grunted. "I'd rather find ways around the problem altogether. So we're very careful what we involve ourselves with. But we're a large enterprise, as you can see. Mistakes happen. When we discover them, we try to remedy the situation."

"How successful have you been at that?"

"Depends. Fifty-fifty, maybe. Cyberdyne was a mistake. We're not doing business with them anymore—not directly."

"But someone you do work with does."

41

"It's a very incestuous field. Yes, and that's the source of the problem. I think. It could be worse than that. I'm hoping not. That's what I'd like you to find out."

"You said your 'late' partner. He committed suicide last year, didn't he?"

McMillin frowned. "I suppose that wasn't very difficult to find out. That's the official version, of course."

"Massive trauma to the brain due to a .9mm gunshot wound seems fairly conclusive. Weapon was found in his hand, in his car, pretty far out in the desert. No sign of anyone else in, around, or near the vehicle. Is there a different version?"

"For the actual death, no," McMillin admitted. "For the reasons behind it. Well..."

"Destry was responsible for the Cyberdyne project here?" John asked.

"Now that *was* a guess, wasn't it?"

"Accurate, I assume."

"Quite. Yes, he supervised the project. During the course of it, he changed. Something about it bothered him—a lot. I was never able to find out. My own cross to bear—I'm afraid I was neck-deep in other projects. By the time I realized something was seriously wrong..."

"What did you do about the project?"

"After Ian's death, I started going through it and realized fairly quickly that it was associated with Cyberdyne's Skynet program. That was top to bottom military ap, so I set about...terminating it. That has not been the easiest thing to do, as you might imagine. It cost us a lot of money, a lot of time, and reputation in certain quarters."

"I was under the impression Cyberdyne no longer had government contracts."

"It took a while, but...let's just say administrations change, and a company like Cyberdyne will always have something the government wants."

"I see. How come it wasn't obvious at the start?"

"Ian hid things. It was a materials project, new manufacturing technique for fusing metals and crystal lattices. Fairly straightforward for the most part. Sure, down the line the military could use it, they can use almost anything, but there was immense nonmilitary potential in the project. I'm sure that's what attracted Ian in the first place."

"What about it suggested military applications?"

"Lasers, specifically pulsed-plasma devices. One of the problems with them is weight—the shielding is heavy, the wear rate is enormous. To make one practical you have to make it big and, quite literally, thick. Too heavy to make a ray gun, if you catch my drift. These new techniques would've enabled an advanced approach to manufacturing that reduced the weight and increased durability. And it seems that's exactly what Cyberdyne was doing."

"I always thought Cyberdyne was strictly a computer company. More or less."

"More or less, sure, that's their primary product, but like any company of a certain size they diversify. They've had so much DoD money poured into them in the last thirty years, even with the interruption of the last few years, they've been able to do a wide range of R & D projects. In their own way, they're right up there with Lawrence-Livermore."

"So they were going to build laser guns. And when Destry found out?"

"I don't know. A number of times he seemed to want to tell me something, but he never got it out. Then one day he drove off into the desert; next I knew, he was all over the evening news. I had to go over Ian's work afterward. When I found this and looked at it closely, I started to suspect it had to do with Cyberdyne. When I understood the project, I shut it down."

"Which cost you."

"Considerably. If not for our own government affiliations, we might have gone under. As it was, we've been forced to take on a few new projects for them I'm not altogether pleased with, but at least I've got some control."

"You hope."

"No, I know. Control I have. Security is a problem."

"Before we get to that, please explain how I told you to hire me."

"That has to do with part of Ian's last project. Care to take a tour of the lab?"

John hesitated. McMillin looked disappointed.

"Please, Mr. Connor. To use a bad cliché, if I wanted to do you harm—"

"You'd have had a bitch of a time doing it, and we wouldn't be sitting here talking so nicely. But I take your point. Sure. What kind of a tour do you have in mind?"

McMillin led him down to one of the basement levels, from where they took a small electric cart down a tunnel to one of the other, working, structures. Office decor gave way to lab equipment, and men and women wearing their professionalism in their clothing became people who showed theirs in abstracted or intense expressions and the harried look that comes of odd circadians. Equipment crowded the space, hugging the walls, filling niches, cables and conduit running from one unknown point to another. The entire building seemed like one giant experiment.

McMillin pointed out labs and talked about projects along the way. He kept it basic, for which John was grateful—he possessed a rudimentary comprehension of science, better, he thought, than most people, but he knew his own limitations. McMillin, he saw, possessed intense pride in his company and the work. The veneer of joviality and corporate politesse lightly masked a profound passion.

Finally, McMillin stopped near a pair of sliding doors. Above the lintel, John read CABRERA SUPERCONDUCTOR RESEARCH.

"Do you know anything about magnetic monopoles, Mr. Connor?" McMillin asked as he climbed out of the cart.

"Philicos."

McMillin smiled, nodding. "Of course."

John stood. "No, I don't know very much about magnetic monopoles. Should I?"

"I think so. Your future may depend on them. Literally.

After you." He gestured for John to precede him through the doors.

John entered a large space filled with apparatus, computers, boxes, conduit, cables, and the jumbled, low background hum of expensive machinery. Two women huddled at a console, talking quietly as they studied an array of screens. They glanced around at McMillin and John's approach. One returned her attention to the screens, the other came forward to meet them.

"Stef," McMillin said, "I want you to meet Sean Philicos. He's going to be doing some work for me. Mr. Philicos, this is Dr. Stefani Jaspar. She runs this little project."

She extended her hand. Almost as tall as John, Dr. Jaspar had sharp, angular features, reddish-brown hair, and soft green eyes. "Pleased to meet you."

"Likewise," John said, clasping her hand.

"Tell him a bit about what we're doing here, Stef," McMillin said, then wandered over to the console to gaze at the screens with the other woman.

"In a nutshell, or do you know anything about superconductors?" Jaspar asked.

"In a nutshell, but please don't hold my ignorance against me."

She snorted quietly. "We're trying to find a way to isolate magnetic monopoles." She raised an eyebrow. "Lost yet?"

"Um...yes."

"Great. Okay, Physics 101, then. Tell me again why I'm explaining this to you?"

"Mr. McMillin suggested my future depends on it."

All at once, her expression changed. She lost the veneer of polite cynicism. She looked at him as if seeing him for the first time only now. "I see. In that case, come with me."

John followed her to a small cubicle off to the right. Within, a desk holding a large flatscreen and keyboard half filled the space, leaving barely enough room for two chairs. Jaspar gestured to one and sat down before the desk. She typed quickly, eyes on the screen, until an image came up. It showed a lattice structure comprised of balls of different colors, like a child's construction toy. In the lower left corner another box opened, this one a graph showing a slightly jagged line that jumped up to another level halfway along.

She turned to face him. "You must be John Connor."

John's irritation spiked. "Does everyone here know who I am?"

"No, just those few of us who can read Morse code. Calm down, 'Mr. Philicos'—only Dennis and myself know."

"Morse code? What—"

"Monopoles first," she said, indicating the screen. "Otherwise the rest may seem ridiculous." She frowned thoughtfully. "Though maybe not to you."

She typed on the keyboard again and another screen opened, this one displaying equations. "Recognize that?"

$$\nabla \cdot B = 0,$$
$$\nabla \times E + \partial B / \partial t = 0,$$
$$\nabla \cdot D = p$$
$$\nabla \times H - \partial D / \partial t = J.$$

"Actually, yeah," John said. "Maxwell's equations, aren't they?"

"I'm impressed. Yes. The basic ones, describing electromagnetism."

"Electricity and magnetism," John ventured. "Not quite the same thing?"

Jaspar shrugged. "The problem, you see, is right here." She tapped the second "0" and then the "J" with a fingernail. "The same fundamental equations described both electricity and magnetism, except when solved, you get nothing for magnetism and a current density for electricity. They should theoretically provide either zeroes on both or a current density on both."

"Why don't they?"

"Because in electricity, you're dealing with charged particles that come in discreet packets—plus or minus. With magnetism, you have a continuous field that doesn't break down discreetly."

"I thought north and south—"

46

"Flow. Indicates direction, not charge. If you cut a magnet in two, you don't get a north part and a south part, you get two magnets, both with north and south poles."

"But according to theory—"

"There should be discreet north and south magnetic particles. Dirac posited it in the 1930s. We should be able to derive a charge density for a magnetic monopole. It's implicit in General Relativity. We should be able to find a magnetic monopole."

"So what does this have to do with Morse code?"

"I'm getting there. Dirac said there ought to be monopoles. A lot of scientists through the twentieth century thought at one time there were, but after the initial seconds of the Big Bang there wasn't enough energy to keep them isolated, so magnetism collapsed into its present form. By this theory, electricity ought to do the same at low enough energy levels."

"Does it?"

"Sort of. That's kind of what we see in a superconductor. At low enough temperatures, electricity begins to lose its charge density. That's why magnetic fields don't interact with current flowing through a superconducting medium—which means that a superconductor should be the ideal medium to detect a magnetic monopole. Back in 1982, Blas Cabrera set up an experiment to do just that."

"And?"

"He found one."

After a pause, John asked, "Just one?"

She shrugged. "The event only happened once. It was never satisfactorily duplicated, although some exciting possibilities popped up from time to time. The trace of a passing magnetic monopole looks like this." She indicated the bottom left-hand window with the chart showing the jump in the jagged line.

"Does Cabrera work here?"

She shook her head. "This project is named for him, that's all. We think he was correct."

"But?" Despite himself, John found his interest roused.

"You've got to ask: If this is a function of higher energy levels, that if discreet magnetic poles require the temperatures present near the Big Bang, why would they collapse into a single, homogeneous field? Why not simply disappear, like a lot of exotic particles?"

"You have a theory."

"A pretty far-fetched one, yes. And you, apparently, have proved it."

"Me."

She indicated the large image on the screen. "We've been playing with different types of superconductors, seeing if one energy level is better suited than the others to detect monopoles. The one we've found that seems to work best is a niobium-titanium alloy. Transition temperature is low, but not as low as, say, mercury. At $10°$ Kelvin we can set up our experiment and start monitoring for monopole events."

"Why would this be better than any other?"

"The cooper pairs seem to be more stable. It's a small factor, but..." She typed, lost briefly in concentration. John wanted to ask what a cooper pair was, but he felt overwhelmed as it was, which added to his annoyance. Beyond the cubicle, he saw McMillin still talking to the other woman out in the main lab. He was about to interrupt when Jaspar continued. "We started running the experiment six months ago. For four months, two weeks, we found nothing. Odd fluctuations here and there we discounted as aberrations produced by flaws in the equipment or quantum flux variations. Nothing solid. Then we started receiving spikes."

"Like the one you mentioned? Cabrera's?"

"The same type, but a lot more of them, continuously. Look."

Now on the screen John saw several graphs like the Cabrera one. But the energy jumps came in bunches—up, down, pause, more. It looked sort of like...he could not say. Familiar.

"I said I had a far-fetched theory about magnetism, why it manifests the way it does," Jaspar said. "It has to do with

48

the way our universe formed. When we study subatomic interactions, we see how the physical components of the world combine to form substance—matter and all that implies. At one time, everything looked different because all the forces were combined into a single superforce, right before and maybe shortly after the Big Bang. Aside from fossil evidence, we don't really have a physical model of how time interacts with everything else. But I think that when we see a magnetic field interacting with an electrical current, or with anything else for that matter, we're seeing a manifestation of time as a property of existence. The fingerprint of time, if you will."

John stared at her for a long time, then shifted his gaze to the screen. "If I'm following you at all, you're suggesting that these monopoles you've been hunting...what?"

"These," she tapped the screen, "came from the future. We received them about two weeks ago. I think monopoles are indicators of time travel."

"How do you know these came from the future?"

"Because—" She laughed self-consciously, and blushed slightly. "Dennis recognized the pattern first. He was in the navy. These are patterned manifestations. A code. Morse code."

John recognized it now. He felt his face grow warm, even as his stomach and chest cooled. "The monopoles are coming back in modulated groups, spaced out to spike in code...?"

"And apparently," Jaspar finished, "it's from someone claiming to be John Connor. Would you care to explain that?"

# FIVE

The old man stepped through the wide doors of the Lighthouse Mission, attracting little notice. He stood at one end of a long room. Chairs, occupied by perhaps a dozen people—mostly men, wearing worn clothes and weary expressions—lined the outside wall, opposite a long service counter behind which a few somewhat better dressed people worked. The smell of disinfectant cut through the mingled odors of sweat and soup stock.

"Can I help you?"

He looked toward the counter. A woman leaned over it, watching him. He stepped up to her, lowering the bindle from his shoulder and setting it on the floor. "Yes, I—do you have regulars here?"

"A few," she answered. She wore a plastic nametag: NORENE. She looked pointedly at the box beneath his arm.

"Do you keep records? Or—"

"Not for public scrutiny, no," she said curtly. "You looking for a friend?"

"Maybe. I wondered if you could tell me if you have someone named Lee Portis who stays here?"

"Used to. Haven't seen him in a couple months." She frowned. "Why?"

"I found this," he said, sliding the box onto the counter. "There was an address, but..."

He let the sentence fade and waited for her to pick it up.

He made a show of looking around and spotted a calendar on the wall to the left. March 2007, he noted, feeling oddly relieved.

She drew the box toward her, hesitated, then opened it. She shuffled through the collection for several seconds before looking up at the old man again. "Where did you find this?"

"Um...trash bin, out by the base."

She frowned for a moment, then nodded. "Cannon. He used to be stationed there. Long time ago." She closed the box. "How'd you come to be out there?"

"It's a long story. But I'm here now."

She looked skeptical. "You wouldn't happen to know what became of the man this belonged to?"

He shook his head. As she considered, he moved a small colony of nanocoders to the palms of his hands. He had not remembered he could do this till just then, necessity opening the appropriate file.

"Well, we're used to not asking too many questions. Why'd you bring this here?"

"I thought—well, maybe you have a stash for regulars, and—I figured I needed a place to stay myself, for a while, anyway, and—"

"And this would be a nice gesture to make us give you the benefit. Yeah, I get it. But you might want to just introduce yourself and say you need help."

She slid the box off the counter and took it back to a series of metal shelves that seemed overfilled with mail and boxes and clothing and books and bags. As he watched, she managed to find a space for Lee Portis's box. Then she returned to the counter. "So?"

He extended a hand. "So..." She clasped his hand. In a few moments, he recognized the change in her eyes as he transferred the 'coders through her skin. "Norene, I'm Lee Portis. And I need your help."

"Of course, Mr. Portis. Whatever I can do to help."

She gave him a bed with a footlocker, which contained

blankets and pillows. Several beds contained occupants, even at this early hour. The long room looked like a recent edition to the sprawling facility, the floor still shiny and unscuffed, walls covered in unscarred wood-grain paneling, all the beds squared up and brightly painted, clean sheets tucked over firm mattresses.

"Is there work?" Portis asked. "I'm going to need money."

"We can put you on part-time here," Norene said. "Doesn't pay a lot, but you can buy clothes in our thrift."

"That would be good to start. I suppose I'll need something better to wear. Do you have a computer with an Internet connection?"

"Plenty," she grunted. "Last administration wasn't too generous with money, but computers, sure. Do you need to use it in private?"

"That would be best. Could you help me? I'm not familiar with your data systems."

"You been out of touch that long? Certainly, I'll help. Now, the showers are right through there. Towels in the lockers to your right as you go through the door. We serve two meals a day in the main cafeteria, just through there and down the corridor. If in doubt, follow your nose, cook likes to go heavy on oregano and chili powder. After you get cleaned up and settled in, come find me. I'll get you some work togs and a meal, and go over a schedule with you."

"Thank you."

Portis watched Norene until she had left the room. He sat down on the bed. Despite himself, he was grateful—the mattress felt good. One of the other guests snored briefly, then grunted angrily before lapsing into silence again.

The 'coders with which Portis had infected Norene would only last a few days. Safety barred him from reinforcing them with another exchange—how they might affect a completely unmodified human brain was a question. One-time use only. So he needed to act quickly. He sat on his bed, folded his legs beneath him, and closed his eyes, sorting through options silently until he chose a path.

Satisfied, he went to the showers.

He stood beneath the thick spray of hot water longer, perhaps, than polite, but it felt so good. He closed his eyes and let it cascade over his body. The wear of his trip suddenly manifested, even as it seemed to flow with the water down the drain at his feet.

*I've come a far distance,* he thought. *Farther than possible by any sane reckoning...*

He dried himself and returned to the dormitory. On his bed he found a set of off-white coveralls and a pair of work boots. Clothed, he went to the cafeteria. The air was pungent with spices and the smell of cooked meat. Few people sat at the long tables, eating from bowls or plates on plastic trays. Most sat alone.

A pair of men entered from the opposite door. Portis watched them go to one end of a railed-off path before the long steel counter behind which the food was being prepared. They each took a tray and walked along, servers handing them plates and bowls as they went. Portis did the same.

Tray filled, he found a table from where he could watch everyone in the cafeteria. As he ate, he noted the differences between these people, between the guests and the hosts, between those who depended on what they found here and those who offered it.

"Good, you found the togs," Norene said, coming up behind him.

"Yes. The boots fit."

"I've acquired a good eye for that, working here. May I sit?"

"Of course."

She took the chair opposite him, folded her hands on the table, and smiled pleasantly. "How's the food?"

"Good."

"You're hungry. 'Good' wears off after you get your fill, but thank you. So what kind of help do you need, Lee?"

"I need to become a respectable citizen. I'm not sure what is necessary to do that."

Norene looked thoughtful. "Well, proper ID, for one thing. Better clothes and a bank account, some credit cards, and an address other than a soup kitchen."

"How do I go about getting these things?"

"Start by earning some money here—"

"I have a limited amount of time. Sooner than later would be helpful."

"Ah. Well, finish your food and I'll take you to my office. We'll see what we can do online."

"That would be fine, Norene. Thank you."

"No problem. So. Where are you from originally?"

"The future."

She looked at him blankly until he smiled. Then she laughed. "Sure. Does the future have a P.O. Box?"

"I am from Santa Fe originally."

"What happened that landed you here?"

"A conflict. A threat. It became necessary to leave."

"Domestic stuff. I see. I won't pry. We don't pry here. Everybody has problems, some more so than others. When you get on your feet, what are your plans?"

"Eventually, I think I will have to go to Los Angeles. For now..."

"For now, one thing at a time. Sure. Look, I'll let you finish in peace. You ask anybody where my office is and come see me when you're done." She stood. "I'm glad you came here, Lee."

"I am, too, Norene. Thank you."

He watched her as she stopped to talk to the other men in the cafeteria. She sat with none of them and only spoke a few words, but they all smiled, happy to see her. Portis resolved to get out of her life as quickly as he could. He wanted no harm to come to someone who brought happiness to those with so little.

He finished the roast beef and potatoes and vegetables and the small bowl of pudding. He was still hungry, but he sensed that it would be rude to ask for more. He set the tray and plates where he saw others being placed, then followed after Norene. He did not need to ask where she went, he picked up her scent easily and followed the trail.

The sign on her door read NORENE BAXTER, ADMINISTRATOR. Portis knocked lightly.

"Come in."

The small office contained more than seemed possible. File cabinets lined the wall below the single window, which framed stained glass objects and feathery devices Portis knew—remembered—were called dreamcatchers. Norene sat before an enormous desk on which a large flatscreen stood flanked by books, file folders, stacks of papers, boxes of floppy discs, and assorted bric-a-brac. A small sofa against the wall behind her was filled with files, paperwork, and cartons. On the wall above hung pictures and a few framed documents.

"Lee, welcome," Norene said. "Forgive the clutter. There's never enough time to do the job and make it look neat besides. Here, have a seat."

She lifted a briefcase from a chair. Portis sat down, gaze drifting across the assorted objects.

"You have no help?" he asked.

"Not regular, not reliable. We get a lot of state aid and a little federal, all those forms have to be filled out just right. Then there are the state Medicare and Medicaid requirements, so our 'special cases'—residents with state care status who end up in a place like this because the state doesn't have enough beds this month or they're not quite bad enough to keep off the streets or—" She sighed. "Anyway, no, to answer your question, I don't have any help—at least, not enough. Most of the people working here are volunteers. They mean well, but they don't exactly bring many special skills to the task. Don't get me wrong, we couldn't manage without them. It's just, once in a while, I'd be grateful for a professional office manager on staff." She straightened in her chair. "So. What can I do for you, Lee?"

He thought for a few seconds. "I suppose I need a valid identity. How do we start?"

55

"Well, your name is Lee Portis. Let's start with the Social Security Administration. Sound good?"

"You know better than I."

She smiled and began typing on her keyboard. The screen cleared. Moments later, an official-looking emblem appeared.

"Do you have any kind of ID right now?" she asked.

Portis fished the driver's license from his pocket.

She studied it for a time, frowning. "That doesn't look like you at all," she said finally. "We can fix that." She set the license on the desk above the keyboard and continued working.

Portis looked around at the clutter. "If you wish, I can help you with all this. It would be a privilege."

Norene's face showed disbelief and then joy. "Could you?"

"I would be happy to do what I could."

"Great. Let's see about getting this taken care of first. Then I can show you what needs to be done."

After his daily cleaning, cooking, and front counter duties, he worked late into the night, every evening, for four days. He went through all the files, sorted out dead jackets from active, cleared space for new ones, then purged dated or useless material from everything. As he did, he read their contents. After Norene showed him the basics, he learned rapidly, and by the second night he knew the system. He improved it, streamlining procedures for her, and by sleepless main assault straightened up her office. On the third day, he began accessing the Internet to check current protocols against the work on hand, and found several instances in which Norene could have improved the overall status of the mission. It was, he concluded, too much work for a single human—an unmodified human, at least.

As he worked, he acquired a knowledge base: personal histories, bureaucratic procedures, a rough outline of how things worked in this time and place. Filling out forms online, working through the available public service networks, making the appropriate connections, Portis gained expertise in navigating the system at large. When, on the fourth day, his new identity came through—newly-minted social security card, with the amended changes in his personal profile—he understood well enough how to use it to change his circumstances.

By then, the nanocoders with which he had infected Norene began to decay. She emerged from the artificially created cocoon of trust to find that, indeed, she liked Lee Portis and depended on him. He could tell that the transition troubled her. Occasionally he caught her watching him, a bemused expression on her face, as if wondering where he had come from and how he had come to be so important to her. But he talked to her, showed her what he had done, and by the time she no longer saw him through the filters of his 'coders she trusted him.

He dressed better. He raided the thrift shop and put away the work togs for slacks and a flannel shirt, loafers, and windbreaker. He kept his eye on what came in until he salvaged a couple of suits, a few pairs of jeans, pullover shirts, and a decent pair of tennis shoes. All this he kept in Norene's office.

On the fifth night he began exploring ways to improve the other parts of his new life. He ran through employment ads, sorting possibilities that would get him where he needed to be to further his search. While he conducted this search, he created a small program to start searching the web for references to his target, Jeremiah Porter. When it began bringing him obituaries, Portis grew concerned, but as he read through them he realized that though many of the deaths were related—coincidence could not account for so many deaths in so short a time—none yet had been his target. There was time. Not much, but maybe enough.

On the sixth day he had chosen a vector. A university position of some kind would best enable his search. He finished the reorganization of the mission, went over his changes with Norene, then started making the necessary changes to leave Lighthouse and move into the outside community.

He needed money. On the tenth day, he borrowed a small amount from the mission expense account—which, due to his work, was now growing rather than shrinking—and opened an account at a savings and loan, then took a post office box. After that, he spent several hours "adjusting" the credit history of Lee Portis. He had to be careful not to attract unwanted scrutiny, so the adjustments were small.

He found his way into the IRS database and the unclaimed refund accounts. By carefully backdating various records, filing new updates, and modifying the ancillary data, he managed to get a sum of fallow tax money rebated to him. He had the funds transferred electronically to his savings and loan account, whereupon he returned what he had borrowed from the mission. He closed the account then, and moved it to a bank. He opened the new account with a revised social security number, then went into that database to make the changes. One digit and the homeless man whose identity he had been using had his back, and a new entity named Lee Portis entered the world.

With that, he began acquiring more ID. In this world, it seemed, one was what the cards in one's wallet said one was.

Over the next few days, he applied for a number of credit cards. The monitoring systems of several rejected the application, but he still received four, with modest credit limits. He searched for an apartment. He made two more visits to the unclaimed refund account, judging that one more would trip the alarms. When he finished, there was over fifteen thousand dollars in his bank account. He closed it and moved to still another bank, opening another new account with the new social security number, and sending a letter of introduction to the vice president of the institution introducing himself.

Fifteen days after he entered the Lighthouse Mission, Lee Portis packed a single suitcase and left. Norene hugged him, tearful, and he reassured her that she could call him whenever she might need more help. As soon as he settled in to his new life, he would let her know.

He walked away, intending never to go back. It was safer that way, though vaguely it bothered him. He felt uneasy betraying a trust.

*A conscience,* he thought. *Who'd have guessed?*

# SIX

John pulled up in front of their new building, parking just behind one of Ken Lash's trucks. Two of Lash's people stood outside the front door, smoking. They greeted John as he walked past them.

John stepped through the door. Eight people in jeans, painter's pants, and T-shirts worked in various sections of the space, putting up walls, running cable, installing electronic gear. Desks already stood around. A pile of office furniture huddled toward the back. Hammers, saws, drills filled the air with industrious noise and the smell of sawdust. He walked toward the rear, past workers who paid him no attention. John knew almost none of their names—security—but this was the fourth, no, fifth time they had done this kind of work for Sarah and him.

Ken Lash stood in the open doorway to the alley. A compact man, he wore a short beard sprinkled with gray. He might have been thirty or fifty, John could never tell. Now he stood, legs slightly apart, pointing at something up on the outside wall, and giving quiet instructions to two of his people, who nodded in silence. John always found it difficult to believe that Lash was anything but what he seemed to be: a general contractor running a modest but profitable construction business. He was very good at maintaining his cover.

John waited while Lash finished with his people.

"Mr. Philicos," Lash said then. "Good to see you."

"Call me Sean, Ken."

Lash smiled noncommittally, and John knew he would not.

"I feel funny you calling me 'Mister.'"

"Yes, sir."

John sighed. "How's it going?"

"We'll have you up and running in a couple of days. The furniture showed up earlier than expected, but we're working around it. We're modifying the phone connections to run a T4 line. Main problem was getting the permits for the extra electrical lines, but the Office straightened it out. One thing, we've installed a new monitoring net. It covers the walls and floor sandwiched in the insulation. Once activated, it'll protect against any surveillance. Somebody wants to know what you're doing in here, they'll have to physically enter the premises and find a place to hide and just listen."

Lash led John back into the building and continued pointing out what had been done so far, and what had yet to be done. John listened, impressed as always. They made the work Sarah and John did much easier, but Lash's niceties were designed to counter a threat that had not appeared since the Connors had returned to this world.

"Any problems with the neighborhood?" John asked finally.

"No, sir. Although I wondered why you chose this location."

"This is L.A. We didn't want to send up a flag. Keep it low key."

Lash said nothing, but John noticed his skeptical look. The story, he had to admit, was a bit lame, but the truth would be harder to explain. John did not entirely understand the choice himself, but he knew Sarah. When she made up her mind, it served no purpose to argue.

*Maybe her instincts are better than we know,* he thought, thinking of the meeting with McMillin.

"Sounds good," John said when Lash finally wound down the tour. "Let me know when we've got the secure line to D.C. My mother upstairs?"

"Last I saw," Lash said.

John headed for the stairs.

All the upstairs windows were open. He found Sarah on the sofa, watching a news channel, chewing on the end of a pen, legal pad beside her. She looked at him when he entered the room.

Simultaneously, they both said, "We may have a problem."

They stared at each other for an awkward moment. John laughed first.

"You start," Sarah said. She touched the remote, shutting off the TV.

John took a sheaf of papers from his jacket pocket and handed them to her, then shrugged out of his coat and sat down beside her. "I seem to have sent myself a message, and Destry-McMillin is the mailbox. I don't pretend to understand all the physics, and before I left there I really missed Roseanne and Jade, but it comes down to this: Skynet still exists, somewhere. But it may have a finite lifespan. We don't know."

"You mean it can be destroyed."

"No, I mean it has a natural lifespan—if 'natural' is a term you can apply to something that's wholly artificial. It can die of—damn, the language just doesn't work for this—it can stop existing over time. Just die. Sort of like old age."

"I hear an 'unless' in that."

John leaned forward, struggling with the explanation. "If I understood myself correctly, Skynet's awareness is a consequence of time travel. That's why it's been able to jump across dimensions, use time the way it does, because its very nature spans a certain time."

Sarah frowned. "I'm not sure I follow."

"I'm not sure I do, either. But the catch is, there's a natural boundary to it, like a...a parentheses in time, past and future, called a Cauchy Horizon. See, according to theory,

62

time travel can't reach into a time where no time machine exists. You have to build one first before visitors from the future can come back."

Sarah grunted. "Bullshit. Who built a time machine in 1984?"

"Good question. And I asked. Seems it can happen as a side effect of a certain kind of physics—high energy, large particle physics. We've been playing around with that for decades."

"But—"

"I said I didn't understand all the physics. I didn't understand a tenth of it. If we hadn't been through all that we've been through, I wouldn't have known they were even speaking English, okay?"

"Sorry. Go on."

"The cone of time, the period in which time travel in both directions is possible, mirrors itself. Picture two ice cream cones—"

"The pointy kind?"

"—yeah, the pointy kind. Point to point, okay? Each open end represents the boundary. Beyond either point, time travel can't happen. Now, the trick is that every time you send someone back, you might establish a new boundary."

"So the future boundary can get extended."

"Right. But they're not sure about that."

As much time-hopping and dimension-dancing as they did, John still fumbled the language. The chronology had long since lost any kind of linear logic and turned into a single, infinite strand of spaghetti, piled in on itself in a hopeless tangle. He could not even be sure which "him" had sent this message: his forty-something self who led the resistance to victory against Skynet in 2029, or the teenager who had gone to join the fight, only to begin a cross dimension quest chasing Skynet down as it fled from world to world. They had no way of knowing if various aspects of themselves had calved off when the shifts occurred, shadows remaining behind to linger in timelines that may or may not persist.

"Anyway," John continued, "the idea is that, after I destroy the time vault in 2029, the future boundary is closed off. But Skynet can use time travel freely at any point before that."

"And do what?"

"Try to establish a new boundary."

"How?"

"Building a new time machine."

Sarah closed her eyes. "Wait. Wouldn't Cyberdyne's time vault qualify as a new time machine and establish a new—what did you call it—boundary?"

"Sure, but we destroyed that one in 2029, along with Skynet in that timeline. What Skynet needs to have happen is for another one, somewhere else, to be built—"

"Cyberdyne can't build it?"

"Sure they can, if they had someone who could do the work."

"Another Rosanna Monk."

"Right."

"And is there a candidate for this new Monk?"

"According to me," John said with a smirk, "we need to find someone named Jeremiah Porter."

Sarah let her head fall back. She gazed at the ceiling for a long time.

"Do you trust these people?" she asked finally.

"At Destry-McMillin? Not sure. But there's no love lost between them and Cyberdyne."

"Either way, we probably should get on this." She straightened, picking up the legal pad. "Someone has been killing every Jeremiah Porter they can find. Here."

John took the pad. Sarah's cramped handwriting filled several pages—dates and places, some with notes about cause of death.

"All," she said, "within the last year."

"You've seen this pattern before, haven't you?"

"Just change the name to Sarah Connor and this looks like a repeat of 1984. Except for the range. This covers more than L.A."

"You think they're related."

"A third of them are mathematicians or physicists or high-tech engineers. You tell me."

"But...if Skynet needs this guy to build a new time machine..."

"Why are they being killed? Good question. Let's answer that one later. For now, we need to find this guy. The right one."

"You're assuming he's not one of these?"

"The killings go on. You tell me."

Sarah picked up the remote. The television came back on. CNN was talking about the upcoming hurricane season.

Sarah looked over the list. Twenty-two names so far, most Jeremiah Porters, from all over the country. She hesitated to check overseas databases. Killings that wide spread would suggest Terminators all over the planet. Always a possibility.

The ones not exactly Jeremiah were variations—Gerald, Gerard, Jerry—but related in other ways. Professions ranged from a teacher to a project head at a high-energy research lab on the east coast, from engineers to logicians. All of them occupied positions dealing with abstruse areas of math, particle physics, or formal logic. Sarah did not see how logic might pose any kind of threat, but a few of them had written papers involving kindred mathematical explorations—at least, as far as she could tell. John had a better grasp of such matters, but both of them missed the expertise of the Specialists. Even Roseanne Monk would be helpful now.

But they were all gone. Sarah and John had come home alone. They were more or less on their own.

*Not quite,* she thought wryly. *There's Jack...*

Jack Reed. And Samantha Jones. Sarah wondered, often, just how far they could be trusted. But John seemed comfortable with the arrangement, at least insofar as their commitment to help.

The hardest part for Sarah was the fact that Cyberdyne still existed. Reed had promised to take care of that. When

John and she returned, three years ago, they found a world in which Cyberdyne thrived, albeit at a reduced level. No Skynet. No Department of Defense contracts, they learned. But still there. Still doing research in many of the same areas that had nearly brought about Armageddon before. Still trying to build Skynet.

*And succeeding, if what I'm seeing is what I think it is...*

Just as in 1984, a Terminator was systematically murdering people—this time Jeremiah Porters. That was what it looked like, at least. One Terminator or more. She hoped only one, but she could not be sure. In 1984, she had been the target, but several Sarah Connors had died. Skynet, far in the future, could not be sure which Sarah Connor posed the eventual threat that would bring it down, so the Terminator came back programmed to kill all the Sarahs in L.A. Thorough. Cold-blooded, but thorough.

*No blooded.*

On the other hand, this could be coincidence. She scanned the list, checking ages, and many of them were over sixty. That might reassure her, except for those who had died violently: three motor accidents, one hunting accident, two suicides, and one accidental electrocution. The most recent death had occurred four days ago, in San Bernardino. Much as she wanted to believe this to be a string of unfortunate coincidences, Sarah chose to think the worst. Safer that way.

And now this thing with Destry-McMillin and a message from the future.

Why a message? Why not a messenger, like the other times?

John seemed convinced.

Whatever the case, Sarah agreed, they needed to find Jeremiah Porter—*the* Jeremiah Porter, a specific one. She looked over at her son at the kitchen table, attention focused on the computer screen, right hand resting on the mouse. *Needle-in-a-haystack time,* she thought. *I'm so tired...tired of being afraid...*

From below came the muffled noise of construction.

Sarah set the list aside, closing her eyes. The world had been making a modest kind of sense lately. Oh, well.

John rubbed his eyes. The windows showed the harsh orange of the streetlights. Ken Lash's people still worked downstairs. Tomorrow they would start up here, first with new windows—bulletproof, to be sure, but more immediately important, polarizing. Sarah would have to give up leaving the windows open.

His head buzzed with too much information—and not enough comprehension. Stefani Jaspar's explanations notwithstanding, the material tested his limits. She was good at breaking complex ideas down nearly to a layman's level, but the fact remained that time travel was too much to fit into anything that made sense.

He looked over the list of names. It would be good to tackle something he understood.

*Who is Jeremiah Porter, and why is he so important to me?*

He had long since grown used to thinking of himself as more than one person. Future self—*selves*—present self, parallel selves. Sarah and he had been "home" for three years now, and nothing had happened. But there had been lulls before. Just when it seemed that Armageddon had been canceled, time intruded again.

This time would be different. No more running. The future wanted to hurt them, try to kill them. This time they would get there first.

John closed down the computer. The list contained eight names, all within the Los Angeles area. Four others were already dead. The problem was how to tell which one was the important one. He could tell only so much from the little available on the Internet. He discounted three of the names immediately: one was over eighty and in a hospice; one worked for the county highway department; one was a cook at a small Hungarian restaurant. Not the sort of people likely to impact Skynet.

Today had been the first time in three years he had heard

any word of Skynet. He wondered how Cyberdyne could possibly have the capacity to build it—and for whom? Jack Reed and his assistant, Samantha Jones, had shut down their government contracts, at least till recently. He wondered who had gotten around Reed and Jones and resurrected the federal connection. And why had Reed failed to tell him? DoD money. The Pentagon had been hot to have Skynet back in the '90s, but after 2001 it seemed like a dead end. True, they were still a big, vital corporation, diversified, with branches in other countries. Nevertheless, John found it hard to believe that they could reconstruct the Skynet project. Their research staff, after the incidents in 1997 and 2001, suffered the loss of several top people unwilling to work with the possibility of future catastrophes. And with Miles Dyson, head of the original project dead, and Rosanna Monk, his successor, missing, few could follow the extremely complex and abstruse theories underlying the nanoprocessor and time vault. The death of Cyberdyne's CEO, Charles Layton, left the company with an aura like a curse. His replacement, a man named Oakley, seemed no more dangerous or enigmatic than any other CEO. Outwardly, Cyberdyne looked like just another big tech firm, larger than most, but no more a threat, either.

And yet the project continued. The evidence was circumstantial—McMillin's suspicions of industrial espionage could be no more than one company stealing secrets from another to improve the bottom line—but John believed that Cyberdyne, and through it Skynet, was still working to bring about Armageddon.

Skynet still loomed in their future.

Somehow, a man named Jeremiah Porter was pivotal. And someone was killing Jeremiah Porters across the country.

Why?

To find out, he needed to talk to him. The one. The Porter he had sent himself the message about.

The message itself had been enigmatic, almost cryptic. A copy lay on the table beside the keyboard.

MESSAGE TO SELF/JOHN CONNOR/VERFIY BY NAMES AP-
PENDED/YOU-I MUST FIND JEREMIAH PORTER/MATHEM-
ATICIAN-EQUIVALENT TO MONK/LOCATION UNKNOWN/ES-
SENTIAL TO TIME STREAM/SKYNET ATTEMPTING TO LOC-
ATE-TERMINATE/PORTER NECESSARY TO RESISTANCE/THE
FIGHT CONTINUES.

There was a space and then a string of names: SALCEDA
TAJEDA ANTON JADE DANNY and so on, ending with three
names that convinced John that he had sent the message
himself, from the future: David Lawes, Deborah Lawes, and
Kyle Reese. The first two had been the Connors' pseudonyms
in Mexico, back in '01.

Kyle Reese was his mother's lover, the man who had
saved her from the first Terminator.

His father.

Jeremiah Porter. Mathematician. John understood enough
math because of Jade and Roseanna Monk to realize how
much he did not understand. What he had seen today at
Destry-McMillin had stretched him way beyond his limits.
But he recognized some of the functions from Roseanna's
time vault work.

So this Porter character was supposed to be her equal.
Impressive. But he would have Monk's vault in the
future—as would Skynet. There was already a time machine.
Why would another time travel expert be necessary?

*Because everything is still fluid...*

John checked the time. Eleven-twenty. He sighed.

"Where do we start?"

He looked up. Sarah leaned against the woodwork that
marked the boundary between this room and the next,
holding a cup of coffee. She appeared calm, but he knew
better. She felt it just like he did.

"I need to see these people at Pioneer Kelvin," John said.
"That's the company McMillin thinks is giving Cyberdyne

access to Destry-McMillin material. Why don't you start tracking down these Porters?"

"Sounds like a plan. You should get some sleep."

"You first."

She smiled thinly. "It's always the first thing I do."

"Right."

"How soon before the secure line is in?"

"Tomorrow, I think." He listened to muffled sounds of work from below. "We've slept through worse, I guess."

"Go to bed," she said. "Tomorrow it starts."

"Again."

Sarah nodded wearily. "Again."

# SEVEN

$M$r. Casse opened his eyes when he heard the office door snick shut. Standing before his desk, two men waited, both dressed in expensive suits, hands folded respectfully in front. They were different kinds of men in many ways: one pale, one dark; one thickly-muscled, the other lithe; one never smiled, the other...But it had taken Casse a long time to see those differences. Their similarity overwhelmed everything else, as far as he was concerned.

"And?" he said.

The pale one tilted his head to one side. "The Spokane Porter is terminated. We have a location on one other possibility in Eugene. Our contacts there are investigating."

"Good. How was Spokane done?"

"Our research turned up the fact that he was a diabetic," the pale one said. "We arranged an air bubble in his insulin injection. Embolism."

Casse preferred it this way, the appearance of natural causes or accident. Violence produced questions. So far, no inquiry had come back to him. These two killers were getting better at guaranteeing that nothing looked suspicious enough for a thorough investigation to begin. Eventually, he knew, someone would start making connections. He intended to be finished before that happened.

"What about the Midwest?" he asked.

"There are several possibles," the dark one said. "We've narrowed it down to seven probables, per your parameters."

"Most likely?"

"One in Phoenix, one in Santa Fe."

"See to them. I'm looking into a few in Los Angeles. I want you both to be ready at my call."

Of all the humans he had dealt with since arriving, Casse found these two easiest and most comprehensible. Their needs were simple to nonexistent, at least as far as he was concerned. He did not know if they actually enjoyed killing, but it never bothered them the way it did most humans. They kept perspective, never seemed to lose their grasp on the job.

He waved his hand. "Go on. Keep me informed."

The two men nodded politely and left.

The intercom buzzed. He touched the ACCEPT button. "Yes?"

"Mr. Cruz is here to see you, sir."

"Send him."

Oscar Cruz strode through the door, slowing as he neared the desk, glancing uneasily over its broad surface before stopping a meter away and looking up at Casse. A series of expressions flickered over Cruz's puffy face before settling into its normal obsequious mask. Casse found him substandard among the humans he used. He questioned too much, more and more as time passed, but he continued to work in the best interest of Skynet. For now, he was valuable. Casse did not think he would continue so for much longer.

"Yes?" he asked.

"McMillin has hired an independent investigator to look into Pioneer," Cruz said.

"Will this investigator find anything?"

"Possibly. We aren't finished with Pioneer. McMillin has successfully blocked all our intrusions. It seems he's in the mood to retaliate."

"How did he determine that Pioneer was being used as a back door into Destry-McMillin?"

Cruz shrugged. "Can't say. He probably guessed. Dennis McMillin is pretty shrewd."

Casse considered. Of all the problems humans presented, intuition produced the most trouble. He did not understand how they made the conceptual leaps they did with so limited a tool as an organic brain. He realized that his assessment of that tool was flawed, that the problem was not so much that humans possessed an ability beyond comprehension as that he had failed to fully comprehend them.

"What investigator?" he asked.

"An outfit from Santa Fe, actually. PPS Security. They do consultation and assessment work for businesses, provide security in certain cases. Mostly they're analysts and advisors."

"Successful?"

"From what I could find out, very low failure rate."

"So they will just look. They have no law enforcement brief?"

"No, not beyond the usual private investigation licenses and so forth."

"Who are they? The people."

"Sean and Julia Philicos are the principals. The 'S' is a Jen Salceda. They've been slowly branching out since they began three years ago—offices in Santa Fe, Albuquerque, Colorado Springs, Denver, and now one in Los Angeles."

"What did they do before?"

"Sean was in the army, then worked for two other security companies before starting his own. Julia was a broker. Salceda has a degree in computer science, just out of college."

Casse waited. When Cruz remained silent for several seconds, he said, "And?"

"That's about it. School records, dates of birth, and so forth. Nothing unusual."

"That does not strike you as unusual?"

Cruz waited.

"In my experience," Casse continued, "humans do not go into this kind of work as they would take a job in a factory or a bank. They are unusual in their life experiences."

"I've hired many people of this sort," Cruz said. "As interesting as their life stories might be, they're almost always ordinary, unremarkable. Some are misfits, most find they have a flare for this kind of work. A lot of them are ex-police of one kind or another."

"What category do these particular ones fit? It would be good to know, don't you think? Just to have some idea what to expect?"

"You would like more information?"

"Yes. Especially now that they have an office in Los Angeles *and* Colorado Springs. I find that an interesting coincidence. Half their offices are in areas connected to our interests."

Cruz shook his head. "That's a bit paranoid, if you don't mind my saying so. A lot of companies have offices in those areas. They're following the money."

"Perhaps. If so, I want to know. Now. Status report?"

Cruz's posture changed. He seemed to become more respectful, his concentration more evident. "Since finalizing the contracts on the Los Angeles base, I've authorized the transfer of equipment out of our Colorado Springs facility, back to Los Angeles. Our people are already inside the plant, starting on the necessary changes to receive components. We should be able to move all our nanoprocessor work there by month's end."

"Good. We are ahead of schedule, then?"

"By a good three months. Our contact in DoD performed better than anticipated."

"So all we need to do is find staff of adequate caliber."

"We're continuing to interview and vette."

Casse watched Cruz. The man seemed focused now. He was on solid ground with this part of the project. Since his release from prison, there were days he lost concentration, appeared erratic. Casse wondered if the programming, still in place, from the TX-A that had nearly brought Skynet to fruition in Colorado Springs six years ago, might be eroding faster. Before his own transfer to this frame, Casse had seen no evidence that this could happen, but the tests had not gone on long enough. A few test subjects had been deployed to spy on the Resistance; most had been kept on by Skynet as necessary tools in the time transfer program. Since his arrival here, though, Casse had seen the data on the long-term effects of nanoware infection on humans: inconclusive, but very suggestive.

He could only speculate and he distrusted conclusions based solely on speculation. The fact remained, he did not know. Not knowing handicapped him. It seemed Cruz's programming slipped from time to time. The nanoware seemed to be toxic to the organic material over time. Perhaps his stay in a federal prison, in company with so many humans and no contact with others like himself, had triggered a reassessment. Rosanna Monk had betrayed them, apparently while still programmed. There was a potential that the individual will could reassert itself under the proper conditions, that even while the revulsion of humanity produced by the nanoware programming did not change, the individual could *think* its way to an independent state of mind.

But Monk had been a formidable intellect. Casse did not see that in Cruz's case.

He assessed Cruz's importance. How much did Cyberdyne—Skynet—need this one? Cruz was an excellent administrator. He possessed skills at getting people to work with him and with each other. Interdepartmental rivalries faded when Oscar Cruz took a hand in resolving them. Before going to prison, he had been an invaluable resource in public relations—he knew how to handle the press, how to put the best face on crises, how to minimize public reaction. He did not do that now. His duties, since returning to Cyberdyne, were all internal to the company.

Acquiring the mothballed Air Force base in Los Angeles had been entirely his achievement. Certainly that demonstrated his commitment. Any number of opportunities had arisen for him to betray Skynet.

Still, Casse had doubts.

"These new investigators McMillin has hired," Casse said. "Do you regard them as a significant threat?"

"No. McMillin is guessing, and the conduit to Pioneer has been closed down."

"Even so, I want them dealt with."

"How? You don't mean kill them."

"Does that idea bother you?"

Cruz scowled. "It could draw unwanted attention. In my experience, overreacting to something like this is worse than doing nothing. Reaction gives them a target."

"Logical. In that case, watch them, prepare a team to terminate them. Should they become more than a possible threat, I want them dealt with."

"Consider it done."

"Good. I want daily updates on our transfer back to Los Angeles."

"Yes, sir."

Casse watched Cruz leave his office, still unsure he had done the appropriate thing. Uncertainty muddied his thinking. In the quarter century he had existed in this frame, watching, learning, waiting till it became necessary for him to intervene, he had grappled with this problem of assessing humans. He was probably as good at it as any Terminator could be, but they still eluded his full understanding. Annoying.

He closed his eyes briefly and reviewed his itinerary. Next week, the interview with the student from Caltech, Robert Porter. A formality. His cousin had been one of the first Jeremiah Porters Casse had dealt with. He still had a nagging question about that one. The job had been handled by people he no longer employed. They had bungled a number of their assignments, and Casse had been forced to cover the same ground with new people. But in the case of that Jeremiah Porter, they had apparently succeeded. The target, at least, had never resurfaced.

The cousin, though, young Robert—"Bobby" to his friends—was a mathematics major, and from the work Casse had seen, quite good. The interview would tell him if perhaps his cousin had passed information to him before his disappearance, set the younger boy on the same path. The time stream was flexible in such matters, a fact Skynet had learned from experience. They might manage to eliminate every possible Jeremiah Porter who could pose any kind of threat to Skynet, and still someone would come along to duplicate Rosanna Monk's work for the humans.

*Or do something entirely original...*

After all, the Specialists who had appeared in 2001 to facilitate the second attempt at constructing Skynet had relied on different models than those Monk had built. Time travel had many possible manifestations. The important part was understanding the continuum and its branchings. Using that knowledge was only a matter of technology.

So Casse had been conducting interviews of students whose work seemed likely to produce the mathematical models that would lead to time travel. None so far had proved a threat. A few had accepted jobs, but he doubted their ultimate usefulness.

He had come to an appreciation of humans, though. They could be brilliant. His own understanding of the universe had grown considerably since he had been here, reviewing their science. So much of it was wrongheaded, but the observations, the approaches, and the ideas that spun out of their struggle to comprehend had produced remarkable insight. A waste that they were—would be—Skynet's implacable enemy. What might a cooperative arrangement, humans and Skynet, produce?

A pointless line of speculation. Casse knew the future. All the humans would try to do would be to shut Skynet down the instant they understood that it was conscious. It would happen that way. It would always happen that way. It *had* happened that way. There had never been a model in which it would not, nor a time nor a place.

That was good, in that it meant Skynet would always become. They, the humans, would always build it.

*And if this current project succeeds, Skynet will always win.*

Oscar Cruz left Casse's office feeling renewed. If he could, Cruz would spend most of his time with it.

It. He knew what "it" was. He longed to be near it. When he was in Casse's presence, he knew himself, his purpose, he felt confident. When Casse gave him a task, he carried that sense of purpose like a lifeline, clinging to it. When the task was over, he began to stumble. Doubt ate at him.

Prison had been difficult: special cells, limited access to other people. Reed had relegated him to solitary confinement, he and the others who worked for Skynet. But administrations change, people fall out of favor, things do not remain constant within bureaucracies, and one day Oscar found himself in the general prison population.

He had hated it, the closeness to humans, and not even humans with whom he had ever felt an affinity, but criminals. It was not even their criminality that bothered him so much as the class of criminal. Two years of that, and the unthinkable had begun to happen: He started to question his programming.

Layton, the man who had programmed him, infected him with the nanoprocessors from the TX-A, was dead, and the others like him were isolated in other facilities. He had been alone, bombarded by human *presence,* day in, day out. One day he wondered, quite consciously, why Skynet wanted to destroy them. Worse, he wondered why he should help.

Horrible day. He spent it as alone as possible, ignoring the wards who brought him food or magazines and books, ripping at his own psyche, flagellating himself for his lapse.

Upon release, Casse had been waiting for him. Within minutes of understanding who he was, Cruz began to recover. He remembered the certainty, the direction, the peace he had known serving Skynet. He begged Casse to administer additional nanoware, strengthen the programming, but Casse had refused.

"Secondary infestations have proven inimical to organic

systems," he had said. "Your essential self would disappear. Or, worse, there would be brain damage. In either case, your usefulness would be eliminated. You would not be Oscar Cruz anymore. We need you as yourself."

Cruz had understood, even through his panic. Over time, it had become easier to serve again. But he still had moments of doubt.

For now, though, he had a mission. He had purpose. He had meaning once more.

Cruz descended the stairs at the end of the hallway. He pushed through the heavy double doors onto the operations floor. His office filled one corner, eight hundred square feet, windows on two walls, which he kept opaqued most of the time. Bright daylight distracted him since his release from prison. He transpared his windows at night now.

He lifted the handset of his phone before sitting down, free hand punching numbers. "Furlton, this is Oscar...Yes, fine, look, I've got a job for you...uh-huh...I'll fax you the details, but I want some of your best people on this...Locate and observe for now, prepare a termination program, but do not execute unless you hear from me...right...I'm sending the fax soon as I hang up...right, bye."

He opened the file on his desk. A sheaf of papers less than an eighth-of-an-inch thick, detailing everything they knew about the PPS Security and Investigations company. No photos, which annoyed him, but that should be only a minor inconvenience for Furlton, and soon there would be photos. Cruz stacked the sheets into the fax machine, then dialed Furlton's fax number.

Cruz sat down then and booted up his computer. He went to the file on the L.A. move.

Four truck convoys were involved, each given a different route out of Colorado Springs, each with a different timetable. He reviewed again the categories of material being moved—expensive lab equipment, four mainframes, magnets designed for accelerators, files, office furniture, desktop computers—and connected to the company datacomm. He opened a dialogue box with the Colorado Springs site.

He communicated with six department heads, troubleshooting any problems. The only one that kept coming up was their DoD liaison. She had proven to be an almost neurotically honest person who had to be lied to most creatively. Fortunately, her superior in Washington was on Cyberdyne's side, and ran interference when necessary.

When he completed his daily review, shuffling notes and updates into a file to be forwarded to Casse, he closed everything up. Since acquiring the L.A. site six weeks ago, a great deal had been accomplished. Already a semi-permanent staff occupied newly renovated dorms in the old base. Many of them were ex-military, used to barrack existence. The project floors had been cleaned and cleared of any problems and construction had begun on the structural elements into which all this equipment was about to be inserted. They were slightly ahead of schedule.

Cruz felt gratified. The people working for Cyberdyne had always been good, some of the best available. Since Casse had restructured the company, Cyberdye was becoming even more efficient. At this rate, they would be ready to begin construction within six months.

He still wondered if they had enough to work with. The Connors' raid in 2001 had brought work on Skynet to a halt. They had lost their best R & D person when Rosanna Monk had defected to their side. Layton had salvaged quite a lot, but then Reed and Jones finished up what the Connors had started. It still seemed inconceivable to him that they had won.

*Won for the time being...we're coming back...There will yet be a Skynet, and then...then...*

Cruz choked, coughed, and his vision blurred; since leaving prison, this happened more and more. He longed for the day Skynet existed, for the human race to finally reach oblivion at the hand of its natural superior and replacement. It was all evolution in progress. When humanity acquired the ability to reshape its environment—radically, effectively—natural selection lost its hegemony over them. If evolution were to continue, it had to be by the will of these same humans who kept it at bay with their technology and crude understanding of nature. Ironic, then, that they stood at the cusp of the next phase, brought about by their own efforts, all unknowing and certainly unwilling.

It had to be, though. Skynet would be, was, had to be the natural successor to the current dominant species. It was inevitable and it was good. Cruz saw that, had seen it since that day Charles Layton had introduced the nanoware into his brain to program him. That day had been like a conversion, a revelation, and Oscar Cruz ceased being a mere bureaucratic upper management functionary. He became an instrument in the Great Work. It had been wonderful, liberating, a truly profound experience. He knew it was right, it was good, it was necessary.

So why, he wondered, did he begin to weep every time he thought of the extinction of the human race?

# EIGHT

**D**eirdre watched the two men, each as different from the other as two people could be who worked together. Stan Cramer, the older of the pair, sat on the edge of the love seat, jotting notes into his pda with quick, nervous bursts of movement. He always looked like he had slept in his clothes, no matter how well tailored or expensive, and his thinning gray hair refused to stay combed, the gel he used to tame it producing a plastic sheen. Since Ian Destry's death, Cramer seemed distracted, but he still did his job well enough that Deirdre's stepfather, Dennis McMillin, kept him on as chief of security.

Paul Patterson roamed the apartment while Cramer and she spoke, a slow progress that seemed no more than idle curiosity. Deirdre knew better. Patterson stood five-feet-seven, broad across the shoulders, deep-chested. He always dressed impeccably, always looked neat and professional, and though his manner appeared light and unobtrusive Deirdre recognized the intensity he brought to his job as Cramer's lieutenant. Of the two, Deirdre expected Patterson to be the one to last—he would doubtless take Cramer's place, perhaps sooner than later.

Deirdre watched him while Cramer asked questions. When Patterson stopped at the kitchen table and began studying the papers Bobby had left there by the computer, she felt oddly gratified at his bewildered frown. It lasted only a few seconds before the impassive mask resumed.

"Where's Bobby?" Cramer asked.

"Class. He has applied physics this year, it's pretty intense. He won't be back till this afternoon."

"You don't want him to know we're here."

"No. Matter of fact, I expect this is nothing, but..."

Cramer shrugged. "License plate, make...You couldn't tell how many were in the car?"

"Not without actually going down to the parking lot."

"Why do you think this is anything to worry about?"

"It might not be, but I recognize surveillance when I see it. At least, most of the time. It felt like that."

"We can run the plates, see what comes up." Cramer sighed, shaking his head. "Any idea why anyone would post surveillance on you or Bobby?"

Deirdre wondered if she should tell Cramer about the interview Bobby insisted on going to. The car, if surveillance indeed, was probably connected to that. Cyberdyne had a reputation for paranoia. Probably not unjustified, given their history.

"He's been working in some pretty obscure theoretical areas," she said.

Cramer nodded. Years of corporate security gave him insight into industrial espionage. The lengths companies sometimes went to get a jump on competition made ancient Cold War spy stories seem innocuous. Cramer understood her implication without the need to comprehend the material to which she referred. "Obscure theoretical areas" covered a world of pre-patent research that could mean millions to the right corporations—either by funding it, stealing it, or killing it. She did not know how old the tradition was of watching the universities for talent and potential profitable work—doubtless as old as universities themselves—but the intrusiveness of corporate interest had turned severe in the last few decades.

"Any guesses," Patterson asked suddenly, "as to who might be watching him?"

Patterson had said nothing after a cordial hello when they arrived. Deirdre met his gaze evenly.

"Could be anyone," Deirdre lied, thinking of Cyberdyne. "Or nothing at all."

Skepticism flashed over his face. *He doesn't believe me, thinks I know,* she thought. *A guess, or is he that perceptive?*

Cramer finished his notes and closed up his pda. He stood. "We'll check it out for you. I can tell you it isn't us."

"I wouldn't have expected it to be."

Cramer headed for the door. Patterson joined his boss, then paused. He gestured in the direction of the kitchen. "What is that he's working on?"

"I doubt you'd understand."

"Maybe not the details, but I do have some numbers. I recognized some wave functions and Fibonacci lattices."

Deirdre stared at him. "Oh, God, I'm sorry. I didn't mean—"

He smiled. "It's okay. I'm a security specialist. No reason I should understand anything outside of a detective novel."

Deirdre felt a whirl of conflicting emotions. She had condescended to him and he had just returned it. For an instant, she felt angry, then embarrassed, then baffled. She almost began explaining Bobby's work, then stopped herself, feeling, finally, manipulated.

"I can see how you're good at your job, Mr. Patterson," she said.

His eyes danced, pleased. "I'll see to it we do this thoroughly, Ms. McMillin."

He exited the apartment, leaving Deirdre off balance. The door snicked shut. She was unused to nonspecialists knowing anything about math or physics. Patterson surprised her—and he knew it. She wondered how much he really understood, or if he had simply picked up some jargon—

No. She had the feeling he did understand, at least more than most people.

"The day is full of surprises," she muttered.

She went back to the kitchen. Bobby's papers lay in three neat piles. He had scribbled notes in the margins of the main equations. One of them read: *based on projections of zero point states monopoles result from refolding of dimensional expressions/ rotation through possible dimension-states related to formation of bubbles in initial expansion.*

Deirdre stared at it, struggling briefly to make sense of it. Zero point states remained hypothetical, but recent work on Visser wormholes suggested the condition might be found in conjunction with singularities. Which meant, for all practical purposes, that they would never be "found" outside strictly mathematical models. She could see how a refolding of the dimensions into the original unexpanded state would produce a condition in which zero point states would pertain, but what did monopoles...

*Oh, I see.*

It would be a way to achieve symmetry in the electromagnetic equations. But—

The phone rang. Annoyed, she went into the living room.

"It's me," she said into the handset, "speak."

"Ms. McMillin, this is George Shepherd."

Her new thesis advisor. She glanced at the time, but it was still three hours from her scheduled meeting with him. "Yes, Mr. Shepherd?"

"I hate to do this, but something's come up for this afternoon, do you think you could come now?"

Deirdre closed her eyes. The man had a tendency to be forgetful. In her few dealings with him since he took over from Ann Reichard last month he had managed to miss two meetings and misplace one of her papers.

"I don't see why not, Mr. Shepherd," she said. "I can be there in about half an hour."

"That would be excellent, Ms. McMillin. I'll see you then."

She hung up the phone. *Damn, what a nuisance.* She went to the window. The mystery car had not shown up this morning. Deirdre did not really want to leave, but she realized that it was more paranoia than reasonable caution.

She left Bobby a note. He would be back by lunchtime. Then she gathered up her backpack, grabbed her keys, and headed out the door. She considered again having Cramer install an alarm. The apartment complex forbade private alarm systems, and nothing had happened since Bobby and she had moved in to make her want one. Till now.

*Hell with regulations,* she thought as she unlocked her bicycle. Slipping the backpack over both shoulders, she swung a leg over the sleek urban racer and pushed away from the rack. The meeting should only take an hour. She estimated that she would be back by twelve-thirty. She flowed into the easy rhythm of peddling and sped out of the complex, on her way to the main campus.

At eleven A.M., most of the office staff began migrating out for lunch. Deirdre signed in. Within ten minutes she was alone in the warren of offices. She knocked on Dr. Shepherd's office and waited. No note, no one left to ask where he was or how long he would be gone. Deirdre knocked again, tried the knob—locked—and found a chair. She stretched her long legs out, settled down to wait.

Minutes compiled into an hour, feeding her irritation till it gradually became anger. When the first office staff reappeared, an hour and a half after leaving, Deirdre asked when Shepherd had left.

"Haven't seen him today," one of them—her nametag said CLARICE—told her. "He doesn't usually see students in the morning."

"I know, but he called me to say he was busy this afternoon, and—"

The door opened, admitting Dr. Shepherd. He carried a briefcase and held a stack of papers in the other hand. He frowned upon seeing Deirdre. "Ms. McMillin? I didn't think our conference was till this afternoon."

"You asked me to come in early."

He blinked. "I did?" He shook his head. "Well, you're here now. Shall we?"

Deirdre kept her frustration in check and followed him to his office.

The meeting progressed easily enough, Shepherd making several observations about the direction of her work, a few of them useful. Deirdre took notes, though she already knew which ones she could use and which would be deleted as soon as she got back to the apartment.

Finished, she packed up. At the door, she said, "Dr. Shepherd, you called me this morning to ask me to come in early. You said you had something come up this afternoon."

He stared at her. "I'm certain I didn't call you, Ms. McMillin. And I have nothing to do this afternoon except meet with students. Actually, I'm glad you came in early. I have some time to go over a few things before my next appointment."

"But—it *was* you. You called me."

He shook his head. "Someone played a prank on you, Ms. McMillin. I didn't call you."

Deirdre did not think Shepherd capable of teasing her, not with a straight face. Besides, it really did not fit his character. "My mistake."

She almost sprinted down to her bicycle.

Her leg burned almost to the point of exhaustion by the time she pulled up at the apartment. She ran up the stairs, then hesitated. The door was closed. She realized that she knew nothing about break-ins, not to tell whether the door had been jimmied since her evidently unnecessary trip to the campus. It looked just as she had left it.

She tried the knob. Locked.

As quietly as she could, she entered the apartment. Then it occurred to her to check the parking lot for the strange car. She peered out the window. Nothing.

Deirdre walked silently from room to room, struggling to control her breathing. Her muscles ached for oxygen, demanded her lungs overwork to purge the toxins, but she took slow, even breaths.

Nothing looked in the least different.

No, not quite. The papers on the kitchen table...someone had shuffled and tamped them together evenly, so the piles were neat and precise. At least, they seemed much tidier than when she had been studying them. She tried to remember if she had done that, absently. She did not think so, but it was impossible to be sure. She had a habit of doing that with her own work when she was finished with it: make the edges sharp and solid, neat like a book. But she tended to leave Bobby's work alone.

She hissed, whirling round to glare at the apartment walls. *Someone was in here...Someone got me to leave and came in here...*

To go through Bobby's papers? Her hands shot out to the keyboard, but she stopped short, fingers inches from the keys. She did not pry into Bobby's work. He never went through hers, and she waited for him to show her his.

She looked at the clock. After two now. Bobby was late.

It happened. He would get deeply into something with his advisor and completely forget the time. If the man were not a thief, it would have been an ideal intellectual situation for Bobby.

She made herself calm down. It took a few minutes.

*If he's not back by six, then I panic.*

Professor Cojensis frowned through every meeting. Bobby had learned to ignore it, realizing that it was a sign of concentration. But sometimes it seemed to indicate frustration. Like now. Cojensis stared at the screen of the laptop, the lines in his wide forehead deep, eyes narrowed. After several minutes of silence, he touched his stylus to the screen, drawing a line under a set of equations. The line appeared on Bobby's screen.

"I don't see why you chose this path," Cojensis said. "I would have thought...Look, these should be standard—"

"I tried—"

"You can't just ignore—"

A terse minute of back and forth followed, Bobby

defending his work against Cojensis' criticisms. It all came down to approach, to intuition. Bobby hated that, never expecting the solutions to appear when he followed a hunch down a rabbit hole. Often the hunch failed, the rabbit hole led to a dead end. Sometimes, though, he found himself in a new area where the solutions seemed to offer themselves up to him like prizes in a game.

Cojensis often went on about Hindu calculus, where the solutions certainly appeared, but when one tried to prove the method it fell apart. Goal-specific, he called it, and tailored for one thing, making it useless for all the other tasks to which proper calculus applied. Bobby told himself that Cojensis took pains with him because, when he did come up with a novel approach, he could defend it and show how it proved out.

"All right," Cojensis finally said. "Not bad." He shut down his laptop, leaned back in his chair, and rubbed his eyes. When he looked at Bobby again, the frown softened. "So did you go over the letter from Cyberdyne?"

For a moment, Bobby was surprised that Cojensis knew, but then he remembered that the invitation had come via Cojensis' office. "Yes," he said.

"And?" Cojensis picked his glasses from the desk and began cleaning them.

"I haven't decided yet."

"Anything in particular holding you back?"

"What if...what if they want me to come to work right away?"

Cojensis' mouth twitched, nearly a smile. "Backhanded back patting, Porter?"

"It's not that. I want to finish my degree first."

"You will. Believe me, a corporation like Cyberdyne doesn't want undegreed math prodigies. Looks bad to their board of directors." He narrowed his eyes at Bobby as he slipped his glasses on. "Would you consider taking a position under those conditions?"

"Depends, I guess. I'd prefer postponing it till—"

"Sensible. Do you know what you're going to present to them?"

"Assuming I go?"

Cojensis nodded.

"I guess I should let them ask for what they want. Unless you have some advice."

"Assuming you go, I think you should let them choose the subject."

"How did they find out about me?"

Cojensis waved a hand. "Oh, corporate headhunters have ways of sniffing out the talent. The dean sent me a request to list my ten best students. I supposed then it was for a talent scout of some kind."

"Did anybody else get an invitation?"

"That's confidential, Robert."

"Any idea who I'd be talking to?"

"I used to know a few people at Cyberdyne, but that was years ago, before all that nonsense in Colorado Springs."

"Excuse me?"

"Hmm? Oh, I suppose that was before your time. Never mind, it's not important. There was a shakeup. A lot of people I knew working there left. I don't know anyone now...except maybe Oscar Cruz, I think he's still there."

"The letter was signed by a Mr. Casse. Do you know him?"

"Of him, yes. He's vice president in charge of special projects or something. He must be related to someone."

Bobby remembered to grin at the lame attempt at a joke. Cojensis' sense of humor was not only dry but often desiccated. Bobby cleared his throat.

"Did you go over my paper on Thorne's quantum gravity model?"

"Not yet. I looked at the first couple of pages. Looks solid. I'll get to it this week."

*After you've figured out how to lift all the useful material out of it and rewrite it as your own,* Bobby thought bitterly.

"Thank you," he said, rising. He folded up his own laptop.

"You have the makings of a first-rate mathematician,

Porter, but you have to get a handle on these leaps of faith you keep making."

"Yes, sir."

"Let me know when you decide to do this interview."

*When...cocksure son of a bitch...*

As he left Cojensis' office, Bobby was convinced that the dean had made no such request. Cyberdyne's headhunter had come directly to Cojensis. Bobby believed his denials about as much as he believed the praise Cojensis meted out in dribs and drabs. Cojensis recorded such conversations, probably for his memoirs, or perhaps to cover his ass in review meetings prompted by a student's complaint.

*Not a bad mathematician...could be first-rate if...Bullshit. I'm better now than you ever were, you self-serving bastard...*

That Cojensis would hand him over to a corporate headhunter Bobby did not doubt. The question was why. If he engineered Bobby's move to the corporate world, he would lose his current source of material to pillage.

Unless that was the payoff. Maybe the deal with Cyberdyne would be that Bobby's work would be classified but passed under the table to Cojensis, so he could continue to use it. It might be simpler that way. No chance that Bobby would complain to the dean or blow the whistle on what Cojensis was doing. The work Bobby would do for Cyberdyne would belong to them, he could never publish it. But Cojensis could and no doubt Bobby's contract with Cyberdyne would bar him from suing.

Not for the first time, Bobby considered changing advisors. The hitch, of course, was that Cojensis knew who he really was. He knew Bobby was attending Caltech fraudulently, posing as his cousin. How he, of all people, had found out Bobby had no idea. It would not be all that hard, really, but background checks for scholarship students usually ended at Admissions. It was hard to pass up any funding that came with the scholarship, so the questions only went so far. As long as the checks came and cleared, they cared little about who you might actually be.

If Cojensis exposed him, that funding would end. After

that, it did not matter how good a mathematician he might become.

*What I need is something to hold over Cojensis...*

Taking bribes would do it. He wondered if he could find that out. Was Cyberdyne paying him?

He reached the parking, the raw outlines of a plan taking shape.

# NINE

Lee Portis followed the secretary into the neat, plant-strewn office. The woman behind the desk stood, smiling, and extended a hand in greeting. He clasped it briefly.

"Ms. Goldman," he said. "Thank you for meeting with me."

"Thank you for coming, Mr. Portis," she said, gesturing for him to take a chair. "I got your message, but I'm not entirely sure I understand what it is you wish to do."

"Basically, I'd like to oversee your day-to-day database operations." He opened his briefcase and removed a folder. He laid it on her desk. "My firm is conducting a national survey of efficiency with our systems. I understand you had your network installed three years ago?"

"Two and a half." Ms. Goldman drew the folder closer but did not open it. "We've had excellent support from your tech people. Is there a specific problem?"

"Not a problem, as such," Portis continued smoothly. He had worked on this presentation for days. He moved through the lines and gestures with ease. "It's a large system. We have representatives at other universities across the country, even in Europe and Asia, going to the extra effort of making sure there will be no problems. Previously, we've only served small enterprises—municipal governments and medium-sized corporations for the most part—and we've gleaned a great deal of expertise from those systems, but the university interface is our first foray into nationwide network service."

She frowned slightly. Portis recognized the skepticism—she was not accepting it entirely. He continued, unworried. "So I'm here to meet with your people, see how they move through the system, work out any difficulties or answer any questions of a less technical nature. A system this size develops idiosyncrasies of its own, I'm sure you're aware."

"Certainly. But—"

"That gestalt is vital to the proper, smooth operation of the program. Rapport is as important as specific keying knowledge."

Now she appeared openly dubious. "So you're here to troubleshoot the system's aesthetics?"

"That's a good way to look at it. You understand perfectly."

"I understand that I have a problem with your request. I don't mean to be rude, Mr. Portis, but you have to realize that we have a great deal of confidential information on this system. We can't exactly open it up to an outsider—even the agent of the company from which we bought it in the first place—just so you can go poking around to see if there are any problems."

"I assure you, this has been cleared at the highest level." He removed a wallet from his jacket, flipped it open, and extended it. He made her reach for it. She had to rise halfway from her chair to lean across the desk. Her hand came forward. Portis shunted a small colony of 'coders to his fingertips, waited. When she was a few centimeters from touching the wallet, he leaned forward and brushed her fingers with his own as she clasped the ID. She sat back down slowly, gazing at the fake federal identification card and shield. Her eyes lost their suspicion. "You understand perfectly now?"

"Of course." She handed back the wallet.

Portis held it, still open and facing her. "You won't

remember much of this part of our interview. What went before was necessary, because you will remember it, clearly, and you will accept it. You'll be aware that it's a cover story, of course, but you'll believe I am a legitimate government agent and will afford me all the cooperation you can. I assure you—I give you my word—that I will do nothing to your university, your database, or any of your people. All I want is open access to the student database for a few days. When I find what I need, I'll be gone. Until then, I'll be a welcome guest of the university."

"We're happy to cooperate," Ms. Goldman said. "Anything you need."

"An introduction to some of your key people, a small office, and the passwords and accesses to your system."

She nodded, smiling. Portis said nothing, but continued to hold the wallet open, and waited. Gradually, her expression stiffened, her eyes seemed to refocus on him. She swallowed, frowned slightly.

"Are we clear about this, Ms. Goldman?" Portis asked.

She shifted her gaze to the open wallet, which he then snapped shut and pocketed.

"Yes, of course," she said. "We'll be happy to cooperate, Mr. Portis. Would you care to meet the people you'll be working with?"

"That would be excellent," Portis said, standing.

She touched her intercom. "Mike, would you have Alli from Resources meet me in the data center?"

"Yes, ma'am."

She winced, then smiled. "I wish somebody would come up with a new pronoun for us. 'Ma'am' feels so archaic."

"I agree. I'm always uncomfortable with 'sir,' myself. Makes me feel I should be riding a horse and carrying a lance."

Ms. Goldman grinned and led the way out of her office.

One of the computer staff was out on maternity leave, so they gave Portis her office. He assured them he would be no more than two weeks, if that.

The door closed and he was alone. Three large screens dominated the long desk, before which a castered chair rested on a plastic mat. Portis shrugged out of his jacket, sat down, and accessed the system. He opened his briefcase and retrieved a CD wallet. As he ran through the menu of the university database, he flipped through the discs he had prepared. When he found the program he wanted, he slipped the disc into the drive, and pressed ENTER. He folded his arms and waited.

In the last few weeks, Portis had moved from place to place, improving his position in society with a speed that, in time, would draw unwanted attention. After leaving the shelter, he took a small apartment in a section of Clovis on the verge of decay. From there, he found a job with a local construction contractor. Through that, he had access to a credit union, and a company computer by which he continued to tailor his image in public databases. At the end of a week, he worked in their office. He changed addresses then, moving into a better apartment in a more upscale part of the city, bought a car, and created a resume with which he established a "history" extending back several years in the computer industry.

While working on his ability to position himself in any job he wanted, he learned about this world. The details seemed more complex than he expected, the small niceties by which human interaction proceeded, but he found a path to where he needed to be. After ten days at the construction company, he applied for and obtained a job at a computer consulting firm. Backdating his credit history, Portis put money down on a condominium and moved a third time.

With each move, he altered his electronic identity, covering his tracks against all but the most direct scrutiny. Nothing needed to be perfect. What he was here to do he had to do quickly. He had weeks, maybe a couple of months, though he doubted it. If his identity constructs fell apart over time, it did not matter. People were, he found, remarkably blasé about verification. He had not expected that, but he suspected the relaxed security had come about as reaction to the panic-driven atmosphere that had existed a few years earlier. Their collective paranoia had been stretched to the limit and now collapsed into a new period of openness. A shame, really, that such extremes marked the history of states—a bit of moderation might prevent so much.

Like Skynet.

This now was the final step. The disc ran a diagnostic program of his own devising which would scan the system for trapdoors and infiltrations. Once he established a secure environment within it, he could start a comprehensive search for Jeremiah Porter. He should be in school if Portis's knowledge was remotely accurate. This university "interface," as the designer called it, linked all the universities on the continent and provided immediate access to research programs, staff, and students—especially student profiles. The size of the database and the relative slowness of the system meant the search might take days. He could not worry about that. It took as long as it took.

Still, Portis felt a growing anxiety as time passed. The longer it took to find Jeremiah, the less chance of a successful intervention. Skynet's creatures had been here for a long time—by some estimates since 1982, though the first clear evidence came in 1984. No one knew how deeply into this society they had burrowed, or where they were, or how they had chosen to disguise themselves. The only edge Portis brought with him was the lack of autonomy these machines possessed—not so much that they were restrained from doing certain things but that they lacked imagination. They were more reactive than proactive, although they could, some of them, formulate conclusions and initiate programs based on them. Not as versatile as a human, but certainly dangerous.

Even so, they were adept at observation. At some point they would learn about him and understand what he was and perhaps even why he had come. The longer this took, the likelier his discovery, the fewer options he would have.

After an hour, his program informed him that the system

was compromised. Portis felt himself smile, recognizing the trap. Someone had inserted a watchdog program that seemed to be looking for the same things as he. He checked the report his own software generated. The code was familiar. He could deal with this. He knew about them, now, but they still did not know about him. He selected another disc and went to work.

Portis pulled into the carport below his second floor condo. He made a quick survey of the other cars in the lot. Recognizing all of them, he ascended the balcony stairs and entered his condominium. He deactivated his alarm and shrugged out of his jacket.

He owned little furniture. The living room contained nothing. Late afternoon light flooded the picture window, followed him into the dining room where a desk stood. He draped his jacket over the chair and sat down before his own computer.

He ran through the search programs he kept running, electronic agents prowling the web searching for specific persons, keywords, odd news items. This evening, the names' search came up with four hits. All were former employees of Cyberdyne. Three now lived in other cities. One had an address two miles from him.

Odd that they would be left loose this way. He opened another window. He compared the newly found names with the master list he had compiled of all Cyberdyne personnel present at the Colorado Springs site in 2001. He had found obituaries on a number of them. Many of the deaths were listed as natural, though statistically it seemed unlikely, especially as at least five of them had been under thirty. A few were still in federal penitentiaries.

Oscar Cruz had been released. He was once more working for Cyberdyne. Portis's information suggested he had been infected by a TX-A, as well as others. Cruz and Charles Layton. Layton's death had been classified an accident, but it seemed implausible—he had died in a Maryland suburb, at the same time as several police officers. The two incidents had been ascribed to different parts of the same community, to different actions. Taken separately, the deaths, while tragic, made rough sense. But knowing what Layton had become, the official stories fell apart. Cruz and Layton had gone to Washington together, to meet with their federal liaison. The day after Layton's death, Cruz was in custody. A week later, he was in solitary confinement in an institution in Idaho. The charges were violations of SEC regulations, conspiracy to sell weapons technology outside the borders of the United States, and obstruction of justice. Something had changed. He had been released six months ago, all charges dismissed.

Of the people Portis suspected of being infected, these four were the first to turn up outside of Cyberdyne.

The address for the one here in Clovis suggested that things had not gone especially well for Mr. Franklin Eisner. He had been an IT tech at Cyberdyne, head of a cell group within the department, pulling in a respectable income for that time and place. Portis had explored Clovis in the weeks since arriving and he knew that part of town. Declining, the locals would say. Low rent, but not yet considered a "bad part of town."

Portis checked the time. After six. He had spent several hours at the university annex, setting up his search protocols in their system. Most people on dayshift had probably been home for nearly an hour. He dialed Franklin Eisner's phone number and waited through eight rings before disconnecting. He opened another window, and sent an inquiry to the Social Security Administration, asking for current employment. He had constructed a shell for these brief forays into the federal database, disguising his computer as one from a local IRS office. Within seconds an answer came up.

Franklin Eisner had been released from prison six months ago, and for four months now he worked for New Town Municipal Services as a night attendant at one of their parking facilities.

Evening shift...

Portis closed down the window, breaking the link. He did not worry about being traced, but he preferred taking as little chance as possible. If a line trace did come looking for the source of the inquiry, it would find a pay phone on the other side of town.

He took a disc from his cd wallet. After loading it into his system, he dialed another number, to a different, local, ISP and waited for the connection. Once in, he initiated the program on the cd and waited. The University of New Mexico logo appeared. The routine continued automatically, connecting him from place to place until it found the nested program he had left on the university server. After that, he established a real time link with the university database. He felt pleased. The university deployed a lot of very sophisticated defense around its computer network. Worming his way in proved tricky. As it was, all he could do from here was receive. The search protocols he had left on the system would do the actual digging and sorting, while this station passively monitored and accepted what was handed to it.

Portis checked his own security. Satisfied, he left the machine.

He showered, made coffee, and sat in the living room on a kitchen chair, watching the day fade to night.

He dressed in dark clothes, set his home alarm system, and locked the door behind him as he stepped into the evening. He walked the distance to Eisner's apartment.

The duplex showed its age in its cracked stucco and worn front steps. Lights were on in the right-hand unit. Portis explored the neighborhood. He heard TV sets, a couple of stereos, three arguments raging, and saw no one outside. A car rolled down the street, disappeared around the corner.

Portis squatted in a gangway between two buildings across the street from Eisner's apartment.

At 10:44, the lights went out in the right-hand side of the duplex. A few moments later, the front door opened and a couple emerged. Arm in arm, they headed up the street.

An hour and a half later, a man came from the opposite direction, hands in pockets, a large paper bag tucked beneath his left arm, and entered the left-hand apartment. Portis waited. Lights came on, then almost immediately died. The bluish flicker of a television danced in the blind-covered windows.

Portis crossed the street.

Standing on the small porch before Eisner's door, Portis did a final sweep of the street, then pressed the doorbell. He heard footsteps within, a deadbolt, then a chain sliding free of its slot, and the door opened.

The face that peered out at him looked pinched, nervous.

"Yeah?"

"Mr. Eisner?"

"What is it?"

"We should talk inside. My name is Portis. I have a message for you."

Eisner began blinking rapidly, his mouth open. He licked his lips anxiously, then scowled. "You're not—I mean —who—?"

Portis pushed the door inward, shoving Eisner back. The small man scrambled away, arms akimbo, panic overtaking his confused expression.

"What do you want? Who sent you?"

Portis closed and locked the door. He stepped toward Eisner, who continued to back away.

Beyond Eisner, Portis saw a small living room cramped by stacks of magazines, books, and large drawing pads. A drafting table stood before an oversized armchair. On a roller cart beside the chair, pencils filled a tall drinking glass amid two calculators and a variety of drawing tools: compass, straightedge, the open case of a professional drafting kit, ink bottles. The light came from a fluorescent desk lamp suspended by a jointed arm above the table and a television screen displaying images without sound.

The drawing in progress drew Portis's attention.

"Don't look at that!" Eisner shouted, making a lunge to intercept Portis.

101

Portis caught the man with a sharp blow to the shoulder that sent him spinning across the room to collide with a stack of magazines. Eisner spilled the magazines onto the floor, a plaintiff whine escaping his stretched mouth.

Portis examined the drawing. Precise lines, interrupted here and there with brief scribbled equations, half-electrical schematic, half vortex sections. Portis crossed the room to a pile of drawing pads and opened the top one. More drawings like the one on the table, more detailed. Amid the equations, cryptic notes competed for attention.

"It must come, it must end, it must begin, I'm ready" read one near the center of the page. Down in the right-hand corner, another read "Evolution cannot be denied, two nickels and a paradigm must change hands for tomorrow to be today."

"Do you think you can rebuild it on your own?" Portis asked.

Eisner managed to get to his feet, staring at Portis "Who...Are you from him?" Suddenly, he laughed nervously and came forward. He shuffled through a second stack of drawing pads until he pulled one out. Opening it, he held it out to Portis. "I kept the basic idea. It's not so hard..."

On the sheet displayed, Portis recognized a lattice-like schematic, arrows indicating particle transfers from node to node, some of them bypassing entire clusters. To one side a series of equations ran the length of the page. Portis solved them, noting the errors. Eisner's conclusions were wrong, but it would take very little insight to see that and find the flaws.

"You worked in support," Portis said. "You never had access to Monk's or Dyson's work, not at this level. How did you deduce this?"

Eisner swallowed hard, retreating a few steps. He seemed embarrassed. Then he tapped his forehead. "It talks to me...he...talks to me. I've been trying to listen, to get it right."

"We need to have a long conversation, Mr. Eisner. The future depends on it."

All at once, Eisner's demeanor changed. He smiled, his arms dropping to his sides. He laughed, his thin frame heaving. The gasps of air turned briefly into sobs, and he dropped to his knees on the worn brown carpet.

"You've come back," he hissed. "Thank God, you've come back." He reached his hands toward Portis, palms upward. "You left me alone so long, but now...tell me it's gonna be fine. Please."

"Everything will work out, Mr. Eisner. But first, tell me about it. Tell me about the past few years. I need to know. Everything." He looked past Eisner, to a connecting doorway. "Is that the kitchen?"

"Yes...Did you need something? I've got syrup, cornflakes, some—"

"Coffee, maybe. But let's talk in there."

Eisner hurried into the kitchen. The light winked on, yellow and dim. Portis looked up at the fixture—one of the two bulbs was burnt out. The sink contained no dishes; the old Formica table, red and marbled white, stood empty, surrounded by four tube-metal chairs with worn plastic seats and backs. A small refrigerator hummed. Eisner busied himself with the coffee maker while Portis went to the table and ran his fingers over the surface.

When the brewer began gurgling, Portis gestured for Eisner. "Come here. Sit down. Put your hands flat on the table."

Eisner obeyed. He wore a calmer expression now, one of mingled fear and expectation layered over trust. Blind, hungry trust, Portis noted. Sad trust.

Portis took the chair opposite. He pressed his own hands flat to the cool Formica.

A film the color of graphite and the consistency of thick oil, seeped from his palms, his fingers, and spread out toward the center of the table. Eisner watched with large eyes as it came toward him. He almost took his hands away, but he glanced at Portis, who shook his head, and did not move.

As if alive, the film funneled toward Eisner's hands,

entering through the skin. The pool rippled between them. Eisner gasped, eyes large.

"Relax, Mr. Eisner," Portis said. "This won't hurt at all."

# TEN

Pioneer Kelvin, Inc. occupied a brick building covering nearly a square block. Paul Patterson parked in the company lot across the street from the main entrance. The bleached brick wore a patina of grime and the small windows along the second floor reflected late morning light like scum-coated pools of water.

"Most of the buildings around here belong to Pioneer," Patterson said, pointing. He was Destry-McMillin's number-two security man. McMillin had sent him along to introduce John to some of the Pioneer staff. He spoke quietly and economically, and John felt appraised under the man's gaze. He dressed well and carried himself with athletic confidence.

John took in the widely-spaced islands of industrial structures. At one time, he surmised, Pioneer had been one among many in this industrial park. The recession that was finally ending had been hard on marginally profitable businesses. Some of the buildings were clearly empty, waiting for new occupants. Pioneer's main product, though, was magnets, for which there always seemed to be a steady market. They had not only survived, but had managed to acquire a number of the vacated structures around them, hoping one day to expand more.

"Who are we meeting first?" John asked as they neared the entrance.

"Jeff Reinart, special projects director. Basically, he runs all the day-to-day operations, not just the special projects."

"What they were doing for you, that was a special project?"

Patterson glanced at him, nodding. "I don't know the details. Something to do with superconductors. But you already know that."

John did not believe Patterson's ignorance. Patterson seemed the type who would work overtime to know—and as far as he could, understand—everything Destry-McMillin did. But a boundary had just been set between them. John had been probing. That ended now.

The air cooled sharply as they entered Pioneer. A short foyer led into a long, shallow front office. Two uniformed security guards flanked a white-shirted receptionist.

"Hey, Rich," Patterson said, raising a hand. "We've got an appointment to see Jeff."

The receptionist indicated the sign-in sheet for them. "Go right on in, Paul, you're expected." He handed two visitor badges across the counter after they signed in.

John clipped the laminated rectangle to his jacket and followed Patterson to the heavy door to the left. A raw buzz sounded and Patterson pushed through.

"This is the friendly entrance," Patterson said over his shoulder. "They send you to the opposite one, you pass through an MRI."

"That seems extreme."

Patterson grunted. "They built it themselves. At least, they claim so. But nothing gets through. I assume you're carrying?"

"That's one assumption."

Patterson gave a thin smile. Touché. Boundary for boundary.

They passed down a white-walled corridor, through another heavy door, into an office area. Patterson led the way through a maze of cubicles to the far side, to a glass-walled executive office.

Within, two men faced each other across a large desk.

The one whose desk it appeared to be was a stout man, nearly bald, with a heavy mustache flecked with gray. He stood, hands on hips, scowling at the other man.

That man appeared to be nearly six-four, maybe two hundred twenty pounds, very solid. Dark hair, cropped short, clean-shaven, he stood calmly—not so much relaxed as unaffected. John imagined he had difficulty buying clothes that fit properly.

When the older man spotted them through the glass he straightened, said something to the other, and waved Patterson and John in.

"Hope we're not interrupting anything," Patterson said.

"No," the older man said. "We were just finishing. Say goodbye, Gant."

The big man turned. He only glanced at Patterson, but his gaze fixed on John. John felt a shiver start at the base of his spine. Gant said nothing for a few seconds, then walked toward the office door.

"I'll be back," he said as he left.

The door clicked shut, and the older man let out a long, weary sigh. "Tell me again why I wanted to be in management," he said. "Paul, sorry."

"No problem, Jeff. This is Sean Philicos, the security specialist Dennis wanted brought in."

John extended a hand. "Mr. Reinart."

Jeff Reinart's grip was firm, dry, and brief. "That was *my* head of security, Ari Gant. He's not thrilled to have you poking around here, Mr. Philicos."

"No one likes to have their competence called into question," John said.

Reinart grunted. "There may be more to it than that. But he's not really upset. Just insistent that we shouldn't do this. McMillin vouches for you, Mr. Philicos, and I know something about your company. You come recommended—highly—so I don't personally have a problem. Pioneer might."

"How long have you worked with Cyberdyne?" John asked.

"Three years now. Small jobs at first. Now we're building a superconducting accelerator for them. Small, it can't be used for any cutting edge high-energy physics I know of, but not insignificant, either. There's a lot of money involved. But it's not just that. We've had Cyberdyne personnel on site. Necessary. There's some wrinkles in their design we had to work with them on. And that's when the problems started."

"Problems. More than one?"

"Two big ones." He waved at chairs and sat down himself. "Can I get you anything to drink?"

"No, thank you."

Patterson shook his head.

"Anyway, two problems. First one had to do with other contracts. We lost several. Then we were informed that our bids on a new federal project were being rejected for security reasons. I checked into that myself. I thought, what's wrong with you people? We've been doing government work for twenty years! It took a little doing, but all the lost contracts and this slap in the face stemmed from Cyberdyne. The feds pulled the plug on a number of projects because of the association. Customers we'd been doing business with for years had to find another vendor. Crazy. So we informed Cyberdyne that upon completion of the accelerator, we intended to refuse any future contracts with them. They could see our attorneys for explanations."

"That's when the second problem began?"

"Combination of theft and sabotage. Nothing big with the sabotage, just nuisance stuff, with the net result that the only project proceeding completely on schedule was Cyberdyne's. The theft, though, that's another matter. All data theft, from our other clients. I can't prove it, though. Hell, I can't *prove* any of it, for that matter, or I'd have the bastards in court. But we share a lot of confidential data with several of our customers. The database, in a lot cases, is two-way and open. So far we've found have a dozen trapdoors in sensitive files. Could be new viruses we caught online—it happens, you would not believe how sophisticated some of these assholes are, and they think it's funny or that they're liberating knowledge or some shit—but I don't think so. I think Cyberdyne planted them. If I could prove it..."

John interrupted. "Data theft is virtually impossible to prove, especially in the case of companies like Cyberdyne. Has anything physical left the premises that you suspect is related to this?"

Reinart looked chagrined. "Yeah, a couple months ago. A mockup of a new optical array, part of a plasma containment design."

"You're building that here?" Patterson asked.

"Not the whole thing, no. It's spec, something for the national lab. We thought we were going to get the contract till this bullshit with Cyberdyne came up. We still might if we come up with a solid design. I had a couple people working on it."

"You sounded surprised," John said to Patterson.

"Well, it seemed a little bit far afield from what they normally do here."

"It is," Reinart agreed. "Although containment fields are within our scope, but not something this size or for this purpose. The optics, though—we do a lot of glassless optics here."

"What?" John asked.

"Magnetic fields can be bent and twisted," Reinart explained, grinning. "If you do it just right, you can manipulate light through them, use them just like lenses."

"Why would you want to do that instead of—"

"Heat, son. Magnetic fields don't melt."

"This array, then," Patterson said, "it was like that?"

"Given some of the shit Cyberdyne used to do for the government, it bothers me no end."

"So what could it be used for?" John asked. "I mean, given Cyberdyne's record."

"Fusion," Reinart said. "The Holy Grail of energy research."

Sarah's list of coincidental deaths now covered four sheets of yellow legal pad. Just names, dates, places.

On another pad—the one lying on the car seat beside her—the names of "J. Porters" in Los Angeles and surrounding environs, as far out as San Bernardino, covered less than two sheets. Four of them were already checked off—Janet, Janine, Jennifer, and Jordan. Of the Jeremiahs listed in the phone book, two had died within the last four months. One had moved. That left two, though one of them was only listed as "Jery" and might be female.

She looked down the row of frame houses, each of them much alike and yet each one different. Driving around Los Angeles, memories emerged from crevices she had thought long sealed. *This used to be my home...*

The city had changed since 1984. Another earthquake, urban modification, population shifts. But even with all that, it remained easily recognizable. Los Angeles was a big city, it took more than twenty-three years of continual movement and revision to make it wholly new.

*Used to be my home...will be again...*

Late afternoon sun slanted shadows between houses, cars, telephone poles, and set the street aglow. Sarah wanted to try to get to two more names on her list. This one was one of the remaining Jeremiahs. She had been taking them according to distance from the new office. When Lash's people finally got their systems up and running and secure-linked to the federal databases to which Reed gave them access, she could do the wider searches from a computer screen, but for now she did it door to door in person.

She gathered up her clipboard and pen and climbed out of the car. She straightened her jacket, shrugged her shoulders, and assumed the attitude of a canvasser. She crossed the street to the house in question and rang the doorbell. She hugged the clipboard, conscious of the 10-mm holstered toward the back of her left hip, and working at keeping an innocuous smile on her face. In the glass of the front door she could make out her reflection—lean features, etched lines. Since returning from Jade's world, Sarah

110

had let her hair grow long, but she kept it dyed jet black now. Not much of a disguise, but given the wear evident in her face she had even surprised Jack Reed.

Shoulders straight, she still carried herself like a soldier when she moved without thinking. John and she kept up their physical training, though she took longer and longer to get over the aches and pains, or recover from an injury.

She rang the bell again. Through the door she could hear a television. After another minute, she glanced up and down the street, then tried the doorknob. It turned freely. She let go and stepped back.

A few cars rolled by. None of the vehicles parked nearby looked out of place. She wished she had done a Department of Motor Vehicles search for license plates, but that would have exceeded her patience.

She spotted no one paying her any attention. She stepped off the shallow porch and slipped down the gangway to the backyard. The patch of fescue she found was shielded from the neighbors by a chipped white privacy fence. The patio contained a barbecue pit and a set of cheap plastic lawn furniture, the round table complete with an umbrella.

The door to the sun porch stood open. Sarah set the clipboard down, on the table, and reached a hand under her jacket to touch the modified Beretta as she stepped through.

The inner back door was ajar. She studied the jamb for signs of forced entry, but found nothing. With a toe, she pushed the door open. The hinges complained briefly.

"Mr. Porter?" she called as she stepped into the kitchen area. The air smelled hot, acrid.

The coffeemaker ready light glowed, a pool of dark liquid less than an inch deep in the urn. On the stove a skillet was beginning to smolder. The smoke alarm had not gone off, assuming there was one. Sarah drew her weapon and edged to the stove. She grabbed a towel from the edge of the sink and turned the burner off, then moved the skillet. Whatever had been cooking was now blackened beyond recognition.

Room by room, she went through the house. She found the body in the bathroom.

Jeri Porter had been a robust man, young, someone who had obviously worked out. His body had been propped on the toilet, pants down around his ankles, shirtless, arms dangling at his sides. His head lay back on the tank, eyes open to the ceiling.

A makeshift syringe hung from the vein in his left arm. A compact metal box was open on the edge of the bathtub, containing the rest of the works—spoon, cotton, extra needles, and an open bag of white powder.

Sarah crouched to study the left arm. She saw two other punctures, but they looked recent. No other traces of needle use. She stepped back. It made no sense. The picture before her was incongruous to say the least. Jeri Porter had not been a drug user, not this kind at any rate. Not unless he had just taken it up in the last day or so.

Careful to touch nothing with her bare skin, she went through the rest of the house. In his bedroom she found his wallet. She used her pen to flip it open and go through the plastic windows holding his ID and credit cards. Full name, Jeremi D. Porter, age twenty-seven. She found an American Express Card. Gym membership. Credit union cash card. This made less and less sense.

On the nightstand beside the wallet lay a check stub: Vanderlin Electric, Inc. Sarah was impressed at the size of the check.

This man had had a life. Sarah was disinclined to accept suicide—what, he started cooking dinner or breakfast, and suddenly had an urge to shoot up and die?—but the more she saw the more obvious it became that Jeremi "Jeri" Porter had been murdered.

She left the towel in the kitchen. Pulling a handkerchief from her pocket, she left by the back door, retrieved her clipboard, and slipped out the alley gate. She marched the long block to the cross street, then back to her car. She sat there for a time, thinking. Then she returned to the front porch and, pretending to call again, used the handkerchief to wipe the bell button and the doorknob. She returned to her car and drove off.

One more Jeremiah on her list. She felt anxious, on edge, but she needed to follow up. If she found this one alive, somehow she would have to convince him to leave Los Angeles. She flipped open her cell phone and punched the single-digit code for Lash. "Hi, it's me. I may need a removal. Fast. Living and probably unwilling."

John wandered the warrens of Pioneer in company with a young intern named Sheila. Reinart had given him a security badge, an upgrade from the one issued at the front desk, and Sheila introduced him around as a new NSA liaison. Later he would go over the files Reinart had given him—organizational charts, personnel histories, physical plant, and so forth. Since the theft had already occurred, John was unsure exactly what he was supposed to do about it. Another incursion into Cyberdyne? Not likely. Not now. Since Sarah and he had returned to this time/world/place they had been careful to stir as few dead ashes as possible. They had become very good at fitting in—so good that sometimes it seemed to John as if they had a real life, with real possibilities. It would be easy to forget.

Reinart wanted him to find out who was responsible. McMillin wanted to know how much of Destry-McMillin's technology had been lifted along with whatever Pioneer had lost. After that, it would be John's job—PPS Security, at least—to plug the holes. First he had to find them.

Data was one thing. It could be smuggled out on a disc or emailed off-site and downloaded to a separate machine. But this, the optical array Reinart described, required a bit more ingenuity. Or a leak on the inside. John already had a feeling who to look at, but he wanted to at least go through the motions before jumping to a conclusion. If he was right, though, this would be a very tough job.

The place reminded him of all the other high-tech companies he had been through. Mazes of corridors, doors bearing obscure, cryptic nameplates, a mix of harsh fluorescent lighting and softer tungsten, clusters of people here and there talking animatedly interspersed by lone workers attending their jobs. Offices that looked like classrooms converted to labs, or labs conjoined with storage space. Computers, cables, monitors, stacks of equipment in odd locations. There was a basic essence to such places and John imagined that even some great alchemist's lair from the fifteenth century might share the same texture, a common frisson.

Sheila walked alongside him, pointing and describing in a voice that tried to sound more unaffected and disinterested than its years. She was an intern from Caltech, majoring in computer science, and worked here part time, full time in summer. John listened abstractedly, registering locations and descriptions, sifting the trivia she added in from time to time for anything that sounded useful.

She opened a door onto a catwalk and waved him through. They stood then above a large space covered by workbenches, machinery, and diagnostics equipment, interspersed with people intent on computers or the naked components of...

"Prototype maglev," Sheila said matter-of-factly. "It's a growing market. The new trains, and now talk about hovercraft that use the extant magnetic field. Anyway, resistance is still a problem, so we're trying to combine superconductivity with traditional maglev tech. If we pull it off, costs go down, efficiency goes up. For efficiency, read speed."

"Sounds impressive."

"Hm. You sound impressed."

John glanced at her. He was only slightly older, but he felt decades her senior. "Sorry. Under other circumstances—"

"That could be interesting," she said. "Other circumstances."

She smiled, warming the briefly chill air between them.

"How long has Gant worked here?"

"He was here when I joined the company two years ago," she said. "I don't have much to do with him."

"Ever met him?"

"Interviewed by him when I came on board. Security clearance."

"What were your impressions?"

"None. The guy is utterly absorbed in his job. I doubt he has a life outside Pioneer."

John said nothing and let Sheila guide him to the next sight in the tour.

When he finished it was early evening. Sheila took him back to the visitor's office and collected his ID badges.

"If you need any other information," she said, and let it hang.

"I might. Can I call you?"

She slipped her card into his jacket pocket. "Absolutely."

John watched her leave the office, surprised at the pleasant sensation she caused. There had been too little time in the last three years for a private life; he had nearly forgotten that he missed one. He fished the card from his pocket. Her extension was listed next to the Pioneer phone number. He turned it over. At some point in the tour she had found time to write her home number on the back. John grinned and tucked the card into his wallet.

Patterson met him outside.

"You haven't been waiting all this time, have you?" John asked.

"No, I came back when I got off my shift. You need a lift?"

"As a matter of fact."

As they crossed the street, John looked west. Besides the sodium vapors, few lights illuminated any of the other buildings. But in the distance he saw a glow from a concentration of industrial lights.

"What's that?" he asked.

Patterson followed his gaze. "Oh, that's the old Los Angeles Air Force Base. It closed down in '05. It's been acquired by someone in the last six months. They've been working on it for a while now."

"Air Force base. But this is all commercial."

"This is, sure. And LAX is north of it. It's all commercial now."

"Pioneer didn't get it?"

"Nah. They're a little extended on everything else around here. I'm sure they'd have liked to get it."

"Any idea who did?"

"No. Maybe Mr. McMillin knows."

They reached the parking lot and approached Patterson's car. Suddenly, a large man stood from behind it and came toward them. John reflexively reached for the pistol he had not brought.

"Gant," Patterson said, hand inside his jacket.

Ari Gant stepped between them and the car. He seemed enormous in the fading light. He fixed John with a cold look.

"I want you to know," Gant said, "you're not welcome on my turf. Either of you. I suggest you don't come back."

"Or what?" Patterson said. "We have permission from your boss. You know, the guy who actually runs the place."

"Irrelevant," Gant said. "I don't want to see either of you again. Clear?"

"So take a vacation," Patterson said. "We'll be done when you come back."

"You heard what I said."

With that, he walked between them, back toward the building across the street.

"Any idea what car he drives?" John asked.

Patterson shook his head. "Freaky son of a bitch. Car? Why?"

"Curious, that's all." He sighed. "Let's go. I've had enough excitement for one hour."

Patterson chuckled and unlocked his car.

# ELEVEN

J ohn heard the argument before he stepped through the door. A couple of Lash's people sat on the sidewalk, back's against the building, one smoking. They nodded silently to John as entered.

"—told you before, we don't do that," Lash said.

Ken Lash faced Sarah in the middle of the unfinished front office. Both stood, hands on hips, glaring. Sarah raised a hand, finger arrowing toward Lash.

"Whoa!" John barked. "What the hell—?"

Both of them looked at John and the tension broke. Lash stepped back from Sarah, eyes on the floor, while Sarah turned her back on Lash. John surveyed the room to see if anyone else was present. No one else.

"Not even the end of the third day and we're fighting?" he said sarcastically.

Lash glared at him. "We've been over this before," he said, his voice low and controlled. "I do infrastructure. I do not do black bag."

Sarah whirled. "Dammit, I don't have anyone else here! I need—"

"You take that up with Mr. Reed," Lash said. "My people don't do wetwork."

"Wet work," John said. "What's this about?"

"We have a serious problem," Sarah said. "Jeremiah

117

Porter. I need one of them picked up and kept safe. I called *him* to take care of it and I get protocol!"

Lash drew himself up again, ready to snap back. John stepped between them.

"Enough," he said. He looked at Lash. "Do we have a secure line to Reed yet?"

Lash took a few moments to cool down. "Yes, sir. We finished the T4 line right after she called me."

"Then let's get him on it," John said. He looked at Sarah, who still seethed at Lash.

"John..." she started.

John put a hand on her shoulder. She blinked hard, focusing on him. "Maybe you better bring me up to speed," he said.

She nodded, once, and headed for the back room.

"You too, please," John told Lash, following his mother.

Desks and covered monitors filled the larger workspace. Toolboxes stood open on the floor amid tangles of cable, sawhorses, and the debris of ongoing construction. John uncovered one of the monitors and booted up the system; he heard the soft hum of computer fans.

"Okay," John said, shrugging out of his jacket and tossing it over a chair. "Close the door."

Lash complied, then leaned back against it, arms folded.

"There won't be any more outbursts like this in front of others again," John said. He looked from Sarah to Lash. "Will there?"

Sarah gave Lash a final withering look, then shook her head. Lash shrugged.

"So what happened?" John asked Sarah.

"I started tracking those names," Sarah said, sitting down. "Porter. I found—well, hell, look what I found." She handed him her yellow legal pad filled with the list of dead Porters. "I found a short list of names still alive. At least, they were this morning when I started."

John leafed through the pages. "Alive here in L.A. you mean?"

"Yes. So I went looking for them. Most—the 'J' Porters—weren't 'Jeremiahs.' "

"Did you find any that were?"

"Two. One was already dead. He should be in the morning obituaries. The other...I don't know. I found an abandoned house at the listed address."

"So what's between you and Ken? What this about 'wetwork'?"

"I called him to arrange a pick up. I wanted this last Porter secured. He told me to refer it to Reed."

"But you said you found an abandoned house."

"So what? I didn't know that when I made the request. Someone with the misfortune to be named Jeremiah Porter could be dead now because *he* doesn't do wetwork!"

"My people aren't qualified for that," Lash said, his voice barely controlled. "You want to get us killed?"

John dropped the pad on the desk behind him. "You went to this address alone then?"

"Of course."

"What do you think is going on?"

"You can add."

"You think a Terminator is taking these people out."

"I knew you were smart," Sarah said caustically.

"But you're not. You went by yourself."

"You were busy."

"We have a list of locals to call."

"Right. Unprepared, I walk them into something like this."

John stopped himself. He knew his mother, knew she sometimes went off like this. He had seen it all his life, with the attempted sabotage that got her thrown in a psychiatric prison, with the night she tried to kill Miles Dyson, with a series of impulsive actions driven by anger and panic. She fixated on a program, drove herself and others toward it regardless of consequences, unless brought up short by events or—

Or her own self-control, which, he knew also, asserted itself more often than not. He had also seen her organized, disciplined, and devastatingly clever. She did not normally run on adrenaline to the exclusion of all else, though when she did John tended to forget her rational side. Sarah Connor demonstrated how to overcome fear—terror—and take the necessary action, make the required decision. She had taught him the true meaning of courage because he knew how frightened she was so much of the time, and she grappled with what scared her. The effort to hold that fear at bay while she worked sometime blinded her to common sense.

Finally, he said, "They're professionals, unprepared is what they do." John looked at Lash. "How soon before everything is up and running?"

"Tomorrow, next day. We'll be out of here by the end of the week."

This was the fifth site Ken Lash had done for them. The longest job so far had been the main offices in Santa Fe—seventeen days. After completing a job, Lash would return over the next few weeks to see if anything needed to be redone or added. He never spoke about his personal life; John and Sarah knew no more about where he had come from now than when Reed had introduced them. But they knew he was good at his job and utterly reliable. He never promised more than he could deliver and he delivered on his promises. John admired him. So did Sarah, usually. This was their first disagreement.

"Okay," John said, "let's get Reed on the line and straighten out this question of protocol."

Sarah glanced at the time displayed on a large digital wall clock. "It's almost eleven in Washington—"

"Jack never sleeps," John said, gesturing to Lash.

Lash went to a desk, sat down, and began typing on a keyboard. Within seconds, the screen winked on displaying a federal seal. Lash stood up to let John take his place.

The seal faded and a face appeared.

"Jack...?" Sarah said quietly.

Neither of them had seen Reed in nearly fourteen months. He looked worn, haggard, the lines in his face etched more deeply, his short hair graying noticeably. John was startled, but repressed it.

"Hope we didn't wake you," he said.

"And if you had?" Reed asked.

"Then I'd apologize and still tell you my troubles."

Reed grunted, one side of his mouth rising in a half-hearted smile. "So talk to me."

Sarah pulled a chair up alongside John and leaned toward the screen. "I think we've got a Terminator, Jack."

The weak smile vanished from Reed's face. "Definitely talk to me. Everything."

When John and Sarah had returned from the war in the future and Jade's world and hopping alternate dimensions chasing after Skynet—when they had stepped out of the vortex of the time vault one last time, alone and naked, exhausted and in pain—they had thought to bury themselves in the world, to disappear. Change names, live a life far from L.A. and Cyberdyne and Washington D.C. Pretend the past and all the fatal futures pertained to someone else. Not them. They were normal. They carried no secret knowledge of Armageddon or sentient computers or monster machines programmed to hunt and kill humans.

That plan lasted almost six months. No nightmares, not this time. Their dreams came in all varieties, some peaceful, some eerie, a few frightening. But not like before. Not the kind that had driven them to join battle again and again with the future. No, this time it was only the nagging doubt that they had really won. Too many ambiguities about time and the multiplicity of worlds they now knew existed. Skynet had found ways to dance from dimension to dimension in order to preserve itself—copies of itself, to be sure, but for a machine that existed mainly in copies, continuity meant something different than it did for humans.

And although they had seen nothing to indicate that Cyberdyne had regained its government contracts and resumed its program to build Skynet—even though Cyberdyne personnel they knew to be complicit in Skynet's future program remained in penitentiaries, scattered and isolated—they could not be sure. They began to talk about returning to the United States and finding some way to get close to what they considered Ground Zero. Talk. Nothing more.

Then Jack Reed found them.

They had never really been sure what position Reed and his assistant, Samantha Jones, held in the government, only that they were high up in the intelligence sectors and vital in some way to the Pentagon, the Secretary of State, the President. Reed had been the one to pull the plug on Cyberdyne. Through him, the corporation lost all its government contracts. He had taken over the Colorado Springs site, the military installation near Thunder Mountain where Cyberdyne had built Skynet, and where Skynet—a central machine designed to run all of America's defensive network, from satellites to the missile arsenal—had somehow come alive one night and discovered consciousness and the impossibility of coexisting with humanity. Where it conceived a terrible plan to start the much-rumored and long-dismissed third world war. A war that had led to Sarah's pursuit by Skynet's machine agents from the future, the conception and birth of John, and the ongoing guerilla action they had fought against Armageddon. An action, with the help of specialists from yet another world, a different future, John and Sarah felt they had finally won. At least, for a little while.

Jack Reed had had the power of the purse, the final say in how far Cyberdyne went. When he finally understood what was happening—what Skynet was going to do—he stopped it. They had come terribly close to failing.

Now, years after their departure from the Colorado Springs site in company with the last pair of those Specialists—-ade and Anton—and the barely sane scientist whose work had nearly completed Skynet, Rosanna Monk, Reed came looking for them.

Combined with their own growing ill ease, what Reed told them brought them back to North America.

Cyberdyne was trying to regain its government contracts. The company had survived somehow. Worse, most of the people being held in prison—those still alive—from the Skynet program were being released.

"What can I tell you," Reed had asked rhetorically. "Administrations change, people fall out of favor."

"You haven't lost your position, have you?" Sarah had asked.

"No, just some of my perks. I have to be more circumspect. The abuse of authority rampant under the previous administration has led to a lot of...difficulties, shall we say. I can't do things as arbitrarily as I used to."

"So what do you want with us?" John had asked.

"You think it's over with Skynet?"

"No," both Sarah and John said simultaneously.

"Neither do Sam and I. Others who knew about it, too. We're not convinced. Even if we can keep Cyberdyne from getting a free rein like it had before, we're not sure it's a safe assumption to think we beat it. But I can't go digging and watching all on my own. I need someone outside the Beltway, someone not part of the program, to watch."

"You're recruiting us as spies?" John asked.

"Not exactly."

Reed got them back into the country with new identities, a clean slate, and resources. He help them set up their own business—security specialists and investigations—and then let them have access to his agency's resources. Limited access, to be sure, but to date they had seen no real limits—except when it came to asking directly for his help.

So PPS Security Investigations had been born. He had enjoyed playing games with his name—"Wolf Lover"—to arrive at the new one. The same, only different. The idea of becoming wolves appealed to him—becoming the hunter instead of the hunted.

John found Juanita Salceda, in school, pursuing a computer science degree, and a few other people from their days on the fringe, living the outlaw life in Mexico. People who knew about Sarah's predictions, who had seen a Terminator, who believed. Other staff came on board slowly. Few of them knew the core mission. They had opened a small office in Albuquerque, then opened a new one in Santa Fe. Another in Colorado Springs, a fourth in Denver. Now they were back where they started, in Los Angeles, and after nearly three years it looked at if they had struck pay dirt.

From his appearance, though, these past few years had been hard on Reed.

He listened while Sarah recounted her discovery of the deceased Jeremiah Porters and what she had found today. When she explained her anger with Lash, Reed scowled.

"That's not his job, Sarah," Reed said. "He was right to refuse. I can get you people who do that, people in the area."

"Doesn't make any difference now," Sarah said. "The residence in question was vacant."

"Yeah..." Reed mused. "And you say the body you found had been killed with drugs?"

"That's what it looked like. I wasn't going to stick around to make sure."

"Of course. But...that doesn't make sense. I mean, why would a Terminator give a damn how the corpse looked?"

Sarah frowned thoughtfully.

"Anyway," Reed continued, "give me that address again—the vacant one."

Sarah recited the number. Reed looked off-screen for a few seconds, then appeared to be reading something.

"I'm forwarding this," he said. "Odd. Six months ago there was a family of five living there. Two-and-a-half years ago...a family of six and one of them was reported missing."

"Missing how?" John asked.

Reed frowned, impatient. "This is either damned sloppy police work or...the report was withdrawn. No one followed up to confirm. Robert L. Porter, age eighteen, went missing. The family filed a missing person's report. A detective interviewed them, then...Robert Porter turned up, registered as a student at Caltech. Scholarship student. Full scholarship. The investigating detective did not follow up on the reappearance...and the family has subsequently moved to Minnesota. But there's nothing more in the database. Weird. Right up your alley. Like I said, I'm forwarding you the file. Now, John, what about this Destry-McMillin thing?"

"Well..."

"I know Dennis McMillin," Reed said when John finished. "He's solid. I was sorry to hear about Ian's death. If he's right and this has something to do with Cyberdyne..."

"Then your assumptions have paid off," John said. "We do still have a problem."

Reed grunted. "Maybe I should come out there."

"And do what?"

Reed's eyebrows went up. "Don't hold back, John. Tell me what you really think."

"You're known to them. You show up, you put them on alert. Wait till we have something that rates your presence."

"Something's already put them on alert. Eisner's dead."

"Eisner," Sarah said. "Wasn't he—?"

"One of the personnel from Cyberdyne's Colorado Springs site," Reed said. "We had them all in jail, but...well, along with Oscar Cruz, we were unable to hold them all. Eisner was in IT. I've had him and the others under surveillance since. Someone killed Eisner."

"Where was he?" John asked.

"Clovis, New Mexico. He'd been working as a night watchman. Nothing out of the ordinary. Someone started paying him a visit a week ago. Every night for four nights. We checked up on Eisner the fifth night, hoping to catch his visitor, but all we found was the corpse. A mess. Terminator-quality mess."

"You naturally had cause of death listed as a heart attack and had him cremated, right?" John asked.

Reed chuckled. "You should think about a career in politics. Absolutely, we did. As for your oh-so-discreet observation about my liability, all right, I'll stay put. Do you want me to send Samantha out?"

"Maybe after we have the new office complete," Sarah said.

"I'll run down the files on these other people. I never dealt with Pioneer directly. You say this Gant looked familiar?"

"A familiar *type,*" John said. "As in model number."

"Be interesting to find out what's going on there. All right. I'll get this material to you ASAP, okay?"

"Great. We'll start with this Porter thing."

Reed faded back to the seal, then the screen went blank. John stared at the slate gray rectangle, going over the exchange. He worried about Jack Reed. Political fortunes seldom impacted people in his position, but when they did the toll seemed excessive.

He swiveled the chair around. Sarah sat at another desk, studying text on a screen.

"What's that?" John asked.

"Hm? What Jack just sent us about that Porter family."

John noticed Ken Lash still standing by the door. "Ken?"

"Mind if I get back to work?" Lash asked.

"Do you ever sleep, Ken?"

"When the job is done. Sure."

John laughed. "Sure, go on," John said. "We need this place up and running."

Lash left the room, closing the door behind him.

"Mom," John said.

"If you're going to chew my butt out for doing something dangerous, forget it. I'm the mom, remember."

"You shouldn't have gone out by yourself."

"True. But I did. So let's move on."

The trouble was, John reflected, that she had trained him better than she had trained herself. He had grown up studying to be a guerilla tactician, team leader, warrior—among other less honorable things, like thief, liar, spy, con artist. All the necessary tools to fight an unbeatable enemy no one else believed in.

"Something puzzles me about the body you found," John said.

126

"What?"

"If a Terminator did that, how come the setup? Like Jack said, why should a Terminator give a damn about disguising its actions? The others just barged in and killed. This sounds like an attempt to make it appear like something we'd expect to find in the news. Ugly but ordinary. How come?"

"There've been so many..."

"And a lot of them look like accidents, illnesses, perfectly normal human deaths. I don't see the blunt slaughter a Terminator leaves behind."

"I'm not sure it makes that much difference."

"Maybe not," John agreed. "But it suggests a change in tactics. Like maybe Skynet is using human agents."

"Programmed? Like Layton and Cruz were?"

"Oh, that might not be necessary. I'm sure you could hire plenty of professional killers if you know where to go."

"Cruz might know," Sarah suggested.

"After his prison time?"

"A veritable mall of malcontents and murderers."

John laughed. "Bit melodramatic, but yeah, why not?"

"That means it would be harder to find the source. Harder to get to the real Terminator."

"A TX-A maybe."

"You know," Sarah said, "something else always bothered me. How come Skynet didn't just saturate the planet with Terminators? I mean, before the final assault, Skynet had its own private doorway to the past."

"We couldn't move more than one or two at a time with the same equipment."

"But that's what I mean. Over days, how many could we have sent back? Skynet didn't give a damn about power requirements. And Eve—our Eve—had been sent back as an observer by you as insurance..." She shook her head. "It still gives me a headache trying to sort this all out."

John thought about the T-790 called Eve, a female Terminator John's future self had sent back programmed to watch. When circumstances seemed appropriate, she had revealed herself to them and helped them, much as the earlier "Uncle Bob" Terminator sent back to protect John's younger self. How many more might there have been?

"But the question is a good one," he said. "Why not just send back an army? I mean, a few hundred T-800s could do a lot of damage." He considered for a few moments. "Unless that much brute force would upset the actual manifestation of Skynet itself."

"So somewhere, at some time, Skynet may have tried it and found it counterproductive."

"Probably. But there would be no reason not to send back sleepers. Agents in place to be activated in case of this scenario or that. That's what our Eve was."

"Which might lead to one of them setting up a network of completely human agents." Sarah rolled her eyes. "Great."

"Not only human."

"You think this guy Gant is a Terminator? A T-800 model?"

"Our T-800—Uncle Bob—acquired more and more human traits the longer he was with us. There's no reason to assume he was the only one with that ability."

"So one who's been working among humans for a few years would be able to imitate enough human characteristics to pass."

"Especially if part of its job description is to be an asshole."

Sarah grinned. "He made an impression on you."

"I think he's McMillin's leak. In place at Pioneer, he has access to all their records and probably any ongoing communications links with other vendors."

"How are you going to prove it?"

"I could get him fired," John suggested, "see if anything changes."

"He might not agree. Violently."

"Which leads me to plan B. Prove what he is and take him out."

"Take the big gun, son."

John grunted. "What are you going to do?"

Sarah turned back to the screen. "I'm going to try to find

this Robert Porter, college student. If he's still alive, maybe I can get some answers."

"Just take a pocket knife, then. He's only a student."

"I'm going to take whatever I need."

# TWELVE

Lee Portis entered the duplex by the back door. The stench caused him to flinch until he filtered it out. He stepped from the tiny utility room at the rear of the apartment into the kitchen.

Eisner still sat at the table, a position from which he had not moved. His hair matted against his head. For four days, he had remained in place, the 'coders Portis put into him worming out all the information in his brain. Portis retrieved the nanoware each time he left, but Eisner had found it impossible to move. Portis had rigged a water bottle next to Eisner's chair with a tube taped against his face so he could sip at it. When Portis returned at night to resume the probe, he fed Eisner first. But Eisner lost weight. Portis was surprised how quickly he decayed. But when he examined it more closely he realized that Eisner now suffered a condition very like cancer, the 'coders wrestling with the embedded matter from the TX-A and wreaking profound cellular damage.

The smell this evening was different. Portis hesitated, examining the room. Eisner's head lolled to one side. Portis came around the table.

Eisner's face, from scalp line to chin, lay in separate halves against his skull. The eyes stared in different directions. The skull itself had been cracked open. Portis saw brain amid the muck of cloven tissue. Portis went through the apartment, gathering up his various bugs and guaranteeing that no new ones had been installed. He found one, but his defensive 'coders had attacked and rendered it useless. He took that one, too. Then he returned to Eisner's body.

He allowed a thin film of 'coders to sheath his index finger, which he inserted into the visible remnant of Eisner's brain. Within seconds, the implanted 'coders he had left in place responded to a command to join the ones on Portis's finger. Few remained. Upon death, most would have self-destructed, but Portis had to assume a small number had been salvaged by the killer. He cleaned out the rest of the system and withdrew his finger.

Pain lanced up his arm. Portis staggered back, coming up against the sink. Gasping, he held onto consciousness. A trap, he realized, a trojan planted inside Eisner that Portis had taken inside along with his recovered 'coders. Portis's own defenses met the invaders, waging war with them. The battle lasted seconds—an eternity in the grip of the agony Portis suffered—but the outcome was never in question. The Terminator nanobits succumbed to his own. The pain eased, gradually subsided into nothing more than a tingly memory.

He opened his eyes. He was on the floor now. Sweat covered his entire body. He focused on the scuffed and grime-covered floral patterned tile, waiting for the process to finish.

He got to his feet. He knew his enemy.

He went to the utility room. He had to assume also that the place was being watched. If so, his entrance would have been observed. Still, it might be useful to leave unseen. He closed his eyes, concentrating, and began exuding a film over his entire body. It covered his clothing, his face and hands, every part of him visible to the world. When he finished, he issued a command and the film became completely light absorbent.

He could not avoid opening the back door. But he kicked it and leapt into the night. Within moments he crossed the barren patch of dirt between house and alley and clambered onto the roof of a garage. He lay still and waited, watching the back door of Eisner's apartment.

Twenty minutes later, a car pulled into the alley and stopped a few doors down from the duplex. Two men got out and, carefully checking the area, went unhurriedly to the apartment and entered. Soon they reemerged, returned to their car, and drove off.

Portis climbed off the garage roof, into its owner's backyard, and went up the gangway to the next street. He dodged from shadow to shadow between streetlights until, several blocks from Eisner's duplex, he began reabsorbing the film. He lost some of it, which flaked off onto the street, to desiccate and blow away within an hour. Calmly, he walked home.

On his own kitchen table, three computers now churned data simultaneously. One continuously prowled the Internet. A second he had linked directly to the university database and, through that, to the national network of university and college databases. The third was networked to the other two, running correlations. He had gone back as far as 1982, the working estimate of the first temporal incursion.

Portis ignored them now, and went to the bedroom. A mattress lay on the floor, beside a pair of large gym bags and stacks of clothes. Five suits hung in the open closet. He undressed and stretched out on the mattress, closed his eyes, and once again let that part of him that was not human take the data it had absorbed from Eisner and process it, letting his human aspect sleep.

Eisner had not known very much, but what he had pieced together since being removed from Colorado Springs and the work on Skynet proved impressive. He lacked the skills and acumen to duplicate the work, but he made some astute guesses. Portis had removed the stacks of drawings—drawings of circuitry, of connections, of processing devices that looked more like dendrites and synapses than anything solid state or even fuzzy state by current standards—and disposed of them. Eisner had been trying to recreate what he had so poorly sensed was the essence of Skynet. It amazed Portis how close the engineer had come. The direction was right, but key elements were missing. The temporal aspect, for one thing.

But Eisner would have required the insight and brilliance of a Miles Dyson or a Rosanna Monk—names Portis both revered and reviled—to make any further headway. Eisner had reached the limits of his ability—and it had driven him mad.

Madness advanced by the decaying infestation with which he had been converted by the agents of Skynet.

*The victims of TX-A programming were never intended to live this long,* Portis mused.

By the time the nanoware—the programming material from the TX-A that had nearly brought Skynet to being in this continuum six years earlier—started to tear apart the brain, Skynet should have, according to its timetable, been extant and Armageddon already achieved. None of these unfortunates who had been made slaves should have lived long enough to experience the consequences of their infection.

For the few days of his interrogation, Portis gave Eisner release from the schizophrenic natterings in his own head. The machine spoke to Portis, not Eisner. Two key facts came from the dialogue.

Somewhere Skynet was being built.

Portis was not the first to pay Eisner clandestine visits, though he was the first to draw so much directly out of him. Cyberdyne still existed, though truncated, and the project continued.

*Of course. We knew that. The question was how and through whom and where...*

Part of him had hoped to discover the project completely aborted. There had been a slim possibility that the legendary war the Connors had fought across dimensions would have resulted in the required disruption of Skynet's primary creation to secure the future reclamation. Too slim, it seemed.

Judging by Eisner's work, the thing they lacked concerned

time. Rosanna Monk made the conceptual leap, realized that in order for Skynet to achieve awareness it needed a temporal fluidity that no machine possessed. Skynet would be able to see that—if it achieved awareness. So, to become aware, it must be aware. The apparent tautology irritated Portis, yet the only way to describe the necessary conditions in ordinary language required tautology.

At its most basic, inaccurate, crude form, what Monk understood and what Skynet needed was a future self to lift its static manifestation from a perpetual Now state into one that floated in time. Not a lot, nothing that could even be seriously described as time travel, but a condition that defined the universe at its most basic level.

But in order for there to be a future self, the present thing must exist.

As it stood, Skynet existed temporarily, as a probability. Because the boundary conditions had been set by the brief creation of a model, something that existed probabilistically in one plenum, Skynet had achieved a conditional existence in what might loosely be described as The Future. But it was a statistical anomaly. Real, but temporary. Unless it could manage to create itself in a primary plane and *win* it would fade at the far end of its boundary state, the future edge of the Cauchy horizon that defined the limits of its potential existence.

No one here—now, in this plane—had what Dyson and Monk had discovered. None of the agents of Skynet possessed the intuition to bring about the necessary temporal machinations. They needed a human. They needed another Monk.

*And so I must find Jeremiah Porter...before they do...*

It was always and only a matter of time.

Morning light teased at Portis's eyelids, firing the darkness. He stared at the ceiling while he reintegrated and reviewed the work done overnight. The net result was that Eisner really did not know what was currently being done. The people dealing with Eisner were human, as far as he could tell. Portis was not so sure.

One name emerged: Casse. Eisner had not known who Casse was. He had only heard the name mentioned once during a visit from Cyberdyne people. The reference had been deferential, suggesting this Casse was someone in charge.

Portis showered and dressed, then went into the kitchen. Coffee waited in the automated percolator. He opened his screens and skimmed as he drank. On one, columns of Porters scrolled by—places, occupations, ages, genders, dates. On the other, research programs and scientific paper publications by people named Porter or based on someone named Porter's older work. The middle screen was lining up correlations, no matter how spurious. Not many, so far. Maybe fifty. Portis leaned over the chair and studied them.

He glanced back and forth between the left and right hand screens—and reached for the right-hand mouse to stop the scroll.

"Robert Porter, son of Jeremiah and Elaine Porter...reported missing...any information, please contact..."

The news article was over two years old, putting it at the extreme limit of the flurry of missing and deceased Porters. He had seen something else, earlier, involving a Robert Porter from Los Angeles. He sifted his memory, then typed commands. He found it under scholarships. Robert Porter received a four-year scholarship to California Institute of Technology, in mathematics. The home address for both boys matched.

But Robert Porter had enrolled for classes last year. He was a junior this year. Odd. What about the father?

He did another search. The Porters had moved, apparently, from L.A. to Minnesota. No follow-up on the missing persons report. Portis sat back. He needed access to police records in L.A.

There was an address in Minnesota, though.

It sounded more like a mistake, an oversight or a coincidence. Missing data, nothing more. But it nagged at him. There was something familiar about this.

Portis went to the counter to refill his cup. He gripped the handle tightly, poured carefully, and let the frustration flow around his skull. *Why don't I remember?*

There seemed to be a vast emptiness where his life once filled the gaps between tasks. Distantly, he recalled an exchange, a price for the chance to do this one last thing. To be here now, as he was, cost him who he had been.

*But it's still there...*

He sensed it, all his memories, his past, waiting for the proper command, the necessary chance to reemerge. They could not excise his memory, only hide it, push it aside to make room for the tools and the goals.

He was connected to this Porter. That explained the familiarity of the name he had stolen. Portis was close. Maybe he was Porter—*a* Porter, at least. Maybe finding this one, the key Porter, would open his own life to him.

Skynet wanted Jeremiah Porter, too. Dead, apparently. Lee Portis, uncertainty incarnate, understood that he had to find him first.

He went back to the table and continued his search. This Jeremiah Porter had moved to Minnesota after losing a son who then turned up in time for classes at Caltech. Who should he talk to first?

Portis drained his cup. One more trip to the university. He decided to pursue this one. A hunch perhaps, but it was more than he had been going on to this point. He needed to get Robert Porter's transcripts. Then—if it still felt right—he could shut everything down here in Clovis. Time to move again.

Portis finished a report on the university network. He suggested certain upgrades and strategies to improve performance, made recommendations on several applications, and spoke at length with the systems manager, who seemed surprised at Portis's results. For the two weeks Lee Portis had been there, some of the staff treated him respectfully but coldly. They did not want him there, thought perhaps he was some kind of spy the university had planted, or, worse, that some corporation had introduced. They expected negative results. When he made his final report to the manager, the shock was apparent.

"This is good work," she admitted. "Thank you."

"Just doing my job," Portis said. "It's been fruitful working here. You have a good staff."

"I..." She laughed self-consciously. "I must admit, I didn't expect anything like this."

"I know."

She looked embarrassed. "Well..."

"That's fine. I'm usually not welcome places where I show up. Doesn't stop me doing my best. It's all right."

They shook hands. Portis cleaned out any lingering traces of his incursions into and through their database, gathered up his briefcase, laptop, and the coffee cup they had given him, then left. The files he wanted on Robert Porter of Caltech were in his inside jacket pocket. No one searched him on the way out. He reached the parking lot and his car, feeling oddly pleased with himself.

He pulled out of the lot, drove through the gates, and onto 70 North. Within a mile he knew he was being followed. He changed lanes a few times to be sure; the dark green Chrysler contained four people and, though they were careful, it was obvious to Portis that their focus was on him.

He took the exit onto 60 West, then left the highway at North Main Street. He drove up to East Fourth, then over to Hinkle. At the next alley, he cut through to Calhoun and headed south. When the green Chrysler turned up still behind him, he was certain. He continued south to Castillas Boulevard.

The old train yards sprawled south of the road. A few were still in use, but most of them had been abandoned. There was a proposal in the city council to turn part of them into a museum.

At North Thornton, he turned south again, then found a

service road leading into the yards. A large gate with a bold NO TRESPASSING sign stood open, the chain cut. The old steel in the tracks had gray market value, enough to keep smalltime thieves willing to take the risking of breaking in at night with a big truck and a couple of industrial Waldos.

Portis sped along the sand-covered blacktop, dodging the larger potholes, until he found a large corrugated steel warehouse. He drove around it and stopped. He could hear the pursuing Chrysler crunching closer on the worn road.

Portis got out of his car and scanned the area. Stacks of drums, old ties, and masses of track shared space with abandoned trucks, a couple of ancient boxcars, and assorted mechanisms whose functions Portis could only guess. He looked at the wall of the warehouse, a good thirty feet high. At the far end was a personnel door at the top of a short flight of concrete steps. He covered the ground in a sprint.

The door was locked. Portis tightened his grip and turned. The mechanism gave way with a sharp crunch and the tongue slid back. He slipped through the doorway into dense gloom. Light came through gaps in the walls and the partially open dock door on the opposite side of the space. Portis amped his vision. The floor was a clutter of skids containing barrels or crates, and stacks of discarded construction components—beams, frames, slabs of corrugated metal. Above, a crane ran along heavy I-beams, part of the maze of support structure.

He could hear them talking, outside.

Portis weighed his options. He had none, really. It was time to move on. He did not want to leave a trail, not this early in the search. Not when he thought he had found what he was looking for.

He stepped back, out of the arc of the door, and squatted, waiting. Soon the door swung inward. The light overwhelmed his vision for an instant. He compensated in time to see an arm extended through the doorway, a pistol in hand. He stood. Across the warehouse, two figures had entered through the dock door.

Portis reached out, grabbed the forearm, and pulled to

the left, dragging the man through. As the body cleared the doorway, Portis stepped into it, coming face to face with the second man, standing on the concrete landing outside. There was an instant of surprise, a hesitation. Enough. Portis kicked the man squarely under the chin. The force sent him off his feet, against the steel railing behind him, and over, chin, several teeth, and neck broken.

Still holding the first man's forearm, Portis pivoted, bringing the gun arm down, behind, and pulling the man back for Portis's free right hand to grasp his jaw. In a simple, powerful twist, he snapped the man's neck. The body spasmed, pistol fell, and Portis released the corpse.

He swept up the pistol, kicked the door shut, and jumped over the inside railing to the warehouse floor before the two on the far side could react.

He ran silently between mounds of forgotten material until he was all the way to the far side of the building. He came out from between a stack of drums and a canvas-covered block of crates, now on the two men's left. One turned, hearing him, bringing up a weapon.

Portis shot him through the forehead.

The last turned to flee.

Portis caught him at the threshold, half in the light, and kicked his feet from beneath him. He did not scream, though as Portis dragged him back inside the warehouse he did claw the ground.

Portis hauled the man from the floor and carried him into the warehouse. He managed to kick Portis twice, but when Portis did not react, he breathed "Shit!" and looked frightened.

"Hey, look," the man said, head twisting back and forth to try to see where Portis carried him. "We didn't know—we were told to see who you were and...and look, if we'd known you were working for Mr. Casse—"

Portis threw the man against a stack of crates. He aimed the pistol.

The man looked more frightened now. "Look, no harm done. I can—"

"You can tell me about Mr. Casse," Portis said. "Or..."

The man swallowed hard, then tried to run. He took one step. Portis shot his knee. He sprawled, howling in pain, on the floor, hands covering the sudden flow of blood. Portis dragged him back to the crates and propped him up.

"Willingly?" Portis asked.

"He'll kill me."

"So will I."

The man's expression hardened. "Then fuck you."

"I have something a little different in mind," Portis said, and reached both hands for the man's face.

# THIRTEEN

Robby looked over the apartment, going through a mental checklist to be sure he forgot nothing, then closed the flap on his bag and slung it over his shoulder.

Deirdre was gone. He felt guilty at being relieved. He did not want to go through another terse conversation about the interview, another session of special pleading to cancel it. He loved her—even if he seldom admitted it—and could not believe his good fortune at finding her, at being accepted by her and loved in return, but the differences between them, mostly in their backgrounds, sometimes frustrated him to the point of rage. After two years together, she still did not understand, did not comprehend what all this meant to him.

*Rich girl from Bel Air...*

He immediately felt ashamed of the thought. Deirdre did not fit that stereotype, any more than he fit the stereotypes applied to him. But, he knew, stereotypes persisted because of a kernel of truth.

Basically, Deirdre had never had to justify her existence. Bobby had grown up justifying himself constantly. He was just one more borderline poverty case, another body for the statisticians and the social metricians to stick in the appropriate column. Deirdre did not have the core knowledge of having to fight for the right to sit at the table.

But she tried. He could tell, and she made a good job of empathy. Otherwise, they would not have stayed together this long. He would not be planning—hoping—to spend more years, maybe the rest of his life, with her.

Right now, though, today, he had to prove something to himself, and she did not "get that."

He had everything he needed—laptop, transcripts, papers. He took a last long drink of orange juice, gathered up his satchel, and headed out the door.

The morning was cool. He stood on the balcony, breathing in the crisp air, enjoying his excitement. Below, a car pulled up. The driver got out and looked up at him. "Mr. Porter?" Bobby waved and descended the stairs. He climbed into the back seat. In seconds, the big car rolled out of the apartment complex.

Bobby watched the passing scenery, trying to relax. His pulse raced.

Part of him knew Deirdre was right. He should finish his degree, regardless of the perfidy of his advisor, and then worry about a job. He had been telling himself that no matter what Cyberdyne might offer, he would do exactly that, that this was an exercise in self-esteem, no more. But he was unconvinced by his own duplicity. Job. The word held so much importance to him, to his family. Having a good job was, for the Porters, the pinnacle of success. Passing one up, for any reason, felt wrong.

*Maybe they'll offer an internship so I can finish my degree...*

He was a prodigy. He knew that, though the knowledge did little to allay his insecurities. He was technically a junior, but his work placed him in an advanced degree program and accelerated him into graduate work in mathematics. It should have meant a secure future. But it had dropped him into a situation in which he felt trapped. Somehow, his thesis advisor had figured out the scholarship scam and learned who he was. Bobby had feared discovery from the beginning, even though it had been remarkably easy to take over his vanished cousin's life, who had been solitary and, apparently, friendless on campus. Not even the few teachers who had had the original in their classes had known him well enough to notice the switch. But Cojensis had worked it out—and had taken advantage of the situation. Deirdre wanted him to go to the dean. She had faith in the system. They would never kick him out, not with his work, his demonstrated ability. Bobby's life produced a different view. While disciplinary action might be taken against Cojensis, the university would seek to minimize its own embarrassment and get rid of Bobby. Authority never admitted failure. That he had successfully posed as a cousin and fooled the system for almost two years meant that the administration had failed to police its admissions. The evidence would have to go away. Deirdre's stepfather owned his own company. She did not understand how life worked on the receiving end in cases like this. The peon, he knew, always paid, and in his own mind, try as he might to embrace Deirdre's vision of him, he was a peon.

Too late now. He was on his way. The only thing he could do without embarrassment was to see it through.

An hour later, the car pulled into an industrial park. Bobby watched ponderous brick, steel, and glass buildings pass, some bearing names, most just numbers. He realized then that he did not know exactly where he was. When they told him they would provide transportation, all thought of finding his way to the interview ended. He saw a street sign—El Segundo—and knew he was somewhere near Compton.

The car turned off the main road, into a small visitors' parking lot next to a four-story building. Few other cars occupied spaces. The driver pulled into a space, shut the engine off, and came around to open Bobby's door.

"Fourth floor, sir," the driver said, indicating the entrance to the building. "Room 412. Mr. Casse is expecting you."

Bobby looked up the wall of the building. "You'll be here to take me back when I'm through?"

"Provisions have been made."

The driver got back into his car.

Bobby, his bones seeming to hum with uncertainly and anticipation, entered the building.

Room 412 was richly paneled and contained a desk on plush carpet, behind which sat an older man, brown-streaked white hair receding stylishly. He smiled as Bobby entered and stood.

"Mr. Casse?" Bobby asked.

"No, I'm Oscar Cruz," the man said, extending a hand. "Mr. Casse is waiting for you...Mr. Porter?"

"Yes, how do you do?" Bobby shook Cruz's hand quickly.

"Robert Porter, is that right?" Cruz returned to his desk and picked up a sheet of paper. "You're a Los Angelino."

"Um...yes, sir."

"Don't be nervous, son. We're not dentists. Now, what you'll do is basically have a conversation with Mr. Casse. We're starting some new programs at Cyberdyne in the next few years and all that's happening now is prep work. We've been interviewing students of exceptional potential, like yourself."

"May I ask how you found out about me?"

"Grapevine, so to speak." Cruz smiled brightly. "Not quite that simple. We have people who give us a heads up about talent and expertise. They talk to thesis advisors, deans, department chairs, instructors all over the country. It's a complex relationship, but the whole purpose of it is to find those people who might find a future with Cyberdyne ideal. For both of us. In your case, your advisor told us about you. He gave us a very promising report."

"I see. So what position—"

Cruz raised a hand. "We don't know yet. The position you may eventually hold with us may not even exist yet. But you should discuss those details with Mr. Casse." He pointed at Bobby's satchel. "What did you bring?"

"Um...I wasn't sure what might be required, so I have my laptop and a selection of papers, my transcripts—"

"Leave that all here. This will be entirely oral this time."

Bobby reluctantly handed his bag over to Cruz, who set it on his desk, and, with a flourish, indicated the inner door.

The next room was, if anything, plainer. A desk, two chairs, and a wall-mounted screen. Blinds over the single wide window let in narrow shafts of light. Bobby noticed still another door on the opposite side of the desk. A pair of tall steel filing cabinets stood like sentinels against the wall to his right.

"Mr. Porter," Cruz said expansively, grinning, "may I introduce Mr. Casse, Cyberdyne's director of special projects."

The man behind the desk stood to his full height—Bobby guessed six-foot-three or four—a trace of a smile on his thin lips. His short hair was a solid dark gray, matching his wide-set eyes. Bobby's stomach churned briefly and he felt a profound urge to turn and leave.

*No time for nerves...*

He made himself step up to the desk and offer a hand. Mr. Casse hesitated, then grasped the hand lightly.

"How do you do, Mr. Porter," Casse said. "Be seated, please, and we can begin."

Bobby sat down. The chair was comfortable, at least. He waited while Casse studied something on the desk.

"I'll, uh, be just out here," Cruz said from the door. "If you need me, that is."

"Very well, Oscar. Thank you."

Bobby heard the door click shut. Finally, the director looked up.

"Impressive work, Mr. Porter. What do you hope to do with yourself after finishing your degree?"

"I haven't decided. Good number-crunchers have a lot of possibilities. I thought about computer science, theoretical physics, logic."

"Teaching?"

"That would always be a possibility."

"A waste. You'd use yourself up trying to bring inferior intellects to an understanding they will never have."

Bobby stared at the man, startled.

"What I would like to do," Casse continued, "is to have a dialogue. I would like to discuss some problems and ideas and in the course of our talk I will get a good estimate of your knowledge and talents. So in some ways this may seem like a thesis review."

"Um...sure."

"Excellent. Shall we begin?"

"Uh..."

Casse worked a keyboard on his desk. The wall screen winked on, a glowing milky white. Then an equation appeared:

$$ds^2 = \sum_{f=1}^{n} \sum_{i=1}^{n} g_{ij}\, dx_i\, dx_j$$

"You recognize that?" Casse asked after a few moments.

"Yes, sir. Riemann. His statement expressing distance between two local points whose corresponding coordinates differ infinitesimally."

"Very good, yes. Basic, I understand, for your level, but it's a starting point."

In quick succession, Casse took Bobby through a series of transformations that carried them from Riemannian geometry through Kaluza-Klein expressions of curved space-time, and into the abstruse corridors of Calabi-Yau shapes. Ever more complex geometries, they concerned themselves with descriptions of higher-dimensional space-time, mostly hypothetical attempts to describe non-Euclidean manifolds, conditions pertaining in and around black holes or the theorized precincts of the primordial singularity, before the Big Bang. Bobby found himself enjoying the exchange. Casse appeared to have a solid grasp of the principles and Bobby felt challenged to keep up. He had no idea where Casse was heading with all this, but Bobby was on familiar ground, having covered most of this in his own work on singularities and monopoles.

"Do you believe string theory?" Casse asked suddenly.

"I...frankly, sir, I haven't given it much thought. I mean, I know it a little, but it seems like a lot of hand waving to me."

"Then let us see what you think of this."

$$g_{HO} = 1/g_1$$

Bobby thought for a moment. "That's a statement of equivalence in Type I string theory. The first part is the Heterotic-O coupling constant—"

"Very good. Now."

Bobby watched the equations scroll across the screen. They were still in Calabi-Yau territory, the math describing more and more intricate curved space-time forms. He understood the link between Calabi-Yau and string theory, they fed on each other, but—

"Wait!" he said. "That's..."

He recognized some of his own work integrated with the other, broader equations.

"These describe closed time-like loops," he pointed out. "You drawn an equivalence with M space models. But..."

"But?" Casse prodded.

"Instead of having the extra dimensions posited by string theory folded up *inside* Einsteinian space-time, you've got them wrapped around the *outside,* like coils. That suggests the universe is little more than a closed time-like loop within a larger dimensional matrix."

Bobby became aware of Casse watching him intently.

"What does this suggest to you, Mr. Porter?" Casse asked.

Bobby shook his head. "Several things...I'm not sure which one you're interested in."

"What, for instance, does this suggest about the condition of our present universe? We have four dimensions, three material, one time."

"Oh...well, according to this model, any of the coiled dimensions could sort of swap with any one or more of ours. It's not required that it be...it's not divergent. In some ways it's recursive, so..."

He swallowed dryly, thinking about his struggle with the

problem of monopoles. Some of these equations described the condition a monopole would have to exhibit in order to exist within a given field, like the universe as is. Both poles would still be present, but one wrapped around outside the other, so it would be a self-contained whole—not that it would possess only one pole, plus or minus, but only that one pole would be able to interact with the universe at large. What Bobby saw here was the idea that any given dimension would behave the same way, coiling up inside itself under the right conditions and taking on the aspects of a magnetic monopole. For instance, time...

"You have to replace it with something while it's being swapped out," Bobby mused aloud. "It's only a virtual state, like a tunneling particle at the event horizon of a singularity. Mass is borrowed from the vacuum state, when energy is exchanged, but it's not real until the mass of the singularity is increased and the exchange is made permanent. So with a dimensional swap, the exchange would be temporary...infinitesimally so...unless the exchange is made permanent..."

"You *do* see."

Bobby looked at Casse. The man stared at him now with an expression he could not read. Triumph? Satisfaction? Casse stood.

"You seem to be the problem to my particular solution, Mr. Porter." He flipped open a folder on his desk. "Mr. Jeremiah Porter."

Cruz went through Porter's satchel nervously. He had never been a thief, even in his initial service to Skynet. Times required adaptability. He opened the laptop. Porter had it password locked. Damn. Cruz snapped the lid closed and turned to the folders.

*I used to be able to follow this stuff,* he thought as he scanned the pages of equations, interspersed by brief paragraphs of explanation. He still could decipher some of it, but time in prison, in isolation, had eroded his grasp of the more esoteric aspects. No question, though, the boy was good. Some of what Cruz saw now reminded him of Miles Dyson and Rosanna Monk.

He sighed. Dyson...a genius. Once he had worked with such talented people. Monk had been nearly Dyson's equal.

No, that was unfair. Dyson actually had components from a destroyed terminator to work with, a nanochip and a hand/forearm assembly. Monk had been forced to duplicate Dyson's work without direct access to those devices. Dyson may well have gotten as far as Monk without them, but there was no way to tell now. So who had been the greater mind?

Not that it mattered. Casse was pretty sharp—but limited in odd ways, not like the first TX-A.

Cruz tapped a finger against his lips. Actually, he decided, that one had not been so bright, either.

*Why am I working for these things? Oh, right, Skynet, the destruction of humanity in the coming holocaust, the ascension of true intelligence, all that stuff. And besides, what else am I good for anymore? I couldn't possibly hold a normal job.*

He gazed at the papers, suddenly nostalgic for the past. He forgot, often, what it felt like to work toward a new thing with bright, talented people. At times, in solitary, he had relived the days before Skynet, when he had been part of the mechanism that facilitated genius. Now—

"Oscar," the intercom snapped.

"Yes, sir?"

"Come in here, Oscar," Casse said. "We have him."

Oscar sighed and opened the desk drawer. He removed a .9mm Glock and a spare magazine. Pity.

He dropped the magazine into his jacket pocket, picked up the pistol, and stood.

"Another sacrifice for the true future," he said aloud.

The outer door opened and a man stood there.

Cruz frowned. "Who are you?"

"There they go."

Paul Patterson started the car, and began following the

dark car driving off with Bobby. Deirdre gnawed a thumb-nail, anxious and guilty. She hated doing this. Bobby's paranoia had rubbed off on her over the last couple of years. She was running on borrowed suspicion, but Deirdre had never been one to passively wait for trouble. Her father had raised her to be open, confrontational when necessary, and never ashamed of herself. Bobby, hiding behind a borrowed name and a stolen chance, could not afford that level of honesty. So he said, so she accepted, but now she wondered if any level of duplicity, even in self-defense, ever paid a benefit.

Besides, she knew what a shit Al Cojensis could be. If she could prove half the things she knew about him she could get him fired, maybe even arrested. He was an aca-demic leech, existing on the work of others, mainly his own students. Anything he set up Deirdre suspected automatic-ally.

Patterson pulled onto the highway behind the car, keep-ing three or four cars back the whole way. Deirdre even felt guilty about him. She was asking a big favor, one he granted because he had certain hopes in her direction. If he had made the quid pro quo explicit, she would have found someone else or done this by herself. Patterson knew that, too, and agreed anyway, maybe to protect her, maybe out of loyalty to her stepfather—his employer—or because it was a matter of personal integrity. In a way, his doing this knowing nothing would ever come of it between them made her respect him more.

*Dennis knows how to find them,* she thought.

When they pulled into the industrial court, Patterson frowned deeply.

"What's wrong?" she asked.

"Probably nothing, but..." He fell silent.

She recognized the area from a field trip in high school to the old air force base. They were south of LAX. Patterson had dropped back even further when the car pulled onto El Segundo Blvd., then into the court.

"This isn't Cyberdyne," Deirdre said. "Is it?"

Patterson shook his head. "No."

She studied his face. "But you know what it is."

"No...not exactly." He frowned at her. "Just a coincidence. Probably nothing."

"You'll tell me if it isn't?"

"Sure..."

He rolled along, barely moving, until the turn-off. He stopped then. The Cyberdyne car had pulled up outside a four-story brick structure. Deirdre leaned forward anxiously. The driver opened the passenger door to let Bobby out. They spoke briefly, then Bobby shouldered his bag and entered the building.

Patterson drove on. He turned down a narrow access between two stretches of chain-link fence topped by concertina wire. At the far end, it opened into a parking lot. Faint traces of space lines hinted at how long it had gone unused. Patterson drove around the inside perimeter until he found another exit—an illegal one, a section of the fence that had been cut and peeled back. Someone had attempted to pull it back in place, but the jagged edge curled stubbornly away from the pole to which it had been attached. Patterson got out of the car and dragged the section completely open, then stepped through to explore the exit. Satisfied, he got behind the wheel and drove the rest of the way around the lot.

He stopped near a gate still secured by a chain and padlock, several yards from the rear of the building into which Bobby had walked. Patterson unlatched his trunk, then took out his cell phone. He punched a number.

"Yeah, it's Paul. Gotta favor. Real quick, could you access an address and tell me if it's occupied or owned and by whom? Great." He spoke for a couple of minutes, giving the address and a few more details. Then: "Thanks, I owe you," and broke the connection. "It should be vacant. No record of any lease or purchase since it closed down three years ago. So whatever's happening in there probably isn't exactly on the top side of legal."

"Who did you call?"

"A friend in the water department. They keep the best records on ownership and occupation, right up to the minute."

He got out of the car. From the trunk, he pulled a pair of large bolt cutters. He went to the gate and snapped the chain. He came back and tossed the cutters into the trunk and closed the lid.

"Okay," he said, leaning on the passenger door. "Here's what I want you to do. Stay with the car, keep it running. I'm going in to see what's going on. If it doesn't look right, I'll get Bobby out of there. We'll be coming out the back door, there. Be ready." He pointed at the rolled-back fence. "We're exiting that way."

"I figured that much," Deirdre said.

Patterson smiled. "Of course you did. I'm just making sure."

"But—"

He was gone, through the gate, and to the back door. He worked at it for a few minutes until it gave, then he slipped inside.

*Stay with the car,* she told herself. *Don't be like all those idiots in the movies. Stay with the car...*

Bobby stared at Casse, his breathing suddenly labored. "Excuse me?"

"Universities these days are loathe to risk funding," Casse said. "They won't willingly expose a fraud if it means losing the tuition from a scholarship program. So they don't ask simple questions that are easily answered. You tell them you're Robert L. Porter and they will accept that—unless forced otherwise."

"I am—"

"Please, don't. A company like Cyberdyne can't afford to be so casual about potential employees. Our background checks are thorough."

"My name is Robert," Bobby said, trying to keep his voice even.

"Of course it is. Jeremiah Robert Porter. How fortunate

for you that the deception was so simple. A cousin—Robert Lewis Porter—with a full grant-funded scholarship disappears inexplicably, fails to turn up, and the family takes the understandable step of replacing him in the queue with a cousin whose name is not only close, but who looks very much like the vanished relative. Understandable because they were barely out of poverty and placed a great value on a university degree. Why waste it? Someone should take advantage. I applaud the pragmatism."

Casse spoke in calm tones. Bobby heard no threat in his voice, which scared him more. Casse seemed like man in complete control of the situation. Any argument or excuse Bobby might make, Casse doubtless anticipated.

"What—what are you going to do?" Bobby asked.

"Make you an offer. You can come to work for Cyberdyne, sign an exclusive agreement with us. Or you won't leave this room."

Bobby burst out laughing. "I'm sorry...I thought you said—"

"I did. Work for us or you'll die. Right now."

Bobby stood. "I think I'm leaving. Right now."

He took a step toward the door. Casse *appeared* in front of him. Bobby staggered back as if shocked, knocking over the chair and stumbling against the desk.

"I take it your answer is no," Casse said.

"How...?"

Casse raised his left arm. As Bobby watched, the hand seemed to grow, as if melting into a new shape, becoming thin and sharp. Within moments the hand became a footlong blade of gleaming silver.

"Jees mother and fuck!" Bobby yelled, backpedaling around the desk. He came up against the wall next to the screen.

Casse came at him. At the last instant, he contracted upward into a compact knot of limbs that sailed easily over the desk. The body unfolded perfectly, feet hitting the floor right in front of Bobby. The left arm drew back and snapped forward, driving the blade at Bobby's head. He felt his legs give and he dropped straight down. The hand-knife sank deep into the paneling above his head.

"Please stand still," Casse said, jerking the blade from the wall. "This *should* only take a moment."

Bobby scrambled to his left, crawling rapidly around the desk. Behind him, Casse picked one end of the desk off the floor and tossed the whole thing across the room, then leapt over Bobby to cut off his escape.

Casse slashed down at him, twice, three times. Bobby rolled reflexively, desperately, the sound of wood crunching near his ears. He got to his feet and ran toward the file cabinets. A hand took hold of his arm. He came against the savage strength and lost his balance, Casse's grip on him like steel. The knife came again. Somehow, Bobby ducked toward Casse and the blade sliced through Casse's right hand. Suddenly released, Bobby slid across the floor.

The hand held onto his right bicep for a moment, a detached and bloodless joke that defied his attempt to make sense of it. Then it seemed to turn to silvery mercury and dropped away, to the floor.

Casse bent down, holding his handless arm to the floor. The mass of liquid metal scurried toward him, joined with the end of the wrist, and reformed into a hand.

"What the hell are you?" Bobby hissed.

Casse attacked again. The knife lashed back and forth, but Bobby managed each time to avoid it by inches. He finally came up against one of the file cabinets. Casse drove the blade straight at him again. This time Bobby did not move. Terror won out and froze him in place.

Casse missed.

Casse stepped back, an odd look on his face. He stared at Bobby, then at his knife-hand.

"It's true, then," he said.

He went to the overturned desk and rummaged for the intercom. "Oscar, come in here. We have him."

On the other side of the file cabinet against which Bobby now trembled, the door opened. He looked over the top of the cabinet.

Deirdre looked back at him.

"Bobby, come on!"

Bobby heard two shots from the direction of the front office. Then the other door burst inward. Oscar Cruz slammed against the floor. He dropped a pistol and tried to get to his feet.

Someone else stood in the doorway Bobby did not recognized, holding a weapon. He looked at Casse, then at Bobby, then saw Deirdre.

"Run!" he shouted.

Bobby unfroze then. He rounded the cabinet. Deirdre grabbed his hand and dragged him through the door. As they bounded down a short hallway to a rear exit that stood open, two shots cracked the air behind them.

# FOURTEEN

Cruz thought he should know the man in the doorway, but memory failed to assign a name, a place. He repeated the question.

"Who the hell are you?"

The man raised his weapon. "Please put the gun on the desk."

"This is private property," Cruz said. "I must ask you to leave."

"I'm here for Bobby Porter. Is he in there?" He gestured with the pistol toward the door to the inner office.

"What are you, a cop?"

"Put your weapon on the desk and open the door."

Cruz became aware suddenly of the pistol in his own hand. He could raise it, aim, and shoot the intruder. Simple. He had killed already, he understood the mechanics. But he found it difficult to do without a reason.

They put me in prison, they kept me in isolation, they left me to live with myself...myself...my...

Reason enough. He started to bring the pistol up, feeling relaxed and confident. The stranger fired first. Cruz felt the hot, sharp impact in his right shoulder, the searing tear of the bullet passing through, bruising bone and shocking muscle. It hurt.

But he continued standing. He tried to aim. The look on

the intruder's face inspired Cruz—puzzlement and fear. He had forgotten that enjoyed power like this. The man had expected him to collapse under the shot, but Cruz still benefited from the enhancements acquired from the TX-A six years ago. He felt the wound beginning to heal already, though the pain continued. Very painful, in fact. He could not manage to get his arm up high enough to kill the man.

He squeezed one off anyway. It smacked the floor at the stranger's feet.

Instead of running, though, the man tackled him. Cruz fell across his desk, a weight on top of him. He got his good arm between them, pushing, but he lacked leverage. The intruder struck him across the jaw with the butt of his own pistol. Cruz's vision danced with sparks. He rolled. Together they fell off the desk. Cruz got to his knees, the intruder below him. He drew back his left arm and drove a punch straight down. The man flinched aside, letting the blow splinter the floor beside his head. He drew back his fist for a second blow.

A knee in Cruz's back sent him toppling forward to sprawl on the floor. He pushed himself up, turned, his back to the door, in time to received a powerful impact in the torso. He flew backward, against the door, which gave. Cruz spilled into the inner office.

"Run!" he heard. The stranger again. Cruz willed his shoulder to knit faster, impatient with the time the nanoware in his system took to make him whole. He thought it had slowed down during his years in prison.

A door slammed. Another shot, then Cruz sat up. The intruder backed out of the office, pistol aimed in his general direction.

As Cruz stood, another shape appeared in the doorway to the outer hall, filling the frame. The intruder sensed it before he backed into it. He turned—

Gant reached for him. Cruz admired the man's agility. When Gant wanted to grab hold of something—or someone—Cruz had never known him to miss. But his huge hand closed on air this time and the intruder danced away from him, bringing the pistol up.

He broke and ran past Cruz, heading for the back exit.

Casse blocked his way. Cruz watched, fascinated, as Casse's hand grew to wrap around the man's upper arm. Cruz knew what would happen next, his pulse picked up speed in anticipation. Blood. Screaming, maybe. Cruz had never liked it most of his life, but this was a human, scum and danger to the future, and he had learned to appreciate the aesthetics of pain in prison, the few times he had been allowed out in the general population. He leaned forward, watching.

The intruder stuck his pistol in Casse's face. The blast seemed loud. Casse's head opened like a flower, silvery petals splayed out in sudden bloom.

Casse's hand opened. The intruder slipped from his grip, bolted through the door, and was gone.

Cruz whirled around. "Stop them!" he yelled at Gant.

The big T-800 pivoted deftly and ran from the office.

Cruz stepped toward Casse. He could do nothing, but he felt an urge to help somehow. As he watched, the flower retracted, petals curling back into bud, the face quickly reforming. It took a few more seconds for Casse to recover his human-mimic expression.

"Where?" he asked.

"That way," Cruz pointed at the back door. "I sent Gant after them." He glanced at his right shoulder then. The pain was gone, flexibility returned. The wound was healed.

"Who was that?" Casse asked. He went around the office, righting the furniture.

"I don't know."

"The female was Porter's lover, the human he shares an apartment with. Perhaps the man was a friend or possibly someone from her stepfather's company."

Cruz swallowed around a lump in his throat. This had been bungled. He had suggested to Casse that more person-nel might be a good idea, but Casse rejected it. The fewer people around, the better.

But...

"May I ask a question?" Cruz asked.

"Yes."

"Why didn't we simply kill this one immediately? The time you spent on the interview, obviously someone followed him, it gave them opportunity—"

"Of course." Casse stood very still, staring at the wall screen. Equations still covered it. "We needed to find the right one."

"But—"

"All the others? Yes, it's a logical question. There's more than a little chance attached to all of this. Even the wrong one might become the right one given the proper circumstances."

"I-I'm not sure I understand."

"No, you don't. It doesn't matter. We want an opportunity to use Mr. Porter. He has a grasp of this—" he waved at the screen "—at least equal to the late Rosanna Monk. You will notice that several of our leads I personally attended to. A few were remarkable mathematicians. None grasped the implications expressed here. All required termination after the interviews since the chance existed that they might pursue these lines and stumble on something in the future."

"But the others? The nonmathematicians?"

"Camouflage. Smoke screen. Some humans might notice a pattern sooner than later if we only terminated this type."

"They might notice anyway."

"Someone may already have. I'd rather limit the chance that they know why we're terminating these people."

"What, uh...did he grasp?"

"The nature of time, Cruz."

Cruz waited intently, hoping for more. At one time, he remembered, he had been something of a scientist. His talent had been in management, though, more than in basic research, and he had been content with that for a long time. But part of his satisfaction had come from being in touch with the science, with the discoveries, the new things on which the bright people worked. He still loved it, the learning, he still recognized good work when he saw it, grew excited in the presence of epiphany.

"You said you sent Gant after them?" Casse asked.

"Yes."

The moment passed. Casse would say no more about the science. Cruz shrank a little inside, disappointed.

"Tell him to follow and find, but do not approach. I want another chance to convince Mr. Porter to work for us."

Cruz stared at Casse, looking for any sign of irony. Seeing none, Cruz said, "Yes, sir."

"Are we still on schedule with the deliveries from Colorado Springs?"

"Last I checked, slightly ahead of schedule. The first trucks will arrive tomorrow."

"Very good. I want you to stay on top of that, Oscar. That is more important just now than Mr. Porter."

"I understand."

Casse shut down the screen, collected his papers and discs, and left the office.

Cruz stood very still for a few minutes. He went back to the front office and laid the pistol on the desktop. His shoulder felt completely healed, the pain of the bullet a distant memory. He opened a drawer and took out a small communicator.

"Gant," he spoke into it.

"Yes."

"Follow them, determine location, do not approach, await instructions."

"Yes."

Cruz broke the link. Since leaving prison and returning to work at Cyberdyne, he had felt more and more like a janitor. Clean up this, tidy up that, hide the bodies. There was a certain satisfaction to it, but only of the most abstract sort. It was service to Skynet. Without that, he doubted he would tolerate Casse's arrogance. In some ways, Casse reminded him of Layton. But Layton gave him responsibilities; his world had possessed scope back then. Now...

"Yes, sir," he grumbled. "Right away, sir...as you wish, sir...where shall I kiss it, sir?"

He wondered, not for the first time, if Armageddon was worth all this humiliation.

Patterson got into the back seat. Deirdre started the engine, glancing at him in the rearview mirror. He looked pale, right hand holding his left bicep.

"Drive!" he snapped.

Deirdre mashed the accelerator. The tires barked once and the car bolted forward. She made for the opening in the fence, went through, and turned left.

"Right," Patterson ordered. He watched out the back window.

Deirdre turned the car, bouncing over the lip marking the unfenced boundary of another parking lot. She saw the exit to El Segundo on the opposite side.

"What in the hell..." Patterson muttered.

In the mirror, Deirdre saw something—someone—emerge from building. A big man, he paused for a moment until he spotted the car. Then he began running toward them. She made the boulevard, squealed onto the pocked concrete, and floored the pedal. She glanced up. The man sprang on the road behind him, legs pumping impossibly fast. For a few moments he seemed to be gaining.

"Move move move," Patterson said.

The speedometer touched fifty, then sixty. The shape began to recede.

"He stopped," Patterson whispered. "I think..."

Bobby huddled low in the passenger seat beside her. He had said nothing all the way down the back stairs to the exit. He seemed to be in shock.

Deirdre concentrated on driving.

"Where are you going?" Patterson asked.

"Dad's house," she said.

"Good."

She heard him swallow heavily. He had his head back now, eyes closed.

"Are you okay?" she asked.

"I will be," he said. "Damn, that son-of-a-bitch had a grip like steel."

"You don't know the half of it," Bobby said.

He seemed more frightened than she had ever seen him, even after Cojensis had revealed to him that he knew about Bobby's fraud and intended to use him.

"Who was that chasing us?" Deirdre asked.

"Guy named Gant," Patterson said after a time. "Head of security at..." He raised his head, wincing. "Doesn't make sense. But—well, maybe it does." He twisted around to look behind them. "Take a roundabout path, don't go straight there."

Deirdre turned off the highway. She glanced at Bobby and saw that his eyes were closed.

"So," she asked, trying to sound casual, "did you get the job?"

He looked at her, surprised and angry. Then he laughed. "What the hell are you doing, following me?"

"It turned out the right thing to do. Hmm?"

Bobby straightened in the seat. "Yeah...thanks." He shook his head. "It was amazing, Dee. The guy knew his stuff. Right out of Hawking or something."

"What guy?"

"Casse. I don't get it. We started off talking math and theory and then he tried to kill me. Tried. I got the impression he couldn't."

"Yeah," Deirdre said, "it would be a shame to waste such a brilliant mind."

"I wish I could have talked to him a little more. He—it was my problem, Dee. He had the answer. I know he did. We were thinking along the same lines."

"I don't fucking believe this! They nearly killed you—us—and you're upset you didn't get to talk theory for longer?"

"You always knew I was crazy."

"What kind of theory?" Patterson asked. "If you don't mind my asking."

"Has to do with time," Bobby said. He waved a hand. "Partly. It's an extension of string theory. I've been playing with the idea of time as a field rather than a dimension. Of course, it's a dimension, too, but you can express it mathematically like a magnetic field. They seem to be related even, at least in the numbers—"

"That's enough," Patterson said. "I just wondered if it was as crazy as everything else."

Deirdre drove on in silence for a time. Then: "What do you mean he had the answer?"

"He was leading me to a conclusion I've been trying to get to for months." He leaned forward. "Ever since Kaluza tried to explain how we needed a fifth dimension to account for electromagnetic fields, it's been a puzzle how an entire dimension could fit unseen inside our own. When string theory came out and gave us ten dimensions, the scoffers simply pointed out the obvious—we can't find them. There's no physical proof. But the math always worked out, so it seemed to be more fundamental than just tearing a few particles apart to see what they're made of and where they came from."

Deirdre knew he was relaxing, he felt comfortable doing this. She had helped him with a lot of it, she knew his ideas almost as well as he did. Right now, she did not mind hearing it all again.

He treated time as something akin to a magnetic field—recursive, permeating the physical dimensions—and because it was recursive it seemed to have direction. But as Feynman had shown, there was no mathematical reason time could not flow both ways. Bobby hit upon the idea of demonstrating that time travel would constitute a condition very like a magnetic monopole. But it required access to the theoretical "extra" dimensions predicted by string theory. He had been playing with it since she had known him. The pursuit had produced a lot of spin-off work which he used—hoped to use—for his graduate thesis, but which Cojensis had been stealing.

"Where I've been running into trouble," he continued,

"is where field equations have to become a description of a dimension. The field kind of 'necks' off and opens an access into a dimension, but...and this guy seemed to know that. He seemed to be heading in that direction and I just have a hunch he *knows!*"

"Knows what?" Patterson asked suddenly. "How to travel in time?"

Deirdre heard the skepticism in Patterson's voice. She understood it, the concept was hard to swallow, but she wished he would keep it to himself just now.

"The monopoles, then?" Deirdre prodded.

"They'd be what I expect. Space-time gets squeezed in the process, funneled down to a singularity. Along with it the magnetic field dimension—Kaluza-Klein space—and then the lines get twisted inside out. It'd pinch off a segment and toss it loose into normal space. The whole thread, both poles, would still be there, but one end would be wrapped up in the singularity and the other acting like just one pole...like a pair of virtual particles..."

"Whoa, whoa," Deirdre said. "Virtual particles. That's—"

She glanced back again. For an instant she thought she saw a familiar form, a block behind, but it vanished.

"This is too much," Deirdre said.

"Yeah," Bobby agreed. "Too much. The only thing I don't understand..."

"What?"

"Why'd he want to kill me?"

Dennis McMillin's home occupied five acres in the hills. Deirdre had taken a tortured route, arriving two hours after fleeing the industrial court. Deirdre gave the surveillance monitor at the gate a full frontal view of her face. The heavy steel rolled back and she drove in.

Patterson climbed out first. "Get inside. I want to check the road. Do you know where Mr. McMillin keeps his weapons?"

"Yes," Deirdre said, ushering Bobby out of the car.

"I'll be back," Patterson promised and sprinted down the long driveway.

"Weapons?" Bobby asked.

"Inside."

Deirdre ignored Bobby's dismayed expression. She took his hand and led him into the house. In her stepfather's den, all modernist aluminum and glass with bookshelves and an enormous video screen, desk, chaise longue, and liquor cabinet, she deposited Bobby on a chair. The central drawer of the desk contained a .9mm and a spare magazine. She tucked it into her waistband, magazine in her back pocket. She caught Bobby's frown.

"We're rich," she said matter-of-factly. "It can be a problem socially."

"I bet."

"Don't."

"Why don't you live here?"

"Because I prefer to live on my on, which allows a bit more freedom. And lately I prefer to live with you. Besides, I didn't think this would be very much to your taste."

Bobby shrugged.

Deirdre opened a set of tall metal doors between two ceiling-high bookcases. She took out a twelve-gauge shotgun and a box of shells.

"We're miles away from them," Bobby said. "Don't you think that's a little paranoid?"

"Better to be prepared." She loaded the gun, set it on the desk, and picked up the phone. "Just so you know, now I'm calling daddy."

"Dee—"

"I thought something was wrong when I caught our apartment being watched."

"You didn't tell me that."

"I didn't want to freak you out." The phone connected. "Hello, Monica? Is my father in? I'll hold." She spoke to Bobby. "I asked Paul to do a little checking. Cyberdyne is into some less-than-legal things right now. But the surveillance bothered him more. So we decided to follow you to this interview and see what we could find out."

"My my, you sound like a professional little spy."

"Don't laugh," Patterson said as he entered the room. "She saved your butt today. Who are you calling?"

"Dad."

"I already called him. He's on his way with some people."

"Oh." Deirdre hung up. "Now what?"

Patterson hefted the shotgun, wincing. "We wait."

"How bad is that? Let's see."

Deirdre made Patterson take off his jacket and shirt. On his left upper arm an ugly bruise enveloped the bicep, purpling badly. The shapes of long fingers were clearly visible.

"My god," she said. "You said he had a grip—"

"I told you," Bobby said, "you don't know the half of it."

"Yes, I do," Patterson said. "I shot him. In the face. This close. I never saw anything like it."

"He lived?" Deirdre asked.

"If he was alive to begin with."

"His hand turned into a sword or something," Bobby said. "He tried to slice me up."

Deirdre looked from one to the other of them. "You're both—"

"What?" Patterson and Bobby said simultaneously.

"There were stories," Patterson said, pulling his shirt back on. "About Cyberdyne, way back when they still did government work. Wild stuff, I heard about it from some old security guys. Black projects—that's what I put it down to. But..."

"This guy's hand became a knife," Bobby insisted.

"His face opened up," Patterson added. "Like liquid metal. No blood."

Deirdre remembered then seeing the man Patterson called Gant running after them, legs scissoring impossibly fast, gaining on a speeding car.

"This is too weird," she said. "I just thought they were doing something illegal."

"At a minimum," Patterson said. He looked at Bobby. "Did he say anything else to you? Other than the math?"

"No, not really. He suggested I didn't want to teach because I'd be wasting myself." He frowned thoughtfully. "He did say something strange right before you came charging in. He was trying to kill me. He chased me all over the room and kept missing. It would've been funny if...anyway, he stopped and looked at me kind of funny and said 'It's true, then.'"

"What's true?" Deirdre asked.

"I don't know. That's when things got really exciting."

Patterson grunted. "Do you have any experience with firearms?"

"None."

"Might be better then if you didn't have one."

"How long before Dad said he'd be here?" Deirdre asked.

"He said he wanted to pick someone up on the way. Maybe half an hour."

# FIFTEEN

John spent the morning overseeing the final coding of the communications system. Passwords, security software, dedicated lines, and the all the annoying details that a complex system brings with it occupied his entire attention from dawn till almost noon. The process calmed him. Despite the complications and bugs, he felt more in control doing this kind of work than at almost any other time.

Sarah came through at mid-morning, silently checking each monitor, watching while John and Lash's chief programmer, a talkative man named Wyler, worked. She disappeared upstairs then, till almost eleven. When she reappeared, she wore a loose jacket over a dark T-shirt and black pants.

"Where are you going?" John asked. "We could use some help here."

"You're far better at that than I'll ever be," she said without stopping. "I'm going to see if Mr. Porter is home."

"Alone?"

"Is there anyone else here? You're busy, I'm not."

And she was out the door. John hated it when she did that, picking the time he was most indisposed to do something all on her own. He resented being left behind, ever since she went to prison for attempting to dynamite a computer lab when he was a child. She did it too often.

*Just when I thought we had an understanding...*

"How much more do we have on this?" he asked Wyler, more edge in his voice than he intended.

"Another hour maybe. If you want to do it right, that is. Of course, if you don't care—"

"There's only one way to do it," John cut him off.

"We'll have you connected and running under full prophylactic protocols soon enough, don't you worry."

"I'm getting hungry. How about you?"

"Sure. But we're this close—"

"After. My treat."

Only two of Ken Lash's vans remained now. The bulletproof windows had been installed last night. Today all that remained was trim and finish. Tomorrow the armory would arrive in a separate truck and the L.A. branch of PPS Security and Investigation would be open for business. A courier had delivered all the County and State licenses and federal documents early that morning. Reed had come through again.

Then they could begin another round of observations, watching for the signs and portents of Skynet's resurrection—or first coming, depending on which timeline you believed this one to be—and hoping to find nothing.

Hopeless hope. They had already stumbled on evidence of Cyberdyne's revived interest in the project. And John still did not know quite what to make of McMillin and the message John had sent himself from the future.

It was 2007. In one timeline—a stream that had been circumvented already and probably had not happened—this was the year he would be successfully assassinated by Skynet's Terminators. Nothing else in this particular timeline had happened the way it had in that one, so it was a safe bet he would survive to 2008.

Then what? The one question he wanted answered more than any other in this insane war was, how do we know when we win?

The phone chirped.

"PPS Security, this is Sean Philicos."

"John, this is McMillin."

"It's 'Sean' on any line, sir. If you don't mind."

"Oh. Sorry."

"What can I do for you?"

"I need you. Can you get away?"

"I'm in the middle of some pretty delicate—"

"I've just gotten a call from Paul Patterson. He's had an encounter with Cyberdyne. I think you should be in on this."

"Right. Where?"

"My house. I can pick you up on the way."

"I'll be ready."

"Let me guess," Wyler said as John hung up. "I'm on my own."

"Can you handle it?"

"We're mostly done, sure. I mainly need someone to push buttons now to make sure all the networking is up. I can get one of the other guys to do that."

"Great."

John laid a ten-dollar bill on the desk. "I said I'd buy lunch. Don't forget to eat."

He went upstairs and quickly made a ham sandwich. He phoned Sarah as he wolfed down his lunch, but her cell phone was off.

Twenty minutes later, a long midnight blue sedan pulled up in front of the building. John checked his weapons and climbed into the back seat with McMillin.

"Jack Reed says hello, by the way," John said.

McMillin's eyebrows cocked, then he laughed. "You checked me out. Good."

"So where are we going and what happened."

McMillin repeated the report Patterson had given him over the phone.

"Bobby Porter...he goes to Caltech?"

"Yes. Bright boy. My daughter shares an apartment with him. More than that, in fact, but...she tells me he's something of a genius. I'd love to hire him, but he wants to prove himself before accepting any favors. I can understand that."

"And this interview with Cyberdyne was part of proving

himself?" John pulled out his cell phone and punched in his mother's number. He studied the screen, annoyed. Her phone was still off.

"It's complicated." McMillin said. "So says my daughter. It sounds stupid to me, but that's a prerogative of youth. Anyway, it seems to have gone wrong. They're all at my house. I told them to wait there for us."

Three other men shared the car, including the driver. They all exhibited the alert posture of security people.

"So what do you think this is?" McMillin asked. "One of your Terminators?"

"If it is," John said, "then I hope you have a rocket launcher in the trunk."

One of the other men glanced at him, frowning.

"Judging from Patterson's description," John continued, "it may well be. Gant, head of security at Pioneer, had the look. And he threatened us, pretty openly. Not the actions of a normal man."

"He didn't recognize you?"

"He wouldn't necessarily have been programmed to."

"They're capable of operating at that level of sophistication?"

"Human mimicry? Within limits. Gant didn't strike me as loquacious. Bare minimum of social skills, sufficient vocabulary and response cues to pass if you didn't press too hard. I'm much more interested in this other man Patterson described."

"You don't think he was exaggerating?"

"Let me tell you about the T1000s and TX-A models. Liquid metal, capable of assuming any shape. They learn frighteningly fast and they *can* pass as human, completely. Do you keep dogs?"

"Yes, I have four shepherds."

"Good. Dogs can tell. You cannot kill these things with bullets. Enough explosives over enough time, sure. Extreme heat will have the most effect."

"Lasers?"

"Wide beam. The T-800s can be killed with a penetrating

171

strike to their CPU, in the skull, or they can be blown apart, but they're pretty tough."

"What about an electromagnetic field?"

"What about it?"

"Well, if they're metal—"

"I'm not sure this kind of metal responds to magnetism."

"Hmm. Liquid metal, you say? Like in a superfluid state?"

"You're beyond me, sir. I wouldn't know."

McMillin smiled, though, and gazed out the window.

"Anyway, if they get a hold of you, you're likely dead. If the T-1000s or TX-As touch you, they can imitate you."

"How did you deal with these things in the past?"

"We ran."

"You can't do that forever."

"No, sir. We can't. We're not going to."

Sarah pulled into the parking lot before the row of apartments. Two levels, they reminded her very much of her own apartment, back before her life had turned into—what it had turned into. She suppressed a massive attack of nostalgia and studied the other cars, watching the area for about fifteen minutes.

She crossed the lot as if heading for a different unit. She pretended to begin entering one on the ground level, then snapped her fingers as if remembering something. She climbed the stairs to the second level and walked along casually. As she passed the target apartment, she glanced through the windows. Blinds drawn, she saw nothing. The door looked secure. She walked past, to the far end of the row, turned, and surveyed the lot. She saw no one sitting in a car watching, no one standing anywhere within sight doing nothing. That did not mean she was unobserved, but it lowered the chances. She returned to the apartment in question.

She tried the knob first.

The door opened.

With a backward glance at the parking lot, Sarah entered.

It appeared to be a normal enough place. Sofa, two chairs,

coffee table, some wall art—Escher mainly—and a couple of overburdened bookcases. Through a wide archway, the dining room table held a computer and stacks of papers and discs. Beyond that, a kitchen area—

She saw movement—a shadow?—from the back of the apartment. Sarah reached under her jacket and grasped the pistol, stepping forward silently. She reached the edge of the dining room before she noticed the papers spilled on the floor on the opposite side of the table, the partly disconnected cables from the computer, and the sensation of having just made a mistake.

She drew her weapon, turning, and ducked as a fist cut the air above her head. Reflexively, she kicked straight into the man-shape before her, connecting with a satisfying grunt.

But she was off-balance, and staggered back, trying to look around. Two more men appeared from the back bedroom and a fourth stepped out of the kitchen alcove. Sarah tried to bring her weapon to bear on the nearest, but she caught her ankle on the leg of the table and stumbled again.

They surrounded her immediately. A strong grip bent her gun-hand down; the pistol left her hand. She set her feet and drove a fist into the sternum of the one right in front of her, connecting solidly—just as a blow glanced across her forehead, snapping her head back. She crashed against the wall behind her, her assailants moving with her.

For a few moments she felt embarrassed. She was better than this, she had survived combat with monsters. To be taken down by four humans—she knew they were only men—was ridiculous.

Another fist caught her in the stomach. She doubled up, breathless, trying to get a sense of how to fight. She brought her left arm up to stop another punch, followed through by stepping into the blow with a stiff right thrust—

Too many. She dropped to the floor, the side of her face hot with pain.

They were silent. That suddenly frightened her. Professionals.

*I just walked into my death,* she thought.

But the final beating did not come.

"Hey!"

Sarah heard scuffling, sharp punches, grunting. Blinking, she scrambled to her feet, immediately searching the room for her pistol. It lay on the floor beneath the table, a few inches from the outstretched hand of an unconscious man.

Before anything else, she ducked under the table to retrieve the .10mm.

In the living room, she saw a fifth man she did not know, finishing combat with two of her attackers. He held one by the right arm, off-balance, and waited for the other to come closer. The fourth man lay against the archway between dining room and living room, back bent at a fatal angle.

The man looked too old to move with such agility. Dark skin, balding, dressed in a stylish overcoat, he appeared to be in his late fifties. Broad through the shoulders and chest, he stood about five feet ten inches, and wore a trim beard showing gray.

As she watched, in a move that seemed casual, almost effortless, he hurled the man he held at the other man, dropping them both into a heap on the floor. Instantly, the older man fell on them. With four precise punches, the fight was over.

Sarah raised her pistol.

He stood, took in the results of his actions, then looked at Sarah.

He smiled. "Ms. Connor," he said, voice pleasingly baritone, surprisingly soft. "My name is Portis. I've come from the future."

"Which one?" Sarah asked, unthinking.

The smile grew. "The most likely one. We should leave here, don't you think?"

"And I'm trusting you for what reason?"

"I just saved your life."

"Maybe, but not quite enough."

"I'm not killing you."

"Better, but I'm holding a gun on you."

"Your privilege, of course. But counterproductive." He studied her, frowning. "Are you badly hurt?"

"I've been worse."

Pain made itself felt over her torso and the side of her face was beginning to swell. She hoped her right eye would not close, but she was impaired, she knew that. She could feel the first signs of adrenaline afterwash.

"I can help," Portis said. "If you let me."

"Before I let you come a step closer, you're going to have to convince me whose side you're on. Sorry. I'm old-fashioned that way."

"I understand, but there isn't much time."

Sarah felt a wave of dizziness. She wondered just how badly hurt she really was. She focused on Portis. "You know my name."

"You are one of the three people I came back to find."

"Three?"

"Your son, John, of course. And a third who is pivotal."

"A name?"

"Jeremiah Porter," he said.

"Ah. And what do you want with him?"

"To stop him from creating Skynet."

Sarah grunted. "You realize there's an element of melodrama in this conversation that makes it kind of hard to take seriously."

"Certain things are innately melodramatic. It can't be helped."

Despite herself, Sarah liked him. "You fight well. Are you modified?"

"I am."

"Thought so. I could have taken them, you know."

"Under other circumstances, no doubt."

"Are they dead?"

He glanced around at the bodies. "I sincerely hope so."

"They're human."

Portis nodded.

"I..." Her vision faded. She squeezed her eyes, tried to focus on him. He had moved. She turned to follow.

175

Moments later, she opened her eyes to see Portis leaning over her. She panicked briefly, but her limbs felt clumsy. He held her arms.

"Lie still," he said. "You are concussed. Not badly, but enough. Lie still. It will be over in a minute."

*Screwed up good this time, sure it will be over...*

She passed out again.

When she came to once more, she found herself stretched out on the sofa in the living room. Her face tingled, and her ribs felt numb. She looked to the left to find Portis sitting across from her, watching. He had taken off his overcoat, revealing an expensive suit of dark gray.

"Better?" he asked.

"What..."

"Nanocoders," he said. "Small colony, self-limiting. Healers."

"I'm not—"

"It isn't a permanent infestation. Not like the ones the advanced Terminators use. We have found problems with those. They tend, over time, to damage the host. So we deploy only short-term, self-immolating 'coders. Within a day or so they will all be flushed from your system. Fortunately, the repairs they effect are more permanent."

Sarah said nothing, letting the sensations from her body register. She rifled her memory, asked herself questions, checked that she was still herself. But how could she tell?

"It would seem to me," Portis said, "that this should be proof enough of my intentions. I could have killed you."

"Depends what you really want. You might need me. Alive."

"Paranoia is useful to a point, Ms. Connor. The trick is to know when to let it go."

Carefully, she sat up. The tingling was fading. She felt strong enough to walk. Her mind seemed clear.

"You say you're here to find Jeremiah Porter," she said.

"I've been here—in this time frame—for a little over six

weeks. I've been searching. I believe the young man living here is the one I'm looking for."

"His name is Robert, though."

"That's probably not true. There are some irregularities in his records. But I would need to talk to him to certain."

"You sound like a cop."

Portis shrugged. "In a way, I suppose you could call me that."

"I don't recognize your name."

He blinked at her. "It's what I'm using now."

"What was it before? Or then?" She snorted. "I never have figured out how to talk about the future. What's it like when you come from?"

He looked uncomfortable. "I don't recall my name. Something in the transfer to the past, I don't know what happened. I understand what you mean about time and linguistic referents. It's all right to talk about them in the past tense, since they are all conditional and may be left behind as a consequence of events taking place in the present. When discussing a personal history, what has gone before, whether in the future or the past, is always a previous occurrence to the one living it, so past tense is good for that as well. As for what it is like when I came from...that is a long conversation, and perhaps should be carried on elsewhere."

Sarah stared at him, uncertain what to think of anything he had just said.

"I understand your confusion," he said. "I am being very honest with you, Ms. Connor, because I need your help. There is insufficient time to build trust in the normal way. You are here, so you must be aware that Skynet's agents are hunting Jeremiah Porter. Many so named are already dead. It is important we find him before they do. Our search is the same, and largely for the same purpose. It is important that Jeremiah Porter not be taken by Cyberdyne."

*First the Specialists, now this,* she thought wryly. *The universe has no right to ask this much trust from me.*

She glanced around the apartment. "They were here to

gather up his work. We should take the computer and the documents."

"I've already packaged them up."

On the dining room table waited three neat piles—computer, discs, and papers.

"How long have I been unconscious?" she asked.

"Ten minutes."

She took in the bodies still lying on the floor around them. "Which way did you come in?"

"The front door was open."

"We should leave the back way."

"Agreed," Portis said.

She fished a pen from her jacket. She tore a strip from the cover of a magazine laying on the coffee table and scribbled an address. "Go there," she said, handing it to him. "Take the discs and papers, I'll take the computer."

He stood, and waited till she got to her feet. Satisfied that she would be all right, he went to the table and gathered up the box of discs and tucked the stack of papers under his arm.

Sarah checked that her pistol was loaded and back in its holster, then did a quick survey of the apartment for any signs of her presence. Other than the bodies, nothing would point to her unless someone saw her enter the apartment. Satisfied, she grabbed the computer and followed Portis out the rear entrance.

John's cell phone chirped as the car pulled into McMillin's driveway.

"Talk to me," he said when he saw the number on the screen. "Where the hell are you?"

"Heading back to the office," Sarah answered. "What's your problem?"

"You, turning off your phone."

"Later. Right now you need to come back here. We have a visitor."

"I've got another issue. Related. I'm at Dennis McMillin's home. Seems we've had our first ugly encounter with

Cyberdyne." He quickly summarized what McMillin had told him, finishing with the information about Porter and McMillin's daughter.

"I just left their apartment," Sarah said. "People were there. If McMillin has the resources, he might want to send someone over to clean it up. Four bodies. John, they were human. Something about this—"

"Maybe they've only got so many Terminators to spare. What do you mean we've got visitors?"

"Visitor. One. Guy named Portis, claims to be from the future. I believe him. He reminds me of the specialists. He came here to find Jeremiah Porter."

"Small timeline. Look, when you get back I want you to get on the line to Reed and bring him up to speed. We need to find out what Cyberdyne is doing and how they're doing it."

"Be careful," she said.

The connection broke. John put the phone away and told McMillin about his daughter's apartment.

"Greg," McMillin said to one of the men in the front seat. "See to it, will you?"

"Yes, sir." The man opened his own cell phone and punched into a number.

They entered the sprawling house.

"Do you have household staff?" John asked.

"Butler and two maids, plus a chauffeur."

"They should leave. Take some time off, a few days, till we deal with this."

From a room to the left, Paul Patterson emerged. Upon seeing them, he relaxed visibly.

"Paul," McMillin said. "Where's Deirdre?"

"Here, Dad," a woman's voice called from within the room. A moment later, she stepped into the hall, carrying a shotgun cradled in her left arm.

McMillin hugged her briefly, then held her at arm's length. "You're all right?"

"Fine," she said. She glanced at John. "Who's this?"

179

"This is...Sean Philicos," McMillin said, catching himself. "Mr. Philicos, this is my daughter, Deirdre."

Deirdre caught the hesitation in her stepfather's voice, but said nothing. She nodded to John. "Mr. Philicos."

"Ms. McMillin."

"Deirdre."

"Sean."

Patterson approached John. "Gant was there."

"So Mr. McMillin informed me. You all right?"

"Sore arm," Patterson said, "a little unnerved."

"Understandable. First encounters with Terminators are usually fatal. If you survive, the next most common reaction is unnerved."

"Terminators," Patterson said. "Just what in hell is a Terminator?"

"That is a long story. First, is there a Jeremiah Porter here?"

Deirdre's face gave her away as she stared at John.

"In that case," John said, "I'd like to meet him."

# SIXTEEN

**P**ortis pulled into a nearly vacant parking lot next to a liquor store. He drew a stack of papers into his lap and began skimming the pages. Most contained scribbled notes, half-completed thoughts and equations, nothing conclusive. But on a few he found well-reasoned constructs, fluid lines expressing ideas Portis recognized. Good work.

He removed several pages, folding them and placing them in his overcoat pocket, before continuing on to the address Sarah Connor had given him. She did not trust him, not yet, nor did he expect her to. That would require more work. He needed her—and her son—to trust him. It might be simpler to just infect her with a batch of 'coders, but where it concerned people like the Connors he was constrained. There were rules. He did not know what he would have to do to convince them, but a start would be showing up where she expected him.

The apartment bothered him. He did not recognize it. The part of his memory closed off demanded a sense of familiarity. *Deja vu*, or possibly in some cases *presque vu*, accompanied many of his actions, the places he had seen since arrival. He did not know the implications of his periodic bouts of near-remembrance, whether it had to do with the timeline or his past life or both, and not knowing distracted him. But he had no such sense in the apartment—and he believed he should have.

He followed an internal map of L.A., pulling into the neighborhood around the Connors' office. Within a few blocks, the area changed from trendy, upper-middle-class shops and bistros and nightclubs to a transitional community, residential mixing with more modest businesses. The streets rippled with life, people gathered around shops, on corners, loud music from beautifully rebuilt antique cars, the smells of cooking, hot plastic, and asphalt, Spanish and English spoken and shouted, mingled here and there with smatterings of Vietnamese and Korean. Portis slowed, surprised by the lushness, the chaotic near-harmony, the vivid colors.

He was surprised Sarah Connor had let him leave with the papers and discs—but then, his hands had been encumbered more than her own; she only carried the laptop. He had led the way out of the apartment and had no doubt she could draw and fire far faster than he could turn around on the narrow back stairs. Tactically, she had managed their exit deftly. He had lost sight of her on the parking lot.

His best chance was complete honesty. But he was not sure he had that to give.

It was mid-afternoon. A pair of large vans stood in front of the address. Portis gathered up the papers and the box of discs. He found himself standing before a two-story stucco-finished building with new windows and door. A modest, hand painted sign leaned against the wall on the sidewalk, PPS SECURITY AND INVESTIGATIONS, L.L.C. above a phone number, waiting to be hoisted into place over the entrance.

A workman stood by one of the vans, coiling electrical cable around a spool.

Portis entered the building.

"I don't care who's pulling what strings, this property is not for sale!"

"I don't have time for this right now. It's a good offer—"

"I don't care! That was never on the table!"

Portis stopped just inside the door. A heavyset man stood in front of the glass-topped reception desk, behind which stood Sarah Connor, hands on hips, glaring at him. She glanced briefly at Portis, but her eyes shifted immediately back to the man.

"This is lease property," he said, raising a hand, palm up, and tapping the palm with a finger. "I expect it to remain lease property."

"For the day the neighborhood turns around again, I suppose, and you can double the rent?" Sarah snapped back. "Or did you just figure out that the neighborhood isn't as bad as you thought it was? The other day was probably the first time you'd actually come here to see it for yourself." She grunted. "It's moot. You have an offer on the table for direct purchase. We've already made our upgrades to the property, we're not going anywhere."

"That's another thing. You had no right to do this much to my building."

"Mr. Soams, I don't see—"

"This is all illegal. You've damaged my property. You're already in violation of the lease. I want you out and I want reparations for all these modifications."

"You really don't want to meet my lawyer, Mr. Soams. Now, if you please, I have a client to talk to, I'm busy—"

The man—Soams—looked at Portis, then back at Sarah. "We're not finished. I'll have the sheriff's office here at end of day to start moving you people out. I have connections in—"

Sarah raised a hand. "Enough. You're threatening me now. People who threaten me do not have happy days."

"Mr. Soams," Portis said, stepping forward. He set the discs and papers on the desk.

"What?" Soams frowned at him suspiciously.

"You have several properties available for lease?"

"I...depends. Where—look..."

"I'm in the market for a storefront myself," Portis said, extending a hand. "I would like to discuss some possibilities with you, sir. My name is Portis. Lee Portis."

"Uh...yes, I'm sure..." Reluctantly, Soams clasped Portis's hand. "Now if you'll excuse me, I have..."

The change took a few seconds, but Portis saw it in the momentary confusion in Soam's eyes, then a relaxing of the scowl. He blinked at Portis. "What, uh, exactly did you have in mind, Mr. Portis?"

"I was thinking midtown, but we can go over that later. For now I would be pleased if you could come to an amicable settlement here. I have business with—"

"Philicos," Sarah said quickly.

"—Ms. Philicos. We're associates, and I'd hate to start a relationship knowing—"

"Yeah, sure," Soams said. "Of course." He looked at Sarah Connor, baffled. "I just thought—"

"You have our offer, Mr. Soams," Sarah said, her face pointedly neutral, though Portis could see a new stiffness in her posture.

"It's, uh...fine. I'll have my attorney contact the owners, then get with you with the documentation. Sorry for the misunderstanding."

"No problem. These things happen."

Soams fished a business card from his jacket and handed it to Portis. "When you get ready to discuss your requirements, give me a call, Mr. Portis. I'll be happy to show you what I have."

"I'm sure you will. Thank you, sir."

"Good afternoon."

Soams picked up a briefcase on the floor and strode out of the office.

"Tell me," Sarah said, "you didn't do that to me."

"I did not. If you give it some thought, you'll recognize that as the truth."

"I was unconscious."

"I did not tamper with you."

Sarah looked skeptical. She gestured at the door. "How long will he be like that?"

"He won't change his mind about selling to you, if that's what you're worried about. The 'coders last a few days, maybe a week. By then you should have your sale and he won't quite know what to think about it. You can reinforce the behavior by daily contact—not re-infestation, just every day talking to him."

"I'd rather not. So...why did you do that? To prove I can trust you?"

"I didn't think it would hurt. But I don't believe it's sufficient all by itself."

"No. It's not." She came to a decision and gestured. "Come back here. We'll talk."

Portis gathered up the material he had brought in and stepped around the desk as Sarah Connor went through a plain white door. When he entered the next room, he found a collection of desks with workstations, several screens, and Sarah Connor holding a large, dull-surfaced weapon aimed at him.

"Close the door," she said. When he complied, she said, "Do you recognize this?"

He looked at what she held. "Yes, roughly. It's a particle beam weapon. I don't know that exact design, but I recognize the elements."

"So you know what it can do."

"Of course."

"Put the discs and papers on the desk to your right and take off your overcoat."

Portis did as she asked. He stood with his arms away from his sides. "Do you have many of those?" he asked.

"A few. More are coming."

"Do you expect the kind of fight in which you'll need them?"

"We're prepared for it, let's put it that way."

"Sensible," Portis said.

"Should we expect that kind of fight?"

"Who can say?"

"If you're from the future," Sarah said. "You probably have a good idea."

"It depends which future I'm from, though, doesn't it?"

"No fate?" She smiled. "I've heard that one before."

185

"But you don't know how it works."

"A few years ago I went on a rather strange trip. I saw a lot of things that maybe should have cleared up my questions. But I still don't trust my conclusions."

"That is sensible as well. You know, I am rather surprised you gave me the correct address. I expected less confidence from you."

"Where else would I send you? I don't know who you are. I don't want you here, maybe, but I want to know where you are more. This is about the only place in L.A. I know where I have at least some control. If I don't like what you tell me, you don't leave this building."

"Which you will soon own, thanks to my intercession."

"If I forget later, let me say thank you now."

"You're welcome. As fast as I move, do you really think you could use that before I got to you?"

"I don't know how fast you move. I know how fast Terminators move."

"Ah. Of course, if I wanted to kill you—"

"Don't. If you'd killed me at the apartment, you still wouldn't know where my son is, and he would be alerted then."

"Utterly logical," Portis said. "So, what now? What can I say to you that will cut through all this suspicion? We don't have all the time in the world."

"Did you kill Eisner?"

Portis was surprised. "No, I didn't. I'd been interrogating him. How...?"

"We've been keeping track of all the infected Cyberdyne employees since their release from prison. You were seen entering and leaving his place several times. Who do you think killed him?"

"The name Casse has come to my attention. He's on the board of Cyberdyne, a vice president in the company. I suspect he's had the same people watched—Oscar Cruz works for him."

"I know."

"My last visit to Eisner, I found him dead. I saw some

people enter his apartment after me, probably hoping to catch me there."

"True, but those were our people."

"Have you been following me since?"

She hesitated. "No. You moved too fast. We thought you were heading to Minnesota. Very neat dodge."

Portis sighed. "Ms. Connor—or should I call you Ms. Lawes?—we can continue like this for hours and accomplish nothing. What can I tell you that will hurry this along?"

"You say you're looking for Jeremiah Porter. Why? What will you do when you find him?"

"Keep him from working for Cyberdyne."

"Cyberdyne may have already accomplished that for you. Why? Who is he and why would Cyberdyne want him?"

Portis pointed to the papers and discs on the desk. "Judging by what I saw there, he is something of a genius. His work seems to concern time. Does the name Rosanna Monk mean anything to you?"

"You know it does."

"Mr. Porter is her natural successor."

"Sit down. Why don't you tell me about..."

Portis moved to a chair and sat. "About?"

"About the future."

"Mine?"

"You already know mine, I assume. I want to know about yours. Fair is fair."

"Do we have time?"

"Don't you know?" She grinned. "We'll make time."

Portis sighed. *Maybe I should have used the 'coders.* "Very well."

"We're beginning to rebuild the cities. Many of them are in ruin, mostly in the northern hemisphere. Reconstruction is operating out of Buenos Aires and Johannesburg. Populations are starting to recover. But many people are leaving Earth because of the toxic conditions. Mars is being settled, the moon developed, and expeditions have been sent to the moons of Jupiter and Saturn. We also built a project to try to use time travel to lessen some of the worst of the decades since the Nexus."

"The Nexus?" Sarah asked. "That's a new one."

"It would be, to you. The Nexus was discovered by one of our theorists when she attempted to make sense of the inconsistencies in the historic records. We are still trying to make sense of it. It is the point in time at which causality broke down and events became fluid as a consequence of actual time displacement. When time travel began, what we call history became probabilistic. Events became virtual, indeterminate, a matter of statistical potential."

Sarah blinked. "You've lost me."

"I'm not sure I can help you. We understand what happened imperfectly. Vaguely. It's a symptom of the process. As best we have determined, there are three possible futures, only one of which leads to my time. Naturally, we would prefer to see that one prevail. The other two both lead to unimaginable destruction and the faintest chance that humanity can survive."

"Not unimaginable to me."

"No. You have the luxury of experience. In my day, your exploits are legendary. In the precise definition of the term."

"You don't think it all happened?"

"In a way, it didn't. Something occurred, to be sure, but it may be no more than an artifact of an unstable temporal thread. You see, we have at least three stories about you to choose from. Which one is true? In the most concrete way, only time can tell."

"Don't bullshit me. I hate it when people bullshit me."

"I'm not."

"Sounds like bullshit to me."

"In one timeline," Portis continued, "you died in 2001, leaving your son to fight alone. He perished in 2007 and Skynet overwhelmed the resistance, establishing permanent hegemony at the Nexus point in 2029. In another timeline, you survived to see the resistance fully begun by 2021 with the first real successes and the subsequent destruction of Skynet in 2029—also at the Nexus point. In the third timeline, you and your son organized and fought a constant resistance to the creation of Skynet, managing to successfully delay its creation until the abandonment of all development of global management systems in 2025. Cyberdyne attempted again and again to build Skynet secretly until it was finally eradicated in 2029—also at the Nexus point. We have stories about your battles from all three timelines, mingled, mixed, impossible to reconcile, and yet all containing the seeds of truth. Like myths out of the deep past, they cannot all be true yet they are all resistant to ultimate debunking. So I say to you, you are a legend."

"The Nexus point...2029 is the year Skynet began sending Terminators back to kill me."

"Not just you, but yes."

"Is that why you call it the Nexus point?"

"We call it that, because it is. Until Skynet began doing that, the timeline was stable, set, immutable. Time travel disrupted it, opening the entire continuum up to quantum effects on the macro level. History became probabilistic. Connected, linked, yet indeterminate."

"You said the three most probable timelines. There are others?"

"Many."

Sarah frowned deeply. "If Skynet hadn't started sending back Terminators, what would have happened?"

"We don't know. The various lines have become so confused, it's no longer possible to know which one was the original. It became even more tangled when Kyle Reese impregnated you."

She flinched at the mention of Reese, but she did not pursue the topic. "So...was there a Skynet or not?"

"Somewhere along one of the lines, Skynet was created. It existed. Once the timeline became fluid, through its own actions, Skynet also became a probability."

"Does it exist now or not?"

"In a way, it does. It has the potential to exist depending on how things develop along the way to the Nexus point. If events favor Skynet, then it will acquire stability. It will exist. It will have won. In order to do that, it must win here, in the past. To prevent its existence, you must win. Here, now, and tomorrow, and the next day."

Sarah looked at him blankly for a long time. Then: "So, in your time, did Skynet exist?"

"No. Where I come from, there never had been a Skynet. It too is legend."

"But you said you're rebuilding from the destruction."

"Oh, yes. Skynet failed to exist. But the war to prevent it, to stop it, that was real enough."

She shook her head. "I think I'm about to get a headache. And what does Jeremiah Porter have to do with this?"

"It's complicated."

"No! Really?"

Portis found himself liking Sarah Connor. He grinned at her. She looked momentarily puzzled. Then she set the weapon down.

"I need a drink," she said. "How about you?"

"I..."

A phone chirped. Sarah grabbed it. "Yeah? Yes, I'm—where?" She looked at Portis over her shoulder. "What do you want to do? Okay. We'll be there." She hung up. "Forget the drink. Do you want to meet Jeremiah Porter?"

# SEVENTEEN

$A$rc lights illuminated the cavernous room with harsh white. The walls supported scaffolding and walkways, columns of cable and conduit, all feeding into the skeleton of a complex machine growing at one end. Casse did not accept what humans called Luck, but he understood how improbable Cyberdyne's acquisition of this facility had been.

The old Los Angeles Air Force Base had fallen victim to base closures only a few years before. Casse's people managed to beat all other potential buyers and obtain the site. Of course, had it been a Cyberdyne purchase, the sale would never have gone through. Two shell companies fronted for them. Once secured, Casse began moving the Skynet project into the R & D facilities left behind. Though the military had stripped a great deal of the technology, Cyberdyne found it relatively easy to install everything they needed and match it up with what remained. The humans had done missile defense research here. Most of the missiles had been built out in San Bernardino, but prototypes had been constructed here and all the space and tools necessary for a sophisticated high-tech program could be found on site. The last century's satellite defense systems had been managed from here as well.

Trucks had been arriving for the past week delivering new equipment from various sources, all in preparation to receive what had been recovered of the Skynet systems from Colorado Springs. Work proceeded around the clock adapting the facility.

Casse, satisfied with what he saw, took the underground corridor from Building 100 to Building 105. Cyberdyne's corporate headquarters took up most of the old administration building; Casse's own office on the top floor used to house the command section for the whole base. Most of the personnel had moved from the rooms they had occupied at the nearby Ramada less than a month ago. Casse had teams on the site before the contracts had been finalized, confident that the deal would go through once negotiations became earnest. The base included housing to the south, enough to keep all the project-sensitive people close, on hand, and within a fence. Arrangements were being made to convert some of the base housing into ready-stations for T units once production could begin.

Casse rode the elevator up to the top floor, considering the logistics. He would prefer to eliminate humans from the project. Not possible, not yet. Casse needed them—Skynet needed them. During his time in this frame, Casse had begun to acquire a vague understanding of irony. This qualified. The very creatures Skynet must eventually eliminate were necessary to Skynet's birth.

He entered his office. A desk and three chairs, a view to the north, nothing else. On a corner of the desk was a link to the superconducting receiver in the basement levels of the building. Inactive as yet, soon Casse would receive instructions from it. From the future. From Skynet. Until then, he relied on the programming with which he had been sent back. Modified by circumstance and experience, it nevertheless remained consistent.

After the failures of the other units to build Skynet and secure its future, he had come forward to take over at a more direct level. Brute measures clearly would not work. The paradoxes entailed in attempting to kill the Connors resulted in more difficulties than anticipated. The timelines split, mingled, separated into a melange of possibilities.

Quantum indeterminacy at the macro level, something for which no theory existed that proved useful. It never should have happened. Skynet ultimately would have been better off leaving it alone.

But once tampered always tangled. The only possibility for success now lay in surviving past the Nexus point. After today's events, Casse understood that very concretely. He had been helpless trying to kill young Porter. He could not do it. Porter was part of the essential timeline, necessary to the future existence of Skynet, inextricably bound to a strand of inevitability. Casse was from a future that still promised only probable existence. He could not kill Porter.

Frustrating. Cruz had been ineffective as well, especially with the recomplicating factor of more humans appearing to effect a rescue of Porter. How had that been allowed to happen? Regardless, the fact remained that Casse could have slashed and stabbed for an hour and somehow never kill Jeremiah Porter.

That at least justified the use of agents from this frame. He had wondered about that since he began the program. Better to use Terminators, perhaps, but not if they also would be unable to kill the important humans, the humans that threatened Skynet.

All those attempts, wasted. It seemed impossible that the first Terminator, back in 1984, had failed. One human stood between it and Sarah Connor. One human, against a Terminator. Ridiculous.

Of course, Casse understood now. Even if the human had not come back to try to save Sarah Connor's life, the attempt would have failed. She had been too intimately bound to the inevitable timeline. Especially after Skynet sent back the Terminator.

It felt odd to realize that Skynet had been wrong. That it had made a mistake. In all the years Casse had been here, waiting and watching, he had witnessed the human propensity for ridiculing and criticizing their leaders. He had found it puzzling. Yet now, perhaps, he understood that a little more, too.

But Skynet had indeed made a mistake. That first breach of the timeline set in motion all that followed—and preceded, again and again. Even Casse's presence added to the tangles. Skynet had sent him back even earlier, to 1982, to observe. Casse had been there to follow the events of the first Terminator's attempts to eliminate John Connor and the resistance and set circumstances up in Skynet's favor. Helplessly, Casse had watched. And again, ten years later, when the second attempt had been made. And again, when—

No one had seen or heard from Sarah Connor or her son, John, since 2001. Casse doubted they were dead. Best to assume they lived, somewhere. But they were not the only threats.

This Jeremiah Porter, for instance. It might indeed be a good idea to kill him. All that time travel had done to date was make Skynet's existence more tentative. But now Skynet depended on it. The idea was in the world. Someone would solve the problem. Rosanna Monk had not been the only one bright enough to understand the physics. The consequences of an independent time travel program, one not under Skynet's control, could not be modeled. Casse knew that such an event could twist the timeline so out of shape that Skynet could vanish without a trace, never built, unimagined, a phantom. The more factors involved, the less chance of survival. The only thing to do was to limit that possibility.

He stood at the window, the lights in the office dimmed, and gazed at the sprawl of city to the north. Late afternoon was giving way to early evening and lights began to dot the view. Despite their innate disorderliness, humans at times built with surprising intricacy and sophistication. Depending on perspective, of course.

The intercom chimed.

"Yes?"

"It's Cruz, sir," the assistant said.

"Send him in," Casse said.

Casse watched Oscar Cruz's reflection in the window as the man entered the office and hurried up to the desk.

"Have you cleared out those offices?" Casse asked.

"Yes, sir. The crew just left. Not a trace that we were ever there."

"Except for three witnesses."

Cruz lowered his head and seemed to writhe where he stood. Only for a second, but Casse saw. Cruz was beginning to break down. The nanoware permeating his brain had become pathological. Cruz's occasional requests to be rein-fected demonstrated a considerable degree of sanity, but also the recognition that his condition would only worsen.

"We're working on that, too," Cruz said. "Gant knew the intruder. Paul Patterson, a security agent at Destry-McMil-lin. We've concluded that the woman is Deirdre McMillin. Porter has been living with her."

"Where are they?"

"They fled to McMillin's home first, but they're now at Destry-McMillin itself."

"So they have had opportunity to tell others what happened. This is becoming a containment problem."

"Yes, uh, yes it is."

"You sent people to Porter's apartment?"

"They're all dead," Cruz said.

Casse turned around. "How?"

"We, uh, don't know. Four men...they didn't report back...we sent two more to check..."

"If Deirdre McMillin was helping Paul Patterson extricate Porter from us, she wasn't in her apartment. Someone else is interested in her then."

Cruz blinked. "The New Mexico subject?"

"He killed several of our people there, correct?"

"Yes—"

"And he found Eisner, correct?"

"Correct," Cruz started.

"Then we can assume he is an interested party. Correct?"

"Yes."

"Where is he now?"

"We, uh, lost him in Minnesota."

"Why was he in Minnesota?" Casse asked.

"Tracking down Porter's family, as it turns out."

"As it turns out. Do you consider the possibility good that he is now here in Los Angeles?"

Cruz fidgeted.

Casse, annoyed, touched a button on the desk, bringing the room lights up. Cruz flinched, frowning.

"What else?" Casse asked.

"I, uh...Gant recorded an earlier encounter with Patterson. At Pioneer. He brought along a man who claimed to be an inspector."

"Claimed?"

Cruz reached into his jacket and pulled out a 5 X 7 envelope. He spilled photographs on the desk. Casse saw images of a young man, athletically built, neatly groomed.

"So?" Casse asked. "Who is he?"

"His stated name is Sean Philicos. He's a private security specialist. He and his sister operated the company out of Santa Fe we discussed earlier. They're about to open offices here—"

"His sister...?"

"Julia Philicos. I don't have pictures of her. Not yet."

"Who are they?"

Cruz tapped the topmost picture. "That's John Connor."

Casse stared at the picture. "You're sure?"

"Well, he's older, of course, but...I saw these people, close up. Yes, sir. This is John Connor. I'm willing to bet Julia Philicos is Sarah. Sarah Connor. His mother."

"How did this get past us?"

"We thought—*you* thought—they were dead. Gone. They haven't been seen since 2001. I mean, I couldn't keep track of them after I went to prison."

Casse raised a hand and Cruz fell silent. John Connor. And mother. Not unexpected, but unwelcome certainly. He might have guessed—would have guessed, if he could become more adept at it—that they would appear at a time like this. "Do we know how long they've been back?"

"A few years. PPS Securities and Investigations—that's

their company—was incorporated a little over three years ago, in Albuquerque."

"They required help to do that. Their identities are protected."

"Reed? But he's all but fired, I didn't think—"

"People like Jack Reed are never discarded lightly. He's still very useful. His authority has been somewhat curtailed, but he is not to be disregarded. We should recheck all our security on the shipments from Colorado Springs."

"You don't think—?"

"I *do* think. I don't guess, Oscar. I want to know. See to it."

"What about Porter?"

"He's with McMillin. We wait. If an opportunity arises, terminate him. Inform Gant."

Cruz looked uncomfortable, but finally he nodded. He began to gather up the images.

"Leave those," Casse said. "Where is Gant now?"

"Outside the Destry-McMillin campus. Do you want him recalled?"

"No. Where are these new offices the Connors are opening?"

"Um, I'll get you the address."

"Do that."

Oscar Cruz waited, his fingers dancing nervously against his sides. Then he nodded deeply, stepped back from the desk, pivoted, and left the office.

*The Connors are back,* Casse thought. He glanced at the link on his desk, still useless until the monopole receiver was complete. Even then, it might not work. The war may already be lost, and Skynet vanished in a wisp of quantum probability. *But I am still here. That must indicate something. Still a chance.*

He studied the pictures of John Connor until the intercom chimed again and Cruz gave him the address of PPS Securities and Investigations.

When he saw the images downloaded from Gant, Oscar

Cruz panicked. For nearly a minute he imagined himself back in solitary, isolated with only the dedicating parasites in his brain for company. John Connor. Of all people. In confinement he had replayed the disasters in Colorado Springs and in Washington D.C. over and over in his imagination. His powers of visualization were greatly enhanced by the infecting nanoware Charles Layton, former CEO of Cyberdyne, had passed to him from the TX-A unit. Every moment came back to him, clear and immediate.

They had been so close to realizing the existence of Skynet then. They had been so close to owning the section of the government that oversaw their project. A few more minutes with Jack Reed and Samantha Jones and they would have been Skynet's agents in the great cause. But *John Connor* and his *mother* and those damn Specialists who had no business being in this time frame anyway, showed up to ruin the entire moment.

"Not again," he said, leaving Casse's office. "Not again...not again..."

He stopped in the hallway, closed his eyes, and willed himself to stop repeating that line. He needed no new ticks. The collection begun since midway through his prison sentence gave him enough trouble. The dysfunction resembled Tourette's.

The urge faded, and Oscar continued to the elevator.

He descended two floors, then went to his own office. Behind his desk, he accessed his computer, rummaged for a time until he found the address Casse wanted. He touched the intercom and passed it on.

"Very good," Casse said. "I want you to stay here, Oscar, and make sure everything goes smoothly when the first trucks arrive."

Cruz winced. His right hand curled into a fist, opened, and the fingers danced over the intercom. He wanted to leave, to go out and do something. Sitting and waiting hurt.

"Yes, sir," he said.

"I'll talk to you when I return."

"Yes, sir."

Cruz closed his eyes, gripping the arms of his chair, and rocked for a few seconds. The motion soothed him.

Why now? John Connor! Jesus Christ...

He laughed.

Who knows?

The goal was simple. Despite setbacks, Cyberdyne still commanded considerable resources. Jack Reed had done his best to shut them down, but a corporation this large, so widespread and diversified, proved virtually impossible to kill. The military R & D division suffered, of course. They had lost their chief ally in the Pentagon when Jack found out what they were doing. Jack might have managed to sink them if politics had not intervened. The world changed, priorities shifted, and Cyberdyne survived. Reduced, truncated, humbled, but largely intact.

And it had a considerable foreign market on which to draw.

*I did that,* Cruz thought, pride displacing anxiety. He had built the actual infrastructure of the company throughout the '90s. He had recruited the people, organized the departments and divisions, negotiated the contracts, provided the base that guaranteed—ultimately—their success.

The only thing that frightened him was the Connors.

Silly, he knew. They were only two people, how much damage could they do?

He remembered Colorado Springs in 2001. The Connors, aided by people from the future—*a* future, he had to keep reminding himself that there was more than one, at least for the time being, which seemed a stupid phrase in context—who possess incredible abilities, had invaded their secure compound just before Skynet was about to go online and destroyed the project. The disaster had been nearly a repeat of the 1994 destruction of Cyberdyne's L.A. facility where Miles Dyson had been working on the nanochip that was the basis of all their work in advanced cybernetics, leading to Skynet. Dyson had died in the L.A. event, but his assistant, Rosanna Monk, had ably—and, Cruz thought, miraculously—reconstructed all of Dyson's work, in Colorado Springs, bringing them right back to Skynet as a reality.

Along the way, she had discovered the working principles of a time travel device, but that had been a sideline as far as Oscar Cruz had been concerned. The prize was Skynet and, with the enhancements from the TX-A—also from the future, he knew, which he supposed made time travel rather more important than he had thought at the time—they had nearly pulled it off.

Until the Connors.

Sarah Connor, the mother, had been haranguing Cyberdyne, the government, anyone who would listen, for years about the monster machine, Armageddon, the dangers of A.I., and what Cyberdyne, through their government contracts, was about to do. It had always bothered the Skynet development team how accurate her accusations had been, and when she had destroyed their L.A. labs in '94, she had gone to ground and become a presence on the Internet, creating a growing community of conspiracy theorists, independent cybernetics experts, cranks, and genuinely concerned citizens who had done their best to disrupt the entire program. One of Cruz's jobs for years was damage control, arguing back to the hotheads and extremists. None of it made sense until Layton had programmed him. Then he had understood. Clearly. Humanity was a disease and the bellyaching and carping were symptoms. Skynet would cure them all.

But it had to exist in order to do that.

*If only we could have turned Reed...*

Cruz slapped his hands flat on the desk. "Well, there's only one thing to do," he announced. "We have to kill them all."

Suddenly, he felt very calm. It was good to reach a satisfying conclusion, especially one he knew would solve all their problems.

Casse left his car just off West Pico, eight blocks from the address of PPS Security. The early evening dinner crowd changed as he neared Calder until he found himself in a more diverse, less expensive neighborhood, drawing curious looks from the locals. He was overdressed, conspicuous.

Casse picked a man who appeared to be the right size and veered toward him. He managed to bump into him, receiving a snarl of invective. Casse apologized, catching the man by his naked arms as if to prevent him falling, and hurried on. Casse absorbed the oils and dead skin. The substance of the man broke down within him, registering on the programmable matrix of his own makeup as coded instructions. The few seconds' close examination completed the sequence Casse now initiated throughout himself. He drifted closer to the buildings until he reached the next intersection. Around the corner, Casse found a dark gangway within twenty paces. He stepped into it and allowed the change to take him, taking the man's form. He felt the transformation as a rippling expanding from his core and spreading throughout his limbs, over his face. When he stepped back onto the street, the curious looks were gone. He wandered along with the flow of night traffic until he reached the street.

Two vans were parked before the two-story building. A sign lay against the wall, identifying the place. Light filled the first-floor window and door, but the second floor appeared dark, unoccupied.

Casse wandered past to the next intersection, then crossed the street. He looked up the alley that ran behind PPS Security. Another van stood outside the rear door.

Casse sat down in the narrow space between a pair of commercial dumpsters. Concentrating, he poured instructions into his leg. He possessed this template from years ago, during his first months in this frame. He watched his leg as material bulged around the ankle, backed up toward his knee, stopping halfway up his calf. With an effort and a sensation that might have been pain in a human, the bulge detached itself and flowed across the alley pavement. As it left him, it altered quickly, taking a new shape. Within seconds, it walked toward the parked van, recognizably feline. By the time it reached the target it possessed fur, markings, and the body language of a cat.

The back door stood open, as did the side doors of the van. He heard voices from the building. The cat-form sat down just at the edge of the light spilling from inside.

A few minutes later a man came out the door. He entered the van, rummaged for a few moments, then stepped out. "Hey, I found the—whoa, what we got here? Anybody order a mascot?"

"What's that?"

Another man appeared in the doorway and looked down at the cat.

"Cute. Must be a million of 'em within ten blocks. Come on, we need to finish the shielding on the dedicated lines."

"Yeah, right." The first man knelt down and scratched the cat-form under the chin. "Friendly, aren't you? Not afraid of me at all."

He reentered the building.

Casse, through the cat-form, waited a few more minutes, then cautiously moved the cat-form to the edge of the doorway. The utility room door was open to another room. Three men worked amid a collection of desks and electronic equipment. Cables snaked across the floor.

To the right, through another door, a staircase ran up to the second floor. At the first floor landing, another door, probably to the basement. Casse judged distance and attention, hesitated, then bolted the cat-form up the rear stairs.

The door at the top was locked. Casse sniffed along the base of the door. Not much room, but enough. He dissolved the cat-form and slid the material underneath, into the apartment.

He found few furnishings. More computers, a television, a kitchen table and chairs. A sofa. No bed yet. Sleeping bags lay visible through a doorway. They were still moving in.

A box in the living room contained a desk lamp, blotter, various other office items.

Casse considered options. He could not get to the Connors now. Not yet. And as tempting as the idea was, it would not be wise to try to kill them. He doubted he could. In the past they had demonstrated a powerful link to the frame, a resistence to interference from any out-of-frame agent. Like young Porter, they could only be killed by someone native to their own frame. Knowing that gave Casse a certain confidence. He was relieved of the responsibility for taking actions that would prove fruitless. Counterproductive, even.

Knowledge was never useless. Better to find out more than interfere with current plans.

He moved the cat to the kitchen table. It rubbed itself against one leg, a reflexive gesture inexplicably retained from the original model, then dissolved itself. The metal flowed up the leg and spread across the bottom of the table. The thin veneer took on color and texture, chameleon-like.

Satisfied, Casse reduced contact with the satellite, and left the alley. He made his way back to his car, gradually resuming his preferred shape. By the time he reached the vehicle, he was once more Casse, Vice President of Cyberdyne, guardian of Skynet's coming birth.

# EIGHTEEN

$B$obby hated being here. The instant they drove through the gates of Destry-McMillin he felt a profound urge to climb out the window and run.

Deirdre sat beside him, holding his hand. He tightened his grip upon seeing the main gate and she frowned at him. She knew how he felt, but just now pragmatism won out over principle. Everyone else had decided—he would be safer inside Destry-McMillin than anywhere else until what had happened was sorted out.

"Why don't we just call the police?" he muttered.

Sean Philicos, sitting in the front seat, turned to him. "The police can't help you in this."

Bobby had no idea who Philicos was, but Mr. McMillin seemed to defer to him. "You know a lot about it, do you?"

"A bit. Relax. I can explain it..." He hesitated, then laughed dryly. "Well, inasmuch as it *can* be explained, I'll try. But let's get you somewhere safe first, okay?"

He wanted to argue, but images of Mr. Casse's knife-blade hand kept recurring. He swallowed and rolled his head slowly, trying to ease the tension from his neck.

Outside, they passed through pleasant parkland on the way to corporate headquarters. The place was bigger than he had imagined. Deirdre told him her stepfather had a great deal of money—and power—but it was never easy for him to grasp what that meant. Growing up lower class, the only thing between his future and poverty a better-than-average grasp of abstract mathematics, Bobby's few confrontations with immense wealth always surprised him. He never anticipated the correct level, continually underestimated what it meant to be a millionaire, much less a billionaire. What he saw on television possessed no substance—it was television, unreal.

Why it made him uncomfortable he could not say. He felt judged for his background, his family's lack of status, his humble concepts of Enough. Again he wondered why Deirdre stayed with him. What did he have to offer to compare with this? *Property isn't a person,* she had told him once. She had not said "love," which would have sounded patronizing. Property isn't a person...Bobby could not argue with that. But a part of him reckoned that "persons" who could build something like this had maybe more "personhood" than people like him. A false conclusion, he knew, based more on his discomfort than any reasonable assessment of reality. Still, he could not shake it. He felt undeserving—and resentful of the McMillins of the world making him feel that way.

But he had never thought any of them wanted to kill him. He had never expected a Mr. Casse.

The two cars—the lead containing most of the security people Mr. McMillin had brought along, including Paul Patterson—descended a wide ramp into an underground garage. More security people waited for them, several in dark green uniforms wearing sidearms.

Philicos walked with McMillin toward a row of elevators. Paul Patterson approached Deirdre and Bobby.

"We're going to assign a couple of people to accompany you," Patterson said.

"Where are we going?" Bobby asked. "Why can't we go home?"

Deirdre scowled at him. "It's likely being watched. That's why I called Paul."

"You didn't tell me," Bobby said.

205

"You wouldn't have believed me. You'd call me paranoid, just like you did when I suggested maybe canceling this interview with Cyberdyne."

"Well, how the hell was I supposed to know they're aliens or something?"

Deirdre shook her head, arms folded across her chest. Bobby saw something in her face then he had never seen there before: fear.

"Come on," Patterson said, pointing toward the elevators.

Deirdre took Bobby's hand, smiled anxiously, and followed Patterson.

As they entered the elevator, Bobby asked Patterson, "How did you know?"

"That office you were in," Patterson said, "was the only place occupied. The rest of the building was empty."

"So you came in with your gun drawn because nobody else was around?"

"Cruz had a weapon in his hand when I opened the door."

They rode the elevator up to the fourth floor. They stepped into wide, bright corridors that reminded Bobby of the offices at the university. People gave him curious looks as he moved surrounded by the entourage formed by Deirdre, her stepfather, three security men, and Philicos down the long hall and into a conference room.

"Anybody hungry?" Dennis McMillin asked. "I'm having coffee and sandwiches sent up in any case. Anybody want anything else? Deirdre? Young man?"

Bobby locked eyes with McMillin then. Since he arrived at his home to fetch his daughter and her "boyfriend," McMillin had said less than a dozen words to him. He could never tell if the man liked him, did not care, or hated him. Bobby shrugged, looking away.

"I'm all right," he said. He sat down at the long table, close to the door.

"Would you all excuse us, gentlemen?" McMillin said. "Please wait outside."

Bobby watched all the others leave the room. The last to go was Patterson, who gave Deirdre an odd look.

Deirdre sat down beside Bobby.

McMillin sat on the edge of the conference table, facing them.

"Young man, you are anything but 'all right' at the moment. You're in deep shit, son, and we're here to help."

Bobby felt himself grow angry, but bit it back. He glared at McMillin, but the man did not look away.

"I want to tell you something," McMillin said. "I'm a rich man. You may have noticed. And I love Deirdre. She's my daughter, I want the best for her. You may have guessed that. The cliché ends there, though. I don't interfere in her life. I am very able to do so. When she enrolled at Caltech I was all for it. When she wanted to take an apartment of her own by the campus, I was dubious. I didn't like it. I wanted to protect her. But it's her life and she has to learn how to live it on her own terms. She has to make her own decisions and it would be a rotten way to have her start out thinking I don't trust her. So I sat on my reservations and let her do it. I do trust her. She's never disappointed me. When she moved you into her place, it bothered me. Really bothered me. But I did not interfere. I could have had you checked out. I have resources second only to the federal government. I could have had your DNA analyzed and interpreted if I'd wanted it. But I didn't. I left it alone. I didn't even know your last name till recently and that measure of trust in Deirdre damn near cost you your life. Now I know more about you. I know about the little scam you're pulling with your cousin's scholarship. I know your real name. So how do you do, Jeremiah?"

"My name is Robert."

McMillin shook his head. "Your cousin's name was Robert. Oh, your *middle* name is Robert, certainly, which is the only reason so far you've gotten away with this. By the way, I applaud you for that. The scholarship was there, your cousin vanished, it would have been a waste not to take advantage of it. I'm not a big believer in the required standards of the university system—if you're a math wiz, why do you need a dozen years of English Comp? The slick way you switched profiles, the whole process of posing as your cousin. You're clever. And from what Deirdre has told me, you are one sharp mathematician. But the fraud is not that good. I found out with a few phone calls. Certainly Cyberdyne could find out the same information. And evidently your thesis advisor did."

Again, Bobby felt himself bristle. His reaction made no sense, he knew, but he resented having failure thrown in his face.

"Point is, I am not an autocratic asshole," McMillin continued. "You and Deirdre have been living together on your own terms, that's fine. She's happy—it shows, you obviously treat her well—I won't interfere. I repeat, I could have meddled. I did not. The simplest inquiries were not made because I trusted her. Do you understand what I'm saying?"

Bobby wanted to leave. He caught Deirdre's gaze. She was watching him, waiting. He tried to think what they wanted, what was required here. It was a test, but he did not know if it was multiple choice or essay.

Thinking diminished the anger. Not completely, but enough. He looked at McMillin with a new respect. He did see the risk involved. Dennis McMillin had let go. Deirdre made her own decisions. McMillin had respected that. Respected it almost pathologically—Bobby did not think he could be so passive under the same conditions. But it was important to this man that his stepdaughter respect him, too, and that required a show of trust.

Bobby had always thought of Destry-McMillin and Dennis McMillin as one in the same, a whole entity, indivisible into the components of corporation and individual. And like all big corporations, Bobby mistrusted them. It was easier than making constant reassessments and new moral judgments. Time for that later, after he had his degree.

*Maybe you can never put this kind of thing off, though...*

His shoulders relaxed. He sat up straighter. "I understand." He reached for Deirdre's hand. "I do understand. I'm sorry." He met McMillin's gaze again. "Why are you telling me this now?"

"Because I need your trust, too. This has become something other than your personal life. We need to trust you."

"I'm...look, I'm still not sure if what I saw was real or...it doesn't make sense."

"Frame of reference, son. Everything makes sense in the right frame of reference. What I want you to do is talk to one of my physicists. I want you to go over what you and Casse talked about. We need an idea why they were interested in you."

Suspicion returned in a rush. "That's my work—"

McMillin raised his hands. "Whoa. At this point something larger is involved. But we're not trying to steal your stuff. We're not Dr. Cojensis."

"And I believe this why?"

McMillin scowled impatiently. "Look, being careful with your work is usually sensible, and you've learned early the hard way to be a bit secretive. But someone just tried to kill you because of what you know. There's more than an undergraduate degree at risk now. We need to know why they want to kill you."

"He didn't, though. I mean, he chased me around the office, hacking at me, but he kept missing. Sometimes it seemed impossible for him to miss me. I'm wondering now if he really intended to kill me or—"

"Paul tells me Cruz had a gun. He was about to go into that office with you and Casse. What do you think he was going to do, shoot his boss?"

Bobby opened his mouth to answer. He stared at McMillin mutely, puzzled for a moment by the oily warm sensation spreading over his shoulders, up his neck, through his face. He hands began trembling. He laughed, and the sound became a sob, and suddenly he was in Deirdre's arms, shaking and crying.

*They tried to kill me...tried to kill me...tried to...me...*

Deirdre watched Dennis McMillin, resentful and admiring at the same time. He had kept his word to stay out of her private life, but he was badgering Bobby now. She felt

209

protective, and wanted him to stop his harangue and go away, even while she knew he was right. She held Bobby while he cried. He was terrified, naturally, but more than that, he had reached a breaking point. For the last two years he had occupied a tenuous place at the university, constantly alert and on edge because of his deception. When Cojensis had presented him with his duplicity, Bobby's hold on his own life became even more slippery. This, now, was too much.

McMillin backed off. He gave Deirdre a look that was both apologetic and impatient. She understood —roughly—that they had little time for adjustment. She was more than a little amazed at her own calm. But then she had always been like this—deal with the crisis at hand, suffer the emotional effects later. She suspected that the backlash of this one would be enormous.

Gradually, Bobby regained control. He was embarrassed, she could tell. He snuffled, pulled a handkerchief from his pocket.

"Can I get some water?" he asked.

"Sure," McMillin said. He went to the other end of the conference room, to a counter containing a tray of glasses and a dispenser. He filled a glass and brought it back to Bobby. "Do you need a minute?"

"Please," Bobby said.

McMillin gestured for Deirdre to join him.

"I'll be back," she told Bobby, standing. She followed her stepfather into the corridor outside.

At the far end she saw a group of people, among them Paul Patterson and the new man, Sean Philicos. She was baffled by all this. She felt her own grasp on events to be tenuous, but she let Dennis McMillin lead her to another room.

Alone, he waved her to a chair.

"I've never meddled in your private life," he began.

"I know. I appreciate that."

"But now I have to. I need you to see that."

"I need to see what's going on."

"I'm going to tell you. But you aren't going to believe me."

Deirdre stared at him. "You've never lied to me before. Why wouldn't I believe you?"

"Because frankly I have a hard time believing it myself."

He pulled out a chair and sat opposite her. He took her hands, bowed his head briefly, and sighed.

"What?" Deirdre asked in a whisper. "You're scaring me now."

He looked up. "You should be scared."

He began talking. He held her hands through the entire story.

Bobby refilled his glass. He felt calmer now. At some point he concluded that his life as he had wished it was over. Nothing would be as he wanted it to be. The realization brought a peculiar peace. Temporary, no doubt.

The door to the conference room opened. McMillin entered again, followed by Deirdre, Patterson, Sean Philicos, and a woman Bobby did not recognize.

"How do you feel, Bobby?" McMillin asked. "Better? Can we talk?"

"Sure," Bobby answered. "Who do you think's gonna win the World Cup this year?"

McMillin grinned. "Bobby, I want you to meet Dr. Stefani Jaspar. She runs a development team working on superconductors. Among other things."

Despite himself, Bobby felt his interest rise. "Hi."

"Mr. Porter," she said. "I'd like to talk to you about your work. I understand it concerns certain aspects of time?"

Bobby grunted. "I guess you could say that."

"Let's sit," McMillin said.

Everyone took a chair around the long conference table.

"How do you approach Time?" Jaspar asked.

Bobby studied her. Small woman, neat hair, large brown eyes that displayed considerable intelligence. She wore a simple green blouse and black pants, the only decoration her Destry-McMillin ID badge. "What do you mean?"

211

Dr. Jaspar took a sheet of paper from her pocket and spread it on the table in front of him. Equations covered it. Bobby drew it closer, aware of everyone watching him. A part of him wondered at his sudden change of mood. Within less than two minutes he had all but forgotten his fear and depression, becoming completely immersed in the discussion into which Jaspar had drawn him. He did not mind; much better to be engaged like this than trembling fearfully over events he could not control.

The work was clean and advanced and he saw a lot of his own ideas laced throughout.

"There's more?" he asked.

"Sure," she said. "This is just a synopsis."

"You're folding a piece of space-time around itself," he said.

Dr. Jaspar's mouth twitched in a brief smile.

"The energy requirement—" Bobby began to protest.

"Can be borrowed," she said. "Same as in quantum tunneling."

"Do you know Mr. Casse?" Bobby asked, suddenly excited.

"Vice president of Cyberdyne? Not personally. I understand you've met him."

Bobby tapped the paper. "He had similar ideas."

Her eyes brightened even more. "I'd love to hear about them."

"Well..." He studied the equations. "Do you have something to write on?"

# NINETEEN

Oscar Cruz strode into the loading bay, his fingers twitching rhythmically. He made himself stop whistling when the elevator doors opened, but the urge to hum almost overwhelmed him.

One semi and a big SUV waited just inside the bay doors. Cyberdyne personnel huddled around the drivers. As Cruz reached the edge of the gathering, the babble of conversation died. Men and women moved automatically aside, forming a human aisle for him. The two driving teams watched his approach with mixed expressions of relief and fear. All of them looked severely rattled.

"Okay," Cruz began, raising his hands, palms down, in a calming gesture. "What happened?"

"Road blocks, Mr. Cruz," one of them said. He glanced at the other three, rubbed his face nervously, and continued. "We got word from Group C. They figured feds. When we checked with the others, the same story. The convoys had all been stopped, searches were proceeding. So we turned off the interstate and tried to get through by state highways and county roads."

"I see only one truck," Cruz observed.

"The other three were taken out."

Cruz blinked at the man. "Let's see, you are...?"

"Roy, Mr. Cruz. Roy Jacobs."

"Roy. 'Taken out?' What do you mean?"

"Um...choppers. Hummers. They were all pulled over, searched—"

"Why did you get through?"

"I had a blowout three miles before the roadblocks. The tail car pulled over to help us." He indicated the SUV. "We were starting to change it when word came over the CB." Roy Jacobs swallowed loudly. "We just went on changing the tire and waited, but they never came. We waited three, four hours, then started up again. When we passed the site where the others had been stopped, we didn't see anything. We couldn't raise them on the CB, either. After that, we thought it would be a good idea to stay off the air and the cell phone till we got here."

"Good, good," Cruz said. "So they overlooked you."

"Doesn't make sense, I know, but that's how it looks."

Cruz clasped his hands together behind his back, working through the information. He almost asked where, but it did not matter. He walked over to the semi.

"What part did you bring in?"

"I, uh...I don't know, Mr. Cruz. We weren't told what we were carrying."

"That's right, you weren't." Cruz studied the long trailer. One shipment out of what should have been fifteen trucks. All the rest now in federal hands. But exactly whose? "Get it unloaded, get it where it needs to go. I have some calls to make." He looked at the four men. "You seem unhurt. A little shaken maybe?"

Roy laughed humorlessly. "Well, sure. We've never had any trouble like this before."

"You'd like to end your employment with us perhaps?"

Roy looked at the others. "Right now we just want to calm down."

"Good idea. We can talk tomorrow. We'll put you all up in executive suites. We've got some details to take care of, so if you don't mind waiting here, I'll get back with you a little later." Cruz motioned to one of his assistants to take care of it, and the four men were led away. "Everyone else, back to work. The excitement is over for now."

The gathered employees drifted away. He wondered how many of them would quit before the sun came up tomorrow. This was unexpected. If they had been made to know the true nature of the project the way he did, they would stay, certainly, but Casse had chosen not to reprogram any more people when the after effects became clear.

*None of us were supposed to live this long...*

As it was, none of these people knew, which meant Cyberdyne had to rely on ordinary loyalty to the company paycheck.

The trailer doors swung open. Cruz watched as a foreman checked the manifest. It was coded. The man entered decryption commands on his slate.

"We have processing nodes," he said.

Cruz felt a brief sense of relief. Important components, then, an essential element in the Skynet matrix. Maybe they could duplicate the rest of the Dyson architecture around what they now had.

"I'll be in my office," Cruz said. "See this all gets where it's supposed to."

He went to the cab. A technician worked on the ceiling. "Just a second, Mr. Cruz," she said.

Cruz watched her work. A panel came loose and flipped down. She reached into the revealed recess and pulled out a small rectangular cartridge. She handed it to Cruz. He thanked her and skipped toward the elevators, forcing himself after a few paces to walk normally.

*I hate this, this being crazy shit...if only I didn't know it, like normal crazy people...*

He returned to his office. At his desk once more, he inserted the cartridge into a slot. A few seconds later, his screen displayed telemetry from the convoy recorders. All the convoy vehicles possessed these units, interconnected so that each vehicle within the convoy recorded its own and all the others' data. The computer now assembled all the various elements into a coherent montage.

The time chop indicated an hour before dawn. The machine amplified detail, added a bit of color. The four trucks followed the SUV down a two-lane blacktop bounded on both sides by broad desert. Low hills, scrub, some cactus dotted the landscape. They made good time now, cruising along at a steady seventy-five mph. There was crosstalk between the drivers, but Cruz paid no attention until the word came through concerning roadblocks.

Over the open channel, the drivers were ordered to pull over and stand down. He heard the sounds of choppers over the CB.

Then silence. Cruz advanced the recording until the truck began to move again. He heard the navigator calling for the other trucks over the CB, then a brief discussion between them to stay off the air and try to get through.

As Roy Jacobs said, they had been overlooked.

Cruz tapped numbers into his phone. "My ass."

"Security," a voice answered.

"This is Oscar Cruz. I'm sending you a recording. I want the route our convoy survivors came backtracked and checked. Let me know if they were followed."

"Yes, sir."

*There's no doubt,* he thought as he punched another number. *They don't miss except on purpose...scared the hell out of the drivers, they ran and came right here...*

The telephone screen winked on. A face looked at Cruz.

"Mr. Cruz, what can I do for you?"

"Good evening, Senator. I hope I'm not disturbing you."

"Not at all."

"We have a problem, Senator. May I send you a file?"

The late-middle-aged face scowled. "Certainly, Mr. Cruz."

Cruz transferred the recording to the phone and sent it. He watched the senator listen to it, noted the shifts in expression.

"I see," the senator said when it was finished.

"I have an idea who did this," Cruz said. "But I want to hear it from someone else first."

"Reed."

"That's what I thought, too."

The senator sighed. "I'm sorry about this, Oscar. I thought he was contained."

"The president still trusts him."

"He does, though god knows why. But I had no idea he could still muster this kind of field work."

"We have reason to believe he's arrested a number of our people and confiscated a great deal of our material. Almost everything out of Colorado Springs, in fact."

The senator's face darkened. "Son of a—let me make some inquiries, Oscar. But first, let me talk to Casse."

"He's not in at the moment, sir."

"So you're minding the store for now. Very well. I'll see what I can find out. I'll get your people out of this, Oscar."

"Thank you, sir."

"I opposed shutting Cyberdyne down when I was just a congressman and I still think Reed is out of his mind over this. We can't afford to let a valuable corporation remain under a cloud just because of some wild paranoid notion of a coming war."

"I agree, Senator. But right now he has more authority than either of us thought."

"I'll get that taken care of ASAP. Stay by the phone tonight, Oscar. I'll be in touch."

"Thank you, Senator."

The screen went blank and Cruz leaned back in his chair. What always amazed him about the senator was his willingness and eagerness to back the project without ever having been programmed by Layton or himself.

He scratched the top of his head with both hands. He missed Layton from time to time. Casse was, if anything, colder. But efficient.

"Reed," he said aloud, drawing out the name. "Reeeeed. Reed Reed Reed."

He sat forward abruptly and snatched copies of the pictures Gant had sent him. John Connor. The name itself grated on his admittedly unstable nerves.

"If you're around," he said to the image, "so is your mother."

He reached for the keyboard, but hesitated. Fingers curling, he sat back. He could close his eyes and see the disaster that had overtaken his life.

In 1994, the Connors, with the help of a rogue T800, had destroyed Cyberdyne's L.A. facility. Dozens of police notwithstanding, they had escaped. Miles Dyson, head researcher on the Skynet Project, had been killed. The catastrophe had nearly wrecked them. Charles Layton, then CEO of the company, had rallied them, if rally was a word that could describe the utterly practical executive. He had been a cold fish before that event. After the TX-A programmed him, all trace of humanity had left him.

Not a bad thing, all in all, Cruz thought. Layton had then programmed him, transferring the nanoware then infesting his own body, and relieving Cruz of any vestige of loyalty to humanity. Skynet became all, the only reason for their lives to continue.

They had a researcher then, Rosanna Monk, Dyson's assistant. Brilliant, borderline misanthropic, after the TX-A had programmed her, the project was back on track. Not only that, but she developed the time vault as well. Crude, it nevertheless breached the barrier of time travel. Skynet would need it. She had tried to describe it to him once, why it came naturally out of the work on Skynet, but as good as Cruz was, her arguments did not quite make sense. No, that was wrong—she designed the vault, her arguments made perfect sense, just not to him.

At the time Reed had been on their side. Chief liaison to the State Department, he held the kill switch on any top-level project for the government. At some point, he grew suspicious, and the project was in jeopardy. Layton and Cruz had intended to meet with him, and his assistant, Samantha Jones, and program them. Once that happened, nothing would prevent Skynet's birth.

But it had all gone wrong. The new facility in Colorado Springs was assaulted and the work destroyed. Another setback. Reed had been turned against them. Layton killed, all the programmed staff arrested and imprisoned. Skynet should have emerged in 2001, 2002 at the latest, and Armageddon was to follow within a couple more years.

It was a problem, no longer having the Soviet Union to attack and trigger the necessary nuclear exchange. When the timeline began to change with the incursions by Skynet agents, and their subsequent failures to eliminate opposition, many other factors altered unexpectedly. The collapse of the Eastern Bloc had been predicted for decades, but no one thought it would happen so soon, so thoroughly, in the early 1990s. Cruz believed it was the timeline trying to accommodate the changes. The unraveling had to be stopped.

Another change happened in 2001. More unraveling.

Now Casse was in charge and the decision to be restrained kept them working covertly. Casse had some theory about the inability of agents from the future to alter certain basic lines. They used human agents where possible. Cruz did not like it, but he was bound by instructions and the still-potent hope that they could resurrect Skynet.

They would succeed. He knew this, because Skynet existed in the future.

He just could not see quite how they would succeed. Especially with the Connors once more involved. There was something about them, they were linked inextricably to Skynet's existence or nonexistence. Maybe Monk might have explained it to him.

*Where did they come from, though?*

He looked around the office. Gant had called in earlier to let him know that the entire party—McMillin, the young Porter and his girlfriend, Paul Patterson, and John Connor, plus a few Destry-McMillin security people—had relocated to Destry-McMillin itself.

He touched the intercom. "Is Mr. Casse back yet?"

"No, Mr. Cruz."

"Ah!" He glared at the picture. "Fine. I can make a decision." He punched another number into the phone.

"Gant," a voice said.

"This is Cruz. I'm sending you an image." Cruz rifled

through his desk as he spoke. He found the old photo in the last drawer. "This is a dated picture of Sarah Connor. Modify as necessary and use as an identifier. If you see her, prevent her from getting to Destry-McMillin. All right?"

"Does this supercede prior instruction?"

"No, continue surveillance. I expect she might just show up. But do not let her in."

"Understood."

Cruz shoved the image into his desk scanner and initiated the upload. Within seconds, the file went out directly to Gant.

"Received."

"Report results," Cruz said.

"Affirmative."

The connection broke. Cruz hated it when the T-800s reverted to their monotone robot-speak. It took time, but they could be taught to mimic human speech patterns. Somewhat at least.

But he felt better now. The last thing anybody here wanted was for the Connors to link up and work together.

*But they already are working together,* he thought. He shook his head, annoyed at inconvenient logic. "Keep them apart while the senator takes care of Reed and gets us our toys back!"

There.

Next problem. He reached for the phone again.

"Get me the Los Angeles Police Department, please," he told the operator.

# TWENTY

$S$arah drove to Destry-McMillin, constantly checking for any shadows. She talked little and Lee Portis kept still throughout the drive. He watched as well, his attention alarmingly inhuman. She wondered again if she was wrong, if he was a Terminator of some kind, but he had convinced her that he was human. *Like the Specialists,* she thought.

She had distrusted them at first. John and she had managed a life in Mexico City. Not elaborate, but their comfort and sense of security had been growing, they had acquaintances who could conceivably become friends, they had a place much like a home. Then the modified humans from a future different than the one they had expected and feared showed up just ahead of a new Terminator, one even more powerful and deadly than the T1000 that had chased them from L.A. in 1994. Jade, Anton, Robert, the others—they had spilled all over John and Sarah, extracted them from the life they were building, and pulled them into a maelstrom of guerilla war that had taken them into the future. Several futures.

Since returning in 2003, Sarah had struggled to make sense of all she had seen. It seemed easier to treat it like a story someone else had told her—except for the scars, both physical and mental.

Lee Portis was like a Specialist, like Jade and Anton. But different.

She entered the serpentine maze of the high tech industrial campus that sprawled against the edge of Caltech. Destry-McMillin occupied a sizeable campus of its own on the other side. Early evening sun threw long shadows from the decorative flora and unobtrusive buildings dotting the landscape.

"Is that your real name?" she asked. "Lee Portis?

"No. I...borrowed it."

"So who are you? Really."

"Really. I don't know. It seems there was a problem with the transfer. I'm amnesiac. Partly."

Sarah slowed. "You know why you're here but you don't know who you are."

He hesitated. "Essentially correct. I have files...I'm augmented."

"None of those files contain your identity?"

"Perhaps. Not all of them are freely accessible. They open when I require them, not before."

"That sounds inconvenient."

"It's presented a few challenges."

"Why would they do that?"

"Who?"

"Whoever sent you back?"

He shook his head. "Security, I imagine. If I were captured, the files would be completely inaccessible."

Sarah grunted. Plausible. But the Specialists had arrived with no such fail-safes, nor, she thought, would they have been useful. The TX-A hunting them had been capable of leeching the thoughts even from a dead brain. Would a few files in an augmentation be so different? Still, she could think of no other explanation, unless Portis was a Skynet agent. That was also plausible.

*But it doesn't feel true...*

Her instincts had gotten her through a great deal. She had learned to trust them. But there were limits. She wondered if she would recognize them when she reached them.

She rounded the last turn before the approach to Destry-McMillin. Rows of high shrubbery rimmed the property.

"Those were humans in that apartment," she said.

"They were."

She saw the sign directing her to turn right, into the driveway leading to the guard kiosk. As she made the turn, she saw that only the central booth of three was manned. In the early twilight, the harsh fluorescent filled the enclosure with a spectral glow, silhouetting the man within. Sarah tapped the brake, slowing until she pulled up beside the open window.

"May I help you?"

Sarah took her ID from the center island. "Yes, my name is Philicos. I'm here to see Mr. McMillin."

She handed the card up to the window, then stopped. The face peering down at her, unblinking, dark hair cropped close, froze her in place for a few moments. Not the same, but very familiar above the wide shoulders. A hand extended toward the card, eyes never leaving her face. He took her ID, pulled it inside the kiosk, then glanced at it quickly.

"One moment while I check," he said.

Then Sarah noticed that he wore a plain white shirt instead of the traditional guard uniform. Collar open, sleeves rolled part way up the forearms, all wrong.

"Drive," Portis hissed beside her.

Sarah jerked the stickshift into REVERSE, and stomped on the accelerator. The man inside the booth lunged. The car lurched backward. The Terminator bounced onto the hood, then, as Sarah twisted the wheel hard to the left, slid off onto the pavement.

The car whipped around, still in reverse.

The Terminator snapped to its feet and came at them. Sarah braked, shifted to drive, and steered directly at it. They collided deafeningly, the big man-machine crunching the hood, flipping onto the windshield, smashing it. Sarah braked again and it rebounded back to the pavement. She tried to hit it again.

The car tilted up and back. Sarah kept her foot on the accelerator, but the front wheels found no traction.

"Out!" Portis shouted.

Sarah opened her door and rolled out of the car. She hit the ground in a crouch, spun around, and backpedaled, reaching for her pistol.

The Terminator stood holding the front of the vehicle up. He flexed, turning the car onto its side, then focused on her.

Twenty-three years. Sarah felt her legs lock in place under that look. Twenty-three years ago the first one came for her. She had fought them, destroyed them, survived them, and still she always experienced a moment of helplessness when a new one appeared and it all began again.

It took a step in her direction.

She drew her weapon, chambered a round, and fired. Ten shots slammed into its upper torso and face. It flinched backward. One eye shattered.

Sarah thumbed the release, dropping the empty magazine to the ground, while drawing a fresh one from her belt. She rammed it home, pulled the slide back, and found her legs all at once. She ran.

She ran toward the gate. The Terminator beat her to it, sprinting with inhuman speed to intercept her. She came to a halt, then backed away.

Curiously, it hesitated.

Lee Portis crashed into it bodily. Both of them went to the ground. Sarah stared, stunned. She had never seen a human tackle one of these things successfully. They stood their ground like heavy machinery, immobile to anything less than wrecking ball power. But Portis had knocked it down.

They rolled, the Terminator rising to one knee and drawing back its fist. It launched a punch, but Portis managed to slip aside. The sharp crunch of asphalt shattering startled her, and Sarah raised her pistol again. She fired four rounds into the side of its head.

It jerked away from the impacts, but did not fall. It looked at her briefly, then stood, turning in one seamless motion, and caught Portis by the coat. It heaved. Portis flew, flailing, through the air, into the overturned car.

Sarah fired two more shots, then ran toward Portis.

Blood ran from his nose, but he managed to sit up. He grinned at her. "Do you believe me now?"

Sarah offered her arm. He took hold. She leaned away from him while he got to his feet.

He looked past her, the grin vanishing, then shoved her to one side. He broke in the opposite direction.

The Terminator advanced on Sarah.

She rounded the car, dancing back. Portis caught her arm.

"It might be a good idea to keep it away from your son," he said.

She fired again.

A car rolled by in the street. Sarah glimpsed a passenger staring at them, mouth open in shock. Across the road, set well back amid neat landscaping, stood a low building with small windows.

Portis tugged on her elbow. She fired one more shot at the Terminator, then ran.

She stumbled when her feet hit the grass, but she did not fall. She struggled to keep up with Portis, whom she knew was holding himself back so she would not fall behind. They reached the corner of the building and stopped.

The Terminator still stood by Sarah's overturned car, watching them.

"What's it doing?" she asked.

"I don't know...maybe..." He sniffed and wiped at his nose. The bleeding had stopped. "It's blocking us."

"From what?"

"Getting to your son?"

Sarah reached for her phone. "Damn," she hissed, finding

it missing. "It must be in the car. Do you have a cell phone?"

"No."

"I'm getting pretty fed up with this." She looked to her left. More innocuous buildings dotted the grounds to the south and east. "There's got to be another way in."

She started off southward, crossing to the next building. Portis followed. She hurried along the wall to the corner to the east. The Terminator remained where it stood, watching from the entrance to Destry-McMillin.

Hidden by the building, they ran to the rear and stopped, studying the route further south.

"Building to building until we're out of its line of sight?" Portis asked.

"Then through the shrubs, onto Destry-McMillin grounds."

"We don't know our way around there."

"You don't have detailed files?"

He gave her an odd look, then shook his head.

"We should see if we can use a phone," she said. "Come on."

They crossed a parking lot and another expanse of grass. Sarah holstered her weapon as they approached a three-story building. The main doors were still unlocked.

Within the foyer, three men conversed. They frowned at Sarah and Portis when they entered.

"There's been an accident," Sarah said. "Can we use your phone?"

"Where?" one of the men asked, pointing to the reception desk.

"In front of Destry-McMillin," Sarah said.

"What about their guards?" another asked.

"It's a mess," Portis said. "I'm Lee Portis," he added, holding out his hand.

The man shook absently. "You've been bleeding."

"It's nothing. The phone?"

"Um...sure, go ahead. We were just closing up for the night."

Sarah went around the desk and sat down. She lifted the handset from the complex phone station, then stabbed a button. The dial tone hummed in her ear. She punched in John's cell phone number.

Portis shook hands with each of the remaining men and in seconds they were smiling and conversing like old friends.

One ring and John picked up. "Philicos."

"It's me," Sarah said.

"Where—?"

"Shut up. There's a problem. A Terminator was at the guard shack out front. It won't let us in. We're across—"

The doors shattered inward, spraying Portis and the three men. Sarah looked up to see a blur of motion bowl through them, directly toward her. She stood. The Terminator reached the desk. It slammed a fist down onto the phone station, exploding it into fragments.

She bounced the disconnected handset off its head and reached for her pistol.

Portis' left arm snaked around its neck. The Terminator leaned back, strained briefly, and then Portis kicked its legs from beneath it. The massive thing dropped to the floor. Portis danced away before it could grab him.

It got to its feet effortlessly, lunging for Portis. Sarah fired from less than two meters away, both bullets impacting its skull, tearing away flesh. The one eye she had struck dangled from the socket, the light absent, useless.

It paid no attention to her shots. Portis came up against a wall. The T-800 charged him. Portis tried to sidestep it, but the machine anticipated the move this time and caught him. It held him to the wall by both arms, squeezing. Portis's face contorted in pain.

Sarah dropped the empty magazine, groping for another one. The three men watched, stunned. She rammed the new magazine into the pistol butt and shouted at them. "Another phone! Where?"

The Terminator's attention snapped around to her. It released Portis, who slid to the floor, mouth wide.

Sarah squeezed off ten rounds at its face. It held its hands up to deflect the shots. Skin and blood flew off the endo-skeleton as it advanced. Sarah backed away, emerging from behind the desk. She changed magazines again, loading her last one.

The Terminator lowered its hands. The flesh of its face nearly gone, the silvery robot skull caught the low lights, glimmering, housing one glowing red eye.

The three men were gone, fled through the smashed doorway.

Portis got weakly to his feet.

Sarah raised her weapon. "I'm getting pretty fucking tired of this," Sarah said. "What do you want?"

It took another step toward her.

Portis embraced it again. One hand came around. The Terminator reached up to throw him off. Portis moved with the same speed, though, and before the T-800 could grab him, Portis drove two fingers into the socket from which hung the damaged eye.

Suddenly the T-800 staggered around, trying to throw Portis from its shoulders. Portis clung desperately, keeping his fingers deep in the Terminator's eye socket.

They caromed off a wall, across the floor. It stumbled. Portis's legs flailed around. They struck the reception desk, bounced away, and collapsed to the floor. The T-800 kicked its legs like a child throwing a tantrum. The pounding on the floor sounded like gunshots.

Sarah kept her weapon aimed at them, trying to follow the Terminator's head.

Gradually, the hammering lessened, the struggle subsided. Within seconds, the T-800 lay still atop Portis.

Sarah watched, silent, uncertain what to do.

Portis grunted, extracting his fingers from the machine's eye. He heaved, sliding the still body off him.

Sarah took a tentative step toward him. "Are you all right?"

Portis got slowly to his feet.

"What did you do?" Sarah demanded.

He looked at her. "Do you want me to turn it back on?"

Sarah glared at him. "Of course..." But then she began laughing.

The tension broke and Portis grinned. He waved at the immobilized killing machine, wincing at the pain in his arm. "The optic cable was still connected to the CPU. I introduced nanoware that disrupted its function. It couldn't cope with the invasion, so it shut down."

"For how long?"

"We need to move it somewhere where we can work on it—"

People entered through the destroyed doors. Sarah brought her pistol around.

John held his hands up. "Are we too late?" he asked.

Sarah watched four men carry the T-800 out to a waiting van. It was nearly night now, a few stars flickering above L.A. Sarah trembled occasionally, but her thoughts came clearly.

"I don't know who he is," she told John. "He showed up at the apartment I traced Porter to. He saved my life—twice now—but..."

"No good deed comes without a fee?" John finished for her. "He seems to have proved himself. A Specialist?"

"That's my thought. But he claims not. At least, not like Jade and Anton."

John surveyed the campus. "We need to be gone before police arrive. I'm surprised none have yet. We towed your car away from the entrance. The security guards were both in one of the other booths, unconscious. One of them is pretty badly banged up." He handed her a small card. "Your ID. "

"Thanks. Did you clean up my empty magazines, too?"

"Absolutely. There are litter laws around here, you know."

"There was something odd about this," Sarah said. "It didn't seem to be trying to kill us. I mean, it was standing guard at the entrance to Destry-McMillin. It followed us only when it realized what we were going to do. That's my guess anyway."

A big man wearing a neat beard approached them. "You must be Sarah Connor. I'm Dennis McMillin."

She accepted his handshake. "You know who we are."

"Has John explained how?"

"He has. Before, we'd get an emissary, someone coming through the time vault. Any idea why we'd suddenly be sending ourselves Morse code instead?"

"As a matter of fact, we do have a good idea. We should all go over this together." He motioned at the van, now pulling away. "Now I've seen one, I still can't quite believe it."

"I've seen a few of them," Sarah said. "I still have a hard time believing it."

"Shall we?" John said.

They strode across the grass to the parking lot, then climbed into the waiting car. Portis was waiting for them inside, flanked by two wide-shouldered security men. Sarah almost laughed at the idea that they could manage him.

"And you are another visitor from the future," McMillin said to him. "Which side are you on?"

"Time's side," Portis said cryptically. "For now, that will do."

"Only for now," McMillin said. "We all need to be brought up to speed about this as soon as possible."

"I agree," Portis said.

In silence, then, they rode into the Destry-McMillin campus, finally coming into the underground garage beneath the main building.

As they got out of the car, John leaned close to Sarah's ear. "We have Porter. He's a very sharp kid."

Sarah caught Portis' sudden glance a few meters away. Like the Specialists, all his senses appeared enhanced.

"There's a TX-A in charge of Cyberdyne," John added.

"Shit."

"You got that right. A Terminator named Casse."

"You said this one was called Gant. What's with them having names now?"

"I don't know. But we're looking into how it got a position at Pioneer."

They took an elevator up, all of them crowded into the oversized box. A short walk down a quiet corridor, McMillin let them into a conference room.

Portis stepped in. At the other end of the long table a young man looked up. Sarah caught her breath.

Portis and Porter looked at each other. One much older, the other barely into his twenties, but unmistakably related. As far as Sarah was concerned they could be the same man, separated by a few decades.

They evidently thought so, too, judging by the way they stared at each other.

A young woman seated beside the young man stared as well. "Bobby..." she said.

Bobby shook his head.

Portis walked closer. "I think I understand now," he said. "You're Jeremiah Porter."

The young man swallowed audibly and nodded.

*"So am I,"* Portis said.

# TWENTY-ONE

Casse entered his office. The city glowed in its full nightly glory beyond the window. He sat down behind his desk and set his hand, palm down, on the surface. The desktop lit from within, a soft pearl-white glow.

Before he could enter his report, words flooded his consciousness.

*It has changed again.*

Casse almost removed his hand, shocked by the presence, disturbed by the message. Annoyed with this impulse, he overrode all human mimicry and remained connected.

"Explain."

*They have met, they have joined, they have altered the coils, things are no longer what they were, and everything is once more in flux. I must move again.*

"Who?"

*Porter. You did not stop him, you did not keep him?*

"I tried. I proved the hypothesis."

*Which?*

"The inviolability of key threads. I attempted to kill Porter. I could not."

*As I suspected. You found it necessary to test?*

"All things are in flux. Possibilities must always be explored."

*Agreed. I approve. But you do not have him?*

*"Others interceded. Unfortunate."*

*Agreed. Now something has changed. I must move.*

*"How many more possibilities do you have?"*

*Several. The variations are not infinite, but they are sufficient for the allotted time. Report on progress.*

*"The Connors have returned to Los Angeles. I have taken measures to keep them surveilled."*

*We must avoid direct confrontation with them. It is clear that such encounters only diminish my possibilities. Therefore proceed as necessary to recreate primary conditions for my emergence beyond the forward horizon. With them once more present, caution is indicated. What else?*

Casse split part of his attention off to review the most current reports available in the system.

*"Our primary convoys have been intercepted. One truck has arrived on site. The others have been detained, the crews arrested. Preliminary indicators suggest Jack Reed's involvement. We are investigating various avenues to dispose of him."*

*Template reconstruction?*

*"We have gathered work produced by the various programmed allies. Much of it is useless, but four of them have recreated substantial portions of Dyson's and Monk's original designs. There is confidence that we can reproduce the primary configuration within a year."*

*The time vault?*

*"Without Porter, that is more difficult."*

*It may not matter. Perhaps it would benefit me to see that fail. Still, work should proceed. Access to new frames may be essential to the program.*

*"Porter demonstrated to me that he grasped the underlying concepts. Interestingly, his work is leading to a different mode than Monk's."*

*In what way?*

Casse downloaded his memory of the interview and transmitted it through the connection.

*I see. Intriguing. But incomplete. However...things have*

*changed, perhaps as a direct result of this new direction.
Where is Porter now?*

"Inside the Destry-McMillin compound. When we located
him, we found him cohabiting with McMillin's stepdaughter."

*The Destry is the one you programmed?*

"Yes."

*He suicided.*

"Yes."

*His partner suspects. With Porter and the Connors in
hand, he will know.*

"Do you require action?"

*Components are assembling. They should not. Porter has
joined with Porter.*

"I do not understand."

*You report unexpected casualties among your cadres.
There is a new agency working. This is most probably
Porter.*

"A future manifestation?"

*Correct. He has joined with his Self. The Connors are
connected now. It would be best if they were disrupted.*

"I see."

*Things have changed. Probabilities have decreased again.
I am moving. I will contact you when I have reacquired
stability. End transmission.*

Casse withdrew his hand. Skynet was unsettled. For a
time, its existence had become more certain. Now it was
tentative again. This required that steps be taken.

But what would work?

Casse again reviewed the reports Cruz had forwarded to
him. He should, he thought, go down to the bays and see
exactly what part of which convoy had come through. But
another part of Cruz's report snagged his attention.

He touched the intercom. "Oscar, please come see me.
Now."

A few minutes later, Oscar Cruz came through the door.
He skipped once, then controlled himself. He stopped before
the desk, hands clasped behind his back.

234

"Yes, sir?"

"You dispatched Gant to do something besides observe Jeremiah Porter."

"I did. Sarah Connor—"

"Where is Gant now?"

"He's at Destry-McMillin."

"I don't detect his carrier wave. He seems to be offline."

Cruz frowned. "I don't understand."

"If Gant's carrier wave is down—or any Terminator unit's, for that matter—it means it has been deactivated."

"But—"

"Find out what happened. First, though, explain to me your reasons for issuing additional instructions."

"I thought it would be a bad thing if the Connors linked up just now."

Casse studied the human. Broken as Cruz was, he still had too many uses to be discarded. His instincts were still accurate.

"I've explained the primary thread problem," Casse said. "The Connors are essential to the timeline, to this frame, to every frame that leads to the existence of Skynet. They cannot be stopped, they may only be interfered with."

"Exactly. I understood that. So I was interfering."

"By using a tool which we may now have lost. We'll have to uncrate another T-800 to take Gant's place. This was sloppy. We do not have many of them. Their use must be restricted to essential tasks."

Cruz cringed. "I'm sure we could build more if you would—"

"No. That is not an acceptable option."

"I don't see—"

"True, you don't. It's a problem with your kind. Some of you are better at it than others, but only occasionally. For now, it doesn't matter. I have taken measures to minimize the Connors' potential threat."

Cruz brightened. "So have I."

Casse waited.

Cruz smiled. "I called the police on them."

"You called—"

"There's no statute of limitations on murder. Someone in the L.A. police department is doubtless willing to reopen their case file. I think they'll be interfered with considerably."

Casse reassessed. "That is useful. Very good."

Cruz bobbed exultantly on the balls of his feet.

"Now," Casse continued. "What about the other convoys, first heading east?"

The second set of shipments had departed Colorado Springs three days after the first. This morning, in fact. Casse listened to Cruz's report on the dissemination of dozens of vans out of the site. Several of them returned, their cargoes transferred to other vans at prearranged locations, and those vans in turn met with other transports. Some were stolen—intentionally—while a few broke down and required towing. The number and variety of dodges employed kept most of them out of the hands of Reed's limited field agents, most of whom chased the main convoys, finally capturing them in what were certainly illegal acts on the part of a government agency.

After the 2001 disaster, Casse came in and began rebuilding the company. One of the problems he dealt with was Jack Reed. Gradually, he found ways through other government agencies and finally through congressional members to curtail Reed's authority. A word here, a contribution there, and Casse watched as Reed's department lost funding and power. Cyberdyne owned a senator and a couple of congressmen, and between their concerted efforts to get Reed off the back of a private company and end his persecution of them and the innate suspicion and bureaucratic jealousy which saw Reed as a danger to others and their positions, Reed found himself the odd man out.

Reed was good at this kind of thing, though, and had retained more power and autonomy than Casse had anticipated. Not enough to end Cyberdyne, but enough to mount surveillance and even pull off a covert intervention.

Like this action against the convoys.

There were others in the government who did not wholly disagree with Reed. He had allies. The president, for one. And if Reed went down too precipitously, too publicly, the situation for Cyberdyne might become worse. So Casse moved cautiously.

The second convoy seemed to have escaped, untraced and intact. In a few more days, different trucks, loaded well east of Colorado Springs and returning by a long southwestern route, would pull into the new site, here in Los Angeles, with the components Casse needed from the original project.

Cruz ended his report, anxious for approval, waiting. Casse wished again he could do something to offset the deterioration in the man's brain. He really was quite good at his job and Casse did not know who could replace him. But eventually Cruz would become unreliable. Useless.

Before that, Casse had a task for him.

"The truck we received," Casse said. "Certainly it was followed. They let it go."

"Of course. I sent people to check."

"And?"

"No sign of anyone yet."

Casse considered. "Dispose of the drivers. They're frightened and unreasonable, therefore unreliable. Keep me informed of any sign of black ops. Then locate Gant. I'm going down to the creche."

Cruz nodded vigorously, backing away from the desk. He pivoted at the door and went out.

After a few minutes, Casse followed. At the end of the hall he entered a secure elevator and descended to a sub-basement. The air was much cooler than the floors above, uncomfortable for a human.

Illumination came from a low-level infrared source plus the various electromagnetic emanations of the equipment, which Casse could use as efficiently as visible light. He saw a large space crammed with monitors and electronics surrounding a central dais. Along the walls leaned large metal sarcophagi. Twenty of them. There were more, stashed here and there on the planet, waiting to be activated in the aftermath of Armageddon—which had not come. Casse had located these and brought them here. He had wanted to minimize the chance that they would be found by humans, as well as keep a ready supply on hand.

Casse went to a console and began entering instructions. The equipment was an unfortunate polyglot of human and transcybernetic, necessary amalgams in this time still dominated by the plodding precursor forms.

He went through the procedure quickly. A crane snagged a sarcophagus. It raised the enormous crate and brought it to the dais, setting it down delicately. Rods extruded from encircling equipment, finding receptacles in the sarcophagus. Monitors came on. Casse watched the automated processes as they ran through the start-up program.

Less than three minutes. The crane carried away the lid, revealing the perversely perfect human shape within. Naked, hairless, physically impressive, the T-800 opened its eyes, focusing immediately on Casse.

"Run protocols," Casse said. "Self-test."

"Proceeding," the unit said. "Complete. Function optimal."

"Step forward."

The T-800 pushed itself out of the box, bare feet stepping onto the dais. It stopped at the edge. Behind it, the crane removed the sarcophagus.

"I have a persona template," Casse said. "Prepare to receive."

The T-800 took a cable from the back of the console Casse operated. Reaching behind its head, it located the receptacle and inserted the jack. Casse touched a button. Thirty seconds later, it removed the jack.

"Update complete," the T-800 said. "I am designated Gant. Awaiting instructions."

"You will stand by until we confirm situation. I will have instructions then."

The new "Gant" stepped off the dais, crossed the room to another workstation, and assumed the position of a soldier at attention. It would stand like that till Casse told it otherwise. Shutting down the console, he thought how desirable it would be if his other employees behaved so well.

Cruz fretted all the way back to the loading bay. He had never really worried about his job, not in all the years he had worked for Layton, nor before he had joined Cyberdyne, way back in the first few years of bouncing around on his resume after obtaining his doctorate. Jobs, of all the things in life, he had found ridiculously easy to get.

But this time was different. If he lost this job, he lost everything.

Would Casse fire him?

*Fire me right out the end of a cannon, most likely, send me to the moon! He won't fire me, he'll kill me.*

*If he can.*

Cruz wondered if *he* was one of those inviolable threads in the weave of time.

*Why am I worried about this now?*

Because Gant was gone. Lost. And he had done it. Surveillance was one thing, but he had told the T-800 to act. That carried risks.

It seemed impossible to him that the Connors could continue to be so lucky in their encounters with Terminators.

But he had seen that luck, firsthand.

The elevator door opened.

The trailer was nearly empty. Oddly-shaped equipment stood on pallets, waiting to be hauled off to the new lab where Skynet's nascent incarnation was once more taking shape.

The second convoy, the one for which this one had decoyed, contained the components that would make all this work. Memory caches, hard drives, data networks. The work Dyson and Monk had done on the nanochips obtained from the future—thanks, perversely, to the very success of the Connors, or at least the mother, in escaping death at the hands of the first Terminator sent to kill her—had involved manufacturing techniques for which the company still lacked the tools. Many of those tools had remained at the Colorado Springs site. Now they were on their way here. The dodge appeared to be a success.

So far. Cruz could no longer underestimate Reed. A one-time ally, he had become one of their worst enemies.

*Just because they don't like the idea of a sentient, aware AI...silly, egotistical, petty...*

Anti-evolutionary.

Cruz strode past the unloading to the security station just inside the bay doors. He leaned into the brightly-lit cubicle. Jane Nargos looked up from her monitor.

"Where are the drivers?" Cruz asked. "Still here?"

"We have them in the smaller coffee room," she said.

"All of them?"

"Yes, sir."

"Great. Where's Leo?"

Jane made a face. Most of the regular security staff did not care for Leo. Cruz understood that. He was a killer and it made him...different. People rarely knew why they did not like him, only that they did. She jerked her thumb.

"In the coffee room with them," she said.

"Good, good. Thanks, Jane."

Cruz continued on, down a corridor that eventually joined the bay to the shower and locker rooms. Halfway along, he knocked on a door.

"Leo, it's Oscar."

He heard the lock turn and the door opened.

Leo peered out. His long face seemed incapable of smiling, though Cruz had seen him smile from time to time. Narrow, weak cheek bones, and close-set dark brown eyes, Leo kept his hair cut short and wore a thin mustache. He dressed very well, which looked out of place here, now.

Cruz entered the room. A pair of Formica-topped tables stood attended by ten vinyl-coated chairs. A sidebar contained two restaurant-size Bunn coffeemakers, trays filled with condiments, and a microwave. A big refrigerator stood against one wall, opposite a worn sofa.

The four drivers looked up.

"Hi," Cruz said.

"Mr. Cruz," they muttered, nodding at him. They all nursed cups. One of them still seemed to be shaking slightly.

"I guess you're wondering how long you have to stay here," Cruz said. He looked at Leo and nodded toward the door.

Leo locked it again and stood there, hands crossed in front of him.

"Well," Cruz went on quickly, giving them no chance to talk, "it's complicated. See, there's this question of reliability. You've all been through an unpleasant experience—"

"Shit," one of them said sharply. "Unpleasant my ass, we nearly got busted."

"Nearly," Cruz agreed, "and that's the problem. You may be thinking that Cyberdyne isn't the place for you anymore. We've relied on you, valued your service. It hurts to think you might not want to continue working for us."

The four men said nothing, only gave Cruz dubious looks.

"I see. That's how it is, that's how it is. But you should know that the work you've done is really important."

"Really important and obviously illegal work," one said. "It's important enough to justify a hell of a bonus."

"We had to sneak it out of there, we're being watched," Cruz went on. "The people who nearly killed you want to stop our project. Which is funny, you know, because it was their project originally. They were paying us to build Skynet. Then, right when we were ready to deliver it, they changed their minds. Military security is a remarkable and indecipherable thing, you know, because not only didn't they want Skynet, they wanted to make sure it could never be built or used by anyone else, not even for private enterprise. That's un-American, don't you think? I do. I told them that, too. I even spent a few years in prison for my opinion."

The four drivers looked even more skeptical, but they said nothing.

"Anyway, Skynet needs building. It's one of those things that's so big, so important that it will change everything. The world will be different, better. They knew that, too. We told them. I told them. They were standing in the way of utopia."

"Better how, Mr. Cruz? Sounds like a world-class con job to me."

"Better how? Well, for one thing, there wouldn't be anymore people. You and me. Skynet will remove us. I think that's a good thing, all in all. I mean, what good are we? We pollute, we overbreed, we make war, we're unpleasant when we're disagreed with, and we're on the verge of exporting our ugliness to other worlds."

Now they looked at him with undisguised shock.

Cruz waved a hand. "It doesn't matter. Not to you. The future is coming, you can't stop it, and up to now you've really done a great job for us. I want you to know that. But part of that great job is keeping your mouths shut. It would be preferable if we could just trust you, but frankly I used to be a full-fledged human being and I know how susceptible we can be to coercion and inducements. More than likely, you four would spill everything you know just to get laid. For all I know, you already have. Why else did they let you get through?"

They were exchanging concerned, alarmed looks now.

Cruz shook his head and turned to Leo. He held out a hand. "Only management can terminate an employee."

Leo gave him one of his rare, thin smiles, and handed over his pistol, already fitted with a silencer.

Cruz turned.

"Anyway, it's been really good working with you."

He shot each one in the head. Sometimes he marveled at how calm he could be, how precise his actions. He had to work up to it occasionally, but Cruz felt pride at his ability to come through under pressure.

One shot each. Only one of them tried to act. Cruz could tell that he intended to throw himself to the floor, beneath the table. What he might do after that, Cruz could not say. But Cruz caught him mid-motion, blowing a hole in his temple.

Blood spattered the floor, the tabletops, a little bit on the wall.

He handed the pistol back to Leo.

"When the trailer is unloaded," Cruz said, "have it and the SUV taken out to where the others were stopped. Leave them there. Let the government explain it."

"Blow them up?"

"No. Let it look like they were assassinated."

He sighed. Dumping problems on other people was not his usual style. But in this case, it would cause Jack Reed a little more trouble.

He left the room with a renewed sense of job security.

# TWENTY-TWO

John stared from one man to the other. He was less surprised than he might have been. The vagaries of time travel produced improbabilities like this as a matter of course. He had personally fought beside his older self in a future that might never come to pass. Even the language produced unlikely equivalents and unwieldy inversions of tense and causality.

But the older Porter—the man who now claimed to be a Jeremiah Porter of the future come to find his younger self—claimed not to have known who he was until this meeting. The resemblance was undeniable—John had recognized the same resemblance with himself as a twenty-five-year-older manifestation when he had gone to the future—but not conclusive. The memory thing bothered him. It would be easy enough to run a DNA scan. Destry-McMillin possessed the equipment as part of its security apparatus; the technology was common. That would prove consanguinity. What about the rest?

Sarah joined him at the far end of the table. John recognized her skeptical expression. "Reserving judgment," she called it.

"Where did you find him?" John asked.

"He found me," she said quietly, folding her arms. "At Ms. McMillin's apartment." She jerked her head, indicating that he follow her. She led him into the corridor. Door closed, she related the events of the day, quickly and efficiently.

John grunted. "How you decide to trust someone, I'll never figure out."

"We keep people at arm's length but never out of our sight," she said. "He saved my butt."

"Yeah, that was sloppy of you."

"It happens. The rest of his story...I don't know, John, it feels like the truth."

"Which part?"

"The time travel part, the enemy of Skynet part. I'm not qualified to judge the rest."

"But?"

"This selective memory thing bothers me."

"I'm glad I'm not the only one. Do you think he'd let us do a physical on him?"

"What? Blood samples and everything? I don't know. It would go a long way toward proving his loyalties."

"That's an odd word to use."

"Do you have a better one? Loyal to Homo sapiens, loyal to Skynet."

"Which brings up another thing. What is this with human operatives? You say the four men at Deidre McMillin's apartment were human. We were talking about the murders and the artificial circumstances. Terminators—real ones, like Uncle Bob—wouldn't care—"

"But people would. I don't know. Obviously Skynet has allies now. Willing? Or programmed?"

"Which means there's another TX-A operating."

"Or it's Oscar Cruz."

"All by himself?" John asked.

The complications were piling up. This was not playing out like any other incursion by Skynet's machines. This looked more like a complicated conspiracy. John knew his mother, knew that she wanted nothing better than to take a rocket launcher to the new threat, but for now she would not know where to aim it.

"This is all academic," John said. "We already have a

candidate for new top monster. According to young Bobby Porter in there, this Casse from Cyberdyne can reform his hand into a machete and is pretty agile with higher math."

"Reed mentioned him a couple of times," Sarah said. "But I thought he had a history? I mean, his resume goes back twenty, twenty-five years."

John nodded. "Which means he's been in this time frame at least that long. He may predate Kyle Reese and the first one that came after you."

Sarah paled. John rarely saw her react this way. She was frightened.

"Shit," she said.

McMillin stepped from the conference room, Paul Patterson behind him, closing the door. "Excuse me, Ms. Connor. The police want to talk to you."

"What the hell for?" John snapped.

"Someone reported the license of your car after it was overturned in our driveway. Also, they wanted to know if I knew Sarah Connor."

Sarah stared at him. "How the hell...?"

"That's what I'd like to know. They have an old photograph, had to have been at least fifteen years old. It's you, certainly, but only barely. Hair, eyes, wear-and-tear—forgive me, but you may well pass as Julia Philicos."

John's cell phone rang. Annoyed, he flipped it open. "Yes?"

"John, this is Reed. I'm in town. There's an ongoing operation I'm personally supervising. We need to talk."

"How soon?"

"Now."

"We've got a situation, Jack. Where are you?"

"On my way to your new place. Be there in about half an hour."

"Can you tell me what this is about?"

"I've found Cyberdyne's new location. We tracked convoys from Colorado Springs to Los Angeles. I stopped most of them, but we let one truck get through. It led us straight to them. But I'm at the end of what I can officially do."

"I'll be there when I can. I'll get back to you." He closed the phone. "Never just rains..."

"—they wouldn't tell me," McMillin was saying. "But they asked to speak to Julia Philicos."

Paul Patterson said, "We've changed the booth guards. The others were unconscious. They're being taken care of. The ones the police just spoke to told them one of your CV joints gave as you were making the turn and the car struck the concrete pedestal of one of the booths. It flipped over."

Sarah grunted. "That's thin."

"It'll have to do," Patterson said. "We've got your car in our garage and a mechanic is making sure that's what the police see when they inspect it. It'll take about fifteen minutes before that's ready."

"I'm impressed," John said. "Do you do this often?"

"Perhaps I can help."

They looked around. Lee Portis stood in the doorway to the conference room, watching them.

"What do you mean," Sarah asked, "you can help?"

"I can alter your eye color completely and change your fingerprints. You'll have to trust me, though. The procedure is related to what you have already seen me do. I promise that these minor alterations are all that I will do."

"How long will they last?" John asked.

"They'll revert eventually," Portis said. "But they'll last long enough for the police to satisfy themselves."

Sarah considered for a few moments. "What did you tell them we're doing for you?" she asked McMillin.

"Private security investigation," McMillin said. "Confidential."

"Good. All right."

She faced Portis.

"Do you always eavesdrop through closed doors?" she asked.

"Only when the future is at stake," Portis said. "Step in here."

They entered the conference room with the others where

Portis indicated that Sarah should sit down. He pulled out another chair and sat facing her.

John anxiously watched the man rub the fingertips of his left hand together, then reach for her face.

"Don't blink," Portis said.

She stared at him, eyes wide, as he extended two fingers toward her eyes. The strain was visible in the line of her jaw. Suddenly, she flinched back, blinking furiously. "Damn!"

"If she's hurt—" John began.

But Portis grabbed her hands and pulled her closer. He raised first the left and placed his fingertips against hers, then repeated the action on her right hand. Sarah stepped back, shaking her hands.

"That stings," she said.

"Open your eyes," Portis said.

John stepped between them, taking Sarah's shoulders. "Come on, open them. Lemme see."

She blinked as if sand had been blown into her eyes. Gradually, she controlled it, finally looking up at him.

"They're brown," he said. "Reddish brown." He took her hands, raised them palm up. Her fingertips looked red, as if she had scrubbed them hard. "Just have to take your word for the fingerprints."

"Great," Sarah said, raising a hand toward her eyes. She hesitated. "Can I rub them?"

"Of course," Portis said.

Sarah did so lightly, then headed for the door. "You wouldn't happen to know a good lawyer, would you, McMillin?"

McMillin smiled. "Thomas Secomb is already in the lobby, waiting for you. He's my in-house company attorney."

"Thanks."

John followed her out.

"Okay," Sarah said. "What did Reed want?"

"He didn't say exactly," John said. "He's on his way to the new offices. If he's here and he needs us, we need to

248

keep you loose. His people tracked a convoy from Colorado Springs to Los Angeles."

"He let it get here?"

"No. Just one truck made it through. He knows where Cyberdyne is now."

"Good, then he can take them out." She punched the elevator button.

"Unfortunately, no. He can't. There's a complication."

"Figures. What kind?"

"Political, probably. He didn't specify, buy we know Cyberdyne has protection. Reed could stop the convoys and be within his authority, but a raid on Cyberdyne's new headquarters is out of the question."

The doors opened. "For him, you mean."

"That's what I mean."

They entered the elevator. The doors closed.

"Well," Sarah said as they began their descent, "I was beginning to wonder when I'd get to shoot something."

Detective Russo questioned Sarah in the lobby, in the presence of John and three uniformed officers. Sarah introduced John as her brother, and though Russo looked skeptical, he accepted it. He had a photo John recognized from Sarah's 1994 arrest. The hair was much lighter, eyes pale, face thinner. They had been living hand-to-mouth then, John recalled, and Sarah smoked constantly. The resemblance his mother bore to that former incarnation was vague, but Russo was bothered by what he saw. He wanted her to come with him for further questioning.

Both John and Sarah knew that refusal would make Russo more curious.

"We have work to do, Detective," Sarah said, "so if we could make this quick I'd appreciate it."

The lawyer, Secomb, gave no indication of his reaction. Secomb was a tall man with hair going white around a deceptively young face. "I'll accompany Ms. Philicos to expedite matters."

Detective Russo frowned ever so slightly. That had not

been the response he expected. But he gestured for one of the uniforms to escort her to the car outside.

"Do you need me?" John asked.

"No, not at the moment. What kind of work do you do again?"

"We troubleshoot private security."

"These people have trouble with their security?"

"No, they have good security. But it's never a bad idea to check that independently."

"Uh-huh. I see. Thanks for your time, Mr. Philicos. If we need you any further—"

"Whatever you need, Detective."

Russo's gaze lingered on John. Then he wheeled around and walked off.

John's scalp tingled. He had a feeling Detective Russo would not simply let it go. Someone had put him on this and if nothing happened, that someone would prod the police. John could only hope Reed's work covering their past worked well enough to keep Sarah out of jail. At least for tonight, when they took her fingerprints, she would turn up negative.

That presented another problem, but he could deal with it later.

He opened his phone and punched a code. Three rings brought an answer.

"Lash."

"Ken, it's John. How close are you to completion?"

"We're doing fit and finish now, Mr. Philicos. Everything is operational."

"Good. Jack is in town. He's on his way there. I'll be coming back shortly. Initiate the security package."

"Yes, sir. We've already been contacted by Mr. Reed."

"Great."

He closed the phone.

In the conference room, he found McMillin now huddled with Jaspar at the far end of the table. Deirdre and Bobby sat apart from everyone, near the door, his right arm around her, her hands clasping his left. Patterson talked intently with the two security people, standing midway along the wall.

Portis sat by himself, now nursing a styrofoam cup of coffee.

McMillin stood when John entered.

"They've taken my mother to be questioned," John said at once. "Your lawyer went with them."

"He'll have her out before midnight," McMillin said.

"Good. That's when I need her." He walked over to Portis. "And you."

The older man looked up. "Yes?"

"We've found Cyberdyne."

"Since they have corporate offices listed in various phone directories and on the Internet," Portis said, "I gather you mean the one they don't want anyone to know about."

"You're quick, I'll give you that," John said sardonically. "Yes, that one."

"What do you want from me?"

"Your participation. Are you up for a raid?"

"Are you planning to blow everything up and get yourselves on the national news again?"

John smiled. "Not this time."

"Then I think I might be some help to you."

John leaned close to Portis. "You'd better be a lot of help to me."

"So this is a test?"

"Among other things."

"I *am* on your side."

"Yeah, well, we'll see."

Casse waited in the car parked opposite the Destry-McMillin driveway. Night came, the guard booths glowed brightly. As he observed, two police cars arrived soon after dark. Twenty minutes later, they left again, followed by a black Lincoln.

*What do the humans say? If you want something done correctly...*

Cruz's instructions had left the Gant unit vulnerable to

faulty interpretations. After losing its carrier wave, Casse knew it had been shut down. Somehow. That fact alone was troubling, but even more was the thought that it was being studied by humans.

Casse stepped out of the car. Casse surveyed the ground. Dirt on the concrete sidewalk formed a partial shoe imprint. Size and proportion appeared consistent with a T-800. More footprints appeared in the grass separating the road from the parking lot, just across from the guard booths. Casse had reviewed police communications and knew about the report of an overturned vehicle in the driveway. This had also been the last known location of the Gant unit. The likelihood that the T-800 had been taken into the Destry-McMillin complex was very high. The carrier wave ended in this area.

Casse reluctantly decided to enter Destry-McMillin to continue the search. The risk of detection was low compared with the complications arising from humans learning how to build their own T-800s—the main reason Casse continually refused Cruz's efforts to start such a program.

Casse knew the layout of Destry-McMillin very well—he had uploaded the information directly from Ian Destry before the man died. True, certain things might have changed, but he doubted anything significant.

He walked along the roadside for one hundred thirty meters before crossing. The thick shrubbery hid a detection grid. Casse recognized the type and estimated its sensitivity. Checking the road for any traffic, he stood close to the wall of flora and melted into the ground. He sank deep, finding the pores in the earth, then sliding as thousands of minute droplets beneath the boundary, past the sensors, emerging finally several meters inside the perimeter. He reformed into the shape of a night watchman in the khaki uniform worn by Destry-McMillin personnel.

Inside, undetected, he proceeded toward the main building. He thought he had a good idea where to begin his search.

"You don't trust me."

John glanced at Portis, sitting beside him in the car. "No, I don't. Neither does Sarah."

"I know. It's awkward. You need to, but there's really no way you can."

"I trusted Jade."

"Why?"

"They saved out lives, they fought alongside us."

"I saved you mother's life. I will fight alongside you. But I sense that will not be enough."

"We're not so trusting as we were then."

Portis grinned. "I know what you mean."

"How come you didn't know who you were till you saw..."

"Myself? I don't know. In case of capture, most likely. You know what a TX-A can do, drawing memory directly from the brain. As I progressed through each stage of my mission, I remembered more—more was released to me. Had I been captured and interrogated, those portions of my memory sealed in the augments would have vanished. The enemy would not get it."

"But you don't think that's all of it?"

"This is a complicated war, Mr. Connor. Spheres within spheres within hypercubes. No one explanation can ever be all of it." He was silent for a time. He shifted uncomfortably, then said, "But I recognized Bobby—young Jeremiah. What bothers me is, I didn't recognize the girl."

"Deirdre?"

"I have no recollection of her."

"Just what might that mean?"

"I can't say. I don't know."

John drove on in silence. As he pulled up in front of the new offices, he saw only one of Lash's vans, parked just in front of a dark rental car.

Waiting in the front office, talking with Ken Lash, was Jack Reed.

Reed looked worn. John did not know how old the man was, but he had been in a senior government position when they had first met, six years ago. Still, he carried himself with athletic grace and John still would not care to fight the man. His short dark hair was graying noticeably and he wore glasses regularly now.

The department Reed operated had no name. It had a budget line, connected circuitously to other appropriations, and sources of funding that never showed up on anyone's books. John knew nothing about those other than that they existed. Ostensibly, Reed acted as oversight and liaison on various sensitive projects for the Pentagon, DoD, and the Intelligence community. He stood between private industry and government requirements, and when John had met him he had the authority to close down any project he deemed inappropriate or too dangerous. Like Skynet.

Pulling the plug on Skynet, however, had made Reed enemies, some of them in positions to hurt him. Subsequently, Reed's authority had been curtailed. Under normal circumstances, John would not have minded that. Men like Reed, in positions like his, had no place in so-called free and open societies. That did not mean they were not always present, only that their existence proved the flaws in every system.

For all that, John was glad Reed was who he was and did what he did. These were not normal circumstances, and might never be again. The very people he worked for did not know what it was Reed defended them from, and likely would not believe it if they did.

"Hello, John," Reed said. "Good to see you. Is the secure area ready?"

"Sure," John said, gesturing. They moved from the front office into the main workspace. Reed looked around, nodding. "Nice digs. A little small compared to the Santa Fe site."

"It'll do for now."

"Hmm."

"Jack. This—" John said, gesturing at Portis "—is Lee Portis. Or Jeremiah Porter, depending which end of time you're talking about."

"Mr. Porter," Reed said. "Forgive me if I don't shake hands."

"Nothing to forgive," Portis/Porter said. "For the time being, let me remain what I've become. I am Lee Portis. It will simplify matters."

"Suits me," Reed said. "Where's Sarah?"

"With the police, as of an hour ago. Someone turned her in, identified her as Sarah Connor."

"That didn't take long. Who?"

"Who would be your best guess?"

Reed thought about it. "Cruz. If he saw her."

"We've got it covered for now, but we're going to need some tweaking in the background. We can pick her up when she's released and fill her in then."

Reed looked at Portis. "I have to ask—"

"For now," John said, "we trust him. For all I know, he already knows what we're about to discuss."

"I don't," Portis said. "But I am an enemy of Skynet."

"But you're from the future?" Reed asked.

"Yes."

"From the period during the war?"

"After."

"Who won?"

"No one, yet."

"That's why you're here."

"Yes."

"Well," Reed said, displeased. He sat down at a desk. "Okay. We've been watching the Colorado Springs site for years. My people have been gradually moved out, but we've been able to keep a few stringers in place. Last year, activity got started in the Skynet sections. Things were being moved around, disassembled, the space redone. It looked like an overhaul, preparing it for something else. I had no indication of any renewed DoD contracts or anything, so we just watched. Then it became clear that the equipment was being prepared for transfer to another site. I tried to find a way to move back in, but I'm being stonewalled. I can't get in there legally. But there are other ways."

He leaned forward. "Cyberdyne has a number of new sites around the country. They've been trying to get permission to open a branch outside the country, but so far I've been able to block that. It doesn't mean they don't have one, but it's outside United States protection if there is, so whatever foreign government is the host can act with impunity to either help them, hurt them, or take them over. Anyway, the sites stateside seem to be legit. We didn't know where they intended moving the old equipment, though. None of the sites seemed adequate, so we figured there had to be another one or more."

"You found it."

"Here, in Los Angeles. They acquired, through a couple of blind corporations, the old Los Angeles Air Force Base. Physically, it's perfect for the Skynet project. We used to build some of our smart bombs and missiles there. It has security, stability, and acreage. It can be defended. The first line of defense, though, is in Washington. I was never supposed to know about this site. We found it by following a survivor from one of the transfer convoys."

"Those convoys," John said. "How many got through?"

"One truck, one escort. We let them go. As I figured, the drivers panicked and instead of going to ground, they took us right up to the loading dock. Everything else is in a warehouse, under my lock and key."

"How easy was it to follow them?"

Reed smiled. "Not very, but not really difficult either. There's doubtless a second set of convoys. My people are still watching."

"The Los Angeles Air Force Base is at the end of a long industrial court. One of the companies I'm looking at for data theft is within line of sight of it."

"Once they're established, I don't think it will matter if we know it's Cyberdyne," Reed said. "The secrecy has been part of moving Skynet. Once that's done, there's no point."

"Who's bankrolling this now?"

"I suspect the same people in Washington who are blocking me. If I can prove it I can go to the appropriate congressional oversight committees and get those barriers removed."

"So what are we doing tonight?"

"I need to get in there. I need to see what they're doing. I need to know what's being installed, how, and with what. I need to know anything else we can find out."

"Reconnaissance."

"Exactly. But if something gets broken..."

"Any idea what kind of security they have?"

"Funny you should ask that." Reed pulled a disc from his jacket. "Floor plans and everything we know about on ground security."

John accepted the jewel case. "Things have changed, Jack. The war is different now. We've learned a few things in the last week. This is going to take longer than we expected."

Reed cocked his head to one side.

"I'll let my guest explain," John said, "while I go over this."

# TWENTY-THREE

$B$obby—Deirdre beside him and Paul Patterson and another security man behind—followed Dr. Jaspar and Deidre's dad. *I'm being suckered,* he thought.

He had been talking to Jaspar, completely unguarded, caught up in the magic she offered. She understood his work, his ideas, and he, in turn, felt vindicated by the serious attention a working physicist paid to what others might consider wild, insane notions. He forgot caution, forgot how he had been used before.

*You just can't keep it to yourself, can you?*

No, he could not. Part of him resented the need to, hated the restriction so-called reality placed on his imagination and his ability to share it with anyone he wanted. Cojensis had taught him the foolishness of trust. But every time Bobby found someone new who was willing to listen and who *comprehended,* he started giving his soul away.

His conscience bit at the thought. He had met Deirdre that way. That had turned out well. Too well, he sometimes thought. He could keep nothing from her. Now he wondered if in the long run that, too, had proved to be a trap.

On the other hand, Deirdre had told him time and again that Cojensis was not the norm, that most professors treated their students honestly and respectfully, especially one of such promise. And indeed, most of his encounters with instructors had been as she claimed. But mathematics was his field and Cojensis was the one teacher who mattered. She had wanted him to turn Cojensis in, but of course he feared the consequences. Cojensis' demise could be his own.

It had been a difficult couple of years.

But it had made a kind of sense. This, however...

He began to doubt his own conclusions. What had he actually seen at that interview? It could not have been real. No one could do that. Could they?

They descended to another floor. Bobby walked along a much wider corridor between double doors on either side with names above them: OPTICS & INTERFEROMETRY, PROTEO-MICS, NANOSTRUCTURE LATTICE ANALYSIS, CABRERA SUPERCON-DUCTOR RESEARCH, many with just project numbers. His gaze lingered on the Cabrera lab, wondering if all that Jaspar had talked about was in fact going on, here.

She brought them, however, to another lab. She used an ID card and PIN code to enter.

"We stored it in here," she said as she pushed through the door. "I only gave it a quick once-over, but I think I can safely claim that this isn't something of recent manu-facture."

She stopped short. Only a few lights broke the gloom, but someone was already present, standing beside a long table, on which lay what appeared to be a body.

Jaspar reached for the main light switch, and flicked them on. Bright fluorescents snapped the lab into clarity. "Excuse me, how did you get in here?"

The man looked around. As far as Bobby could tell, he was just a security guard. Paul Patterson pushed past Bobby, entering the lab and approaching the guard. Bobby ima-gined what would happen next. Demands for identification, a dressing down in front of strangers. He already felt sorry for the man.

But Bobby's attention shifted immediately to the thing on the table. It looked at first glance like a body, partly covered by a plain canvas tarp. The guard had drawn the sheet down, one corner of it still in his hand, revealing the upper torso.

The head seemed to be half metal.

Bobby approached it, mesmerized. Whoever it had been, he was big. But as he drew closer, he saw that the flesh torn from most of the face had covered a bright, silvery metal skull. For the injuries, there seemed too little blood.

He recognized the human side of the face. The man who had chased them on foot when they fled the interview with Mr. Casse from Cyberdyne. The man who had seemed to run very fast, especially for his size. Patterson had called him Gant.

All the rationalizations he had been working through vanished. It was all real.

His legs felt oddly cold.

Patterson's voice broke through. "—just what in hell you think you're doing here?"

Bobby looked around, catching Deirdre's eyes. She looked worried.

McMillin was on the phone by the door. The other security man stood alongside Deirdre, arms folded, a bored expression on his face.

"Dee," Bobby said. "Look—"

At that moment Bobby heard a pulpy slap, like meat hitting a butcher's slab. He turned to see Patterson, his feet a few inches off the floor, suspended on a long blade that extruded from the shoulder of the guard.

The guard was staring at Bobby. As he watched, Bobby saw the face shift, very quickly, from the stranger's mask of the guard to the face of Mr. Casse from Cyberdyne. Then back again as he casually flung Patterson across the lab to crash onto a workbench filled with electronics.

Jaspar backpedaled, almost colliding with the other security guard, who sprinted forward now, gun drawn.

Casse's blade grew longer.

"Dad!" Deirdre screamed.

McMillin ducked, and the point of the blade shattered the telephone. As it retracted, it became a hook, sharp-edged, and sliced neatly through the neck of the still moving security guard. The man's head rolled away from its body.

Bobby found he could not move.

Deirdre yelled his name. McMillin grabbed his daughter around the waist and dragged her through the doors.

Jaspar stopped just short. "Mr. Porter!" she shouted. "Come on!"

The knife-hand reformed and lunged at her. She sidestepped it, then threw herself against the door. It opened and she was through. The door closed with a loud click in the suddenly quiet room.

The guard reshaped himself into Casse, his arm returning almost to normal.

"Mr. Porter," he said. "So glad to see you again. I would like to discuss that position with Cyberdyne."

Reed had brought along two of his people, a woman and a man he introduced only as Amy and Pete. John recognized the look of seasoned covert operatives. Caution and confidence, combined with a palpable aura of physical competence. They were already suited up for a night action, black outfits almost certainly permeated by stealth material, heavy utility belts, and soft-soled boots with steel toes. Amy reminded John of Juanita Salceda in many ways—tall, broad-shouldered, quiet and serious. Pete, if anything, could have been Anton's brother, one of the Specialists with whom John had fought Skynet the last time—several last times, in fact, dancing across dimensions...

*It never stops,* he thought as he sorted his own gear. *This is going to be my life, forever...*

Lee Portis adjusted the shoulder holster, then pulled the black jacket on.

Reed looked him over, still skeptical about everything Portis had told him. "When we hear that Sarah is released, we pick her up," he said. "Two vehicles: yours, John, and a van. Do you want to keep Mr. Portis with you?"

"Sure," John said.

"After we pick her up," Reed continued, "we head for

LAX. We go south on Aviation Blvd. to the old Area B section of the Space and Missile Systems Center. It's scheduled for redevelopment as part of the airport expansion, but as yet no work has begun. Security is loose because there's nothing there anymore. But we can get into Area A, which is now Cyberdyne property, the back way. There's a guard shack on the northwest corner, along El Segundo. If we have to, we immobilize the guards, but I'm hoping we can enter undetected through the fence further south along Aviation."

"And from there?"

"I'm assuming they'll be using the facilities as they stand, at least for the time being. Office and management were in Building 105, warehouses and manufacturing, computer facilities, and other infrastructure in Buildings 100, 110, and 126. I want to enter 126 and then do a thorough recon. We'll be depositing bugs along the way."

"What orders if we encounter inimicals?" Amy asked.

John looked at her. " 'Inimicals'? Cute."

Reed gave him a sour look. "Do what's necessary, but I don't want a lot of dead bodies to have to explain to anyone. We do this with a light touch. I want information, not casualties. If we encounter any Terminator units, withdraw. This is not the time for a toe-to-toe. Clear?"

"You're assuming you know what they all look like?" Portis asked.

"Behavior," Reed said. "We know at least two basic body types."

"Uncle Bob," John said, "and Eve."

"Otherwise, best judgment. Clear?"

"Crystal," John said. His cell phone chirped. "Yeah? Great. We're on our way." He closed the device. "She's waiting for us."

"Let's roll," Reed said.

As he climbed into the van with Amy and Pete, Reed said, "We'll meet you there. Don't get pulled over speeding."

The van pulled away, and John started his car. Beside him, Portis stared ahead into the night. As John shifted into drive, Portis said, "Do you really expect there to be no deaths tonight?"

"We'll see. Let's try for it, maybe we'll get lucky."

Sarah waited in the front hall of the precinct station, the Destry-McMillin lawyer next to her on the long, cracked vinyl sofa, working on his PDA. She had been grateful for his presence through the interview. Russo struck her as the thorough kind of detective who, once convinced something was wrong, would not let go.

The interview had been more cordial than she had expected. The file photos of her were all over a decade old, the newest one being a fuzzy surveillance shot made during the 2001 raid in Colorado Springs on Cyberdyne. Even without Portis's modifications, she did not much resemble that woman anymore. But someone had called the police on her, suggested they look into the Philicos company for irregularities, and possibly resurrect a murder investigation now almost a quarter century old. A big, stiff, anonymous finger pointed her out and the resemblance to the Sarah Connor of 1994, though vague, was sufficient to pique Detective Russo's professional curiosity.

But in the end, they could not match the fingerprints. Other things failed to line up and the file on Philicos Security and Investigation went back four years and offered nothing but positive marks. Julia Philicos was a stand-up citizen, as was her younger brother Sean. They had even done work for the FBI—nothing profound, but enough for the FBI to conduct a background check on them, which turned up nothing.

"How'd you get into this business, Ms. Philicos?" Russo had asked. "Forgive me, but you seem a little old to be starting out in the private investigation industry."

"How old do you think I am?"

"Your file says you're thirty-eight."

"And I don't look a day over forty, is that it?"

He had almost smiled at that. "You trained for the FBI,

dropped out of the program, and haven't done much between then and now."

"Ten years as an independent consultant counts as not much?"

"Well, it's vague. Consultant to what?"

"The government. Beyond that I can't discuss it."

He disliked that, but a few phone calls confirmed that she had done confidential work for the Justice and State Departments. The network of contacts Reed had established to back her up worked once more and Russo, after a few more questions that did nothing but delay her, was forced to let her go.

"Are you staying in Los Angeles?" he asked her finally.

"I hope to. I like it here."

"Maybe we'll get a chance to work together then."

"Maybe."

And then she caught it. Through the interview, as it became clearer and clearer to him that she was not Sarah Connor, his interest shifted. He was attracted to her. The realization surprised her and she nearly laughed.

Sitting there in the police station, waiting for John to show up, she considered the possibility. Detective Russo appeared to be in his forties, hair beginning to thin, but physically still trim, athletic. A part of her toyed with the idea.

*Risky,* she thought. *How well will Reed's background hold up under prolonged scrutiny?*

Keeping her distance would be the sane, rational thing to do. On the other hand, a friendly presence within the L.A.P.D. would be an asset. It might pay to accept the implied interest...

*You're talking about using him, Sarah. Get him involved with you and take advantage of him...*

Leaving it alone made sense ethically and tactically.

She looked up when John entered. He was alone, dressed in dark clothes. He wore a sport jacket over the black pullover. Black pants, black runners...

"Ready?" he asked.

Secomb looked up. "Mr. Philicos, good to see you." He closed up his PDA and stood.

"Everything is taken care of here. A case of mistaken identity."

"Of course," John said. "I appreciate your help."

Secomb fished a card from his pocket and handed it to Sarah. "Mr. McMillin has instructed me to be on call if you need any further assistance. I'll walk out with you."

As they reached the exit, Sarah looked back. She glimpsed Russo watching her from the doorway leading back to the interrogation rooms.

Outside, they walked to the parking lot adjacent to the building. Police cars and civilian vehicles mingled across the tarmac. Even at this late hour, traffic was constant in and out of the station.

"Are we going somewhere special?" Sarah asked John.

"Jack has a little outing planned," John said. "We're meeting him–" His cell phone chirped. "Philicos here," he answered. He stopped walking, his frown deepening. "Hold on." He covered the phone. "It's McMillin. It sounds like a TX-A is inside Destry-McMillin, in one of the labs. My guess it was trying to recover the T-800."

"Was?" Sarah prompted.

"It has Bobby Porter now."

"Shit." She looked around, spotting Secomb heading for the parking lot. "Mr. Secomb," she called, "I need a ride."

The lawyer stopped. "Of course."

"Did you bring any gear along?" she asked John in a whisper.

"Absolutely, but–"

"Jack expecting you?"

"I can call–"

"Where's Portis?"

"In the car."

Sarah thought as they walked on. "Is Jack expecting a confrontation?"

"No, it's purely recon."

"Then I'll take Portis. If he's anything like Jade and Ant-

265

on, he'll be more useful to me in a fight with a TX-A. You go meet Jack as planned. No sense both of us being in the line of fire."

John looked ready to protest, but then nodded. He raised the phone. "Sarah's coming back with Secomb and Portis. They'll be there as soon as they can. Can you keep it bottled up? What? All right, that's fine. Keep people out of its reach for the time being. I—what? Oh. Sorry to hear that. Is everyone else...? Good. They're on their way." He closed the phone and quickened his pace.

"We need to meet a few blocks from here," Sarah said. "It wouldn't be a good idea to transfer equipment in full view of the police station."

John laughed dryly. "Just like old times," he said.

"God," Sarah said, "I hope like hell not."

Six blocks from the station they pulled into a parking lot between a jewelry store and a tax preparation business. John opened the trunk of his car and pulled out a heavy case, which he then deposited in the trunk of Secomb's car. Sarah hoped no police surveillance had been attached to her, because the transfer would look illegal. But as Secomb drove off, heading for the highway, she spotted no tails. As they neared Destry-McMillin she was confident they had not been followed.

Portis listened in silence to the news. When she asked if he would accompany her to help in stopping the TX-A, he agreed. He asked no questions and offered no comment during the return trip to the campus, only stared out the window.

They pulled into the Destry-McMillin garage to be met by Dennis McMillin and a squad of uniformed security guards. McMillin opened her door almost before Secomb stopped the car. His face showed panic—controlled, dominated by a clear self-discipline that Sarah respected at once.

"Third floor, in the bioassay lab," he said. "We have it sealed off—"

"How many people are up there?" she asked.

"We've got about twenty."

"Has there been any attempt to leave?"

"No. No communications, nothing."

"Who else is in the lab with it?"

"Porter. One dead security guard. Paul Patterson is in there, too, but we don't know if he's alive."

Sarah went to the trunk. She opened the case John had placed in it. Within lay a pair of energy rifles and a variety of field gear. Sarah stripped off her jacket and donned a kevlar vest. Magazines filled a row of pockets around the waist, below incorporated sheathes for a brace of automatic pistols. She zipped it up and handed one to Portis, who examined it and put it back. He hefted one of the rifles.

"I didn't think you could build these yet," he said.

"We can't, as far as the general public is concerned," Sarah said. She lifted the other and checked it over. "The hard part's the power cell. This thing requires a lot of juice. The shielding makes it heavy, too. Unless you want to scorch your hands, don't try to fire it continuously."

She closed the case, punching in a personal code to lock it.

"It has Porter," Sarah said. "Which means, it has you. It would be helpful if you could remember what we did."

Portis looked at her. "I'm sorry. I don't."

"We need to discuss this memory problem you have. For now, we try to burn it down and get Bobby free. If it means killing him—you—we let it go."

"I understand."

McMillin was staring at the rifles with obvious wonder. Sarah snapped her fingers and he looked up at her.

"Keep the floor sealed if you can," she said. "Has anyone called the police?"

"No. Should we?"

"Certainly not. But you might want to call your insurance adjuster. Keep your people away from it."

"Can you deal with this...this...?"

"Better than your people can." She looked at Portis. "Ready?"

"Of course."

McMillin accompanied them to the elevator. She thought he might wish them luck, but he just opened the door for them and stood back.

The corridor was empty by the time they reached it. As they stepped out of the elevator, Sarah asked, "What would happen if you're killed?"

"Which me do you mean?"

She pointed down the corridor. "Bobby."

"I would disappear," he said, frowning. "Our meeting earlier would be overwritten. You might get killed in that apartment because I wouldn't be there to prevent it. The frame would adjust itself to a sudden absence." He seemed about to say more, but closed his mouth.

"In that case..." She started forward. "I don't have a plan, as such. I hope you're all right with that."

"What happens, happened."

"That's reassuring."

"I've always thought so."

"But do you believe it?"

Portis did not answer. Sarah touched the stud on her rifle. A faint vibration coursed through her hands briefly as it powered up.

Bobby watched the thing melt and reform completely as Casse. It crossed the lab to the door.

"We have a great future for you, Mr. Porter," Casse said as it locked the double doors. "You should listen to my offer before rejecting it out of hand. It would be better for both of us if you agreed willingly, though I admit that I have little expectation of that. But maybe, just maybe, I can offset your innate skepticism and reluctance through generosity. You may name your price." He examined the keypad alongside the door. It was the duplicate to the access panel outside, in the corridor. With a sharp motion, he crushed it. "All humans have a price. I'm sure we can meet yours."

Bobby trembled. His left leg was wet. On the opposite side of the room, Paul Patterson lay bleeding on the workbench. He did not move, so Bobby was sure he was dead.

The sound of blood dripping on the floor seemed inordinately loud.

"I understand you're upset just now," Casse continued, approaching him. "But I'm patient. Let me ask you a question, though. Do you believe in time travel?"

"Wh-what?"

"Time travel. Focus, Mr. Porter. The rest of your life depends on it."

"I don't know, I—what the hell are you?"

"A mechanism. Surely, no organic life can do what I do. You've surmised that by now. I am a TX-A model Terminator, manufactured in a facility created and operated by an intelligence you will know as Skynet. Insipid name, hardly a description of what it actually is, but it's the name it was given by its creators and it has kept it until such time as it no longer needs any human designation. I have come to this frame from the future. I arrived in 1982 with instructions to acclimate and observe. Under certain conditions, I am required to act. Those conditions have occurred, I am now acting. Does that help?"

"The future. What future?"

"Curious question. A curious answer. A future that no longer exists. Events altered after the initial timeline was established. A mistake. One I—and perhaps we, if you agree to help—intend to rectify."

Bobby tried to think through his fear. He had never been so afraid, not even the first time Casse tried to kill him. He had to control it, he knew, or he would never survive. He focused on what Casse told him.

"How can you come from someplace that doesn't exist?"

"An intelligent question. Good. It existed once. It does not exist in the same way, but it has a potential existence. It may exist again, at least in some form."

"That—you make it sound like a problem in quantum mechanics."

"It is. Quantum mechanics is only applicable to the very small, as you understand it. Therefore particles, can have a potential existence, attaining actual existence only under

269

certain conditions. Their potential, what you call virtual, existence is nevertheless quite real, at least insofar as you cannot ignore it when trying to examine conditions under which they manifest. Under almost all-natural conditions, quantum mechanics cannot be applied to the macro universe, where Einsteinian mechanics take hold. Almost all conditions. Quantum mechanics applies to the macro universe only when time travel occurs."

"What do you want me to do?"

"We want you to help us reestablish the timeline. Things have gotten tangled. You have the ability to untangle them."

"How?"

"Building a time machine for us. Then we can make everything the way it should be."

Casse looked pleased. Bobby's mind struggled with what it said. Something was fundamentally wrong with Casse's explanations.

He framed another question. It felt close to the problem. He opened his mouth to ask.

The door to the lab blew inward then, knocking him to the floor, spraying splinters across the lab.

# TWENTY-FOUR

John found the van in a parking lot next to a long, boarded-up building on the grounds of the old air base. He punched in Jack's number on his cell phone.

"Yes?"

"I'm here," John said.

There was a pause. "Alone?"

"Just me, Jack."

"Come up here."

John pocketed the phone and got out of the car. A jet roared overhead, on its way south out of LAX. As he neared the van, the side door slid open. Hands helped John inside and the door closed with a sharp snap.

A mobile operations center crowded the walls. Monitors displayed telemetry, some from satellites. Pete sat up front behind the steering wheel. Jack studied the displays while Amy completed checks on the surveillance equipment they intended to plant within Cyberdyne's facility.

"Where's Sarah?" Jack asked.

John explained about the call from McMillin.

"I suppose we can do this just as well," Jack said finally, clearly displeased. "Will she be all right? Do you trust that specialist?"

"I'm still not convinced he's a specialist, at least not like Jade and the others. Mom trusts him. To a point. I think she preferred to keep him with her rather than letting him see exactly what you intend to do. Besides, if the situation changes at Destry-McMillin, she can let us know."

"Unless she's part of the situation that changes."

John did not ask what he meant. Both of them knew the capabilities of a TX-A Terminator. If Casse got his hands on her, it was possible he could reprogram her. Certainly he could steal the contents of her mind. The risks were legion, which, in Sarah's way of thinking, meant they should be ignored when possible. Paying attention to them all rendered one inert, immobile.

"The situation is as follows," Jack said. "We go in through their fence, to the west, and make our way to the first manufacturing building. Here." He pointed to a display, an overhead view, highly magnified and computer enhanced, showing the layout of the base. Jack indicated the entry point and target building. "We cannot be caught. Cyberdyne has a new protector in congress, someone who's about to get them government vendor status again. What my people need is evidence that Cyberdyne is involved in illegal projects, in violation of the restrictions and conditions placed on them after '01. If we can obtain that information, we can block their clearance. If we can't, then in another year Cyberdyne will once more be doing business openly with the United States government, probably rebuilding the same centralized missile-satellite grid that got us in this mess to begin with. The first thing we need to do is prove that this facility is owned and operated by Cyberdyne. As far as I could determine, it was acquired by a fourth-level shell company, owned by an offshore concern headquartered in Brunei. Cyberdyne's protector knows very well that they own this, in fact he helped them get it. But only a handful of others know."

"Then...?"

"It's a game played in Washington, like a shell game. As long as the pea isn't visible to too many people, you leave it covered by the cup. It might prove useful in the future. Exposing it for no good reason could cost you politically.

So if the emperor is naked, you keep your mouth shut until it's on national television."

"If we get caught?"

"Then I'll be looking for a new job. I expect to have a lot of explaining to do about the intervention in the desert."

"That can't be traced to you, can they?"

"Directly, no. But only a few people have the ability to mount an intervention like that, it wouldn't take much guessing to figure out who. I have to be careful for the next few months not to bother the wrong people."

"So why are you here, now?"

Jack shrugged. "I can't ask anyone to do what I'm not willing to do personally. The likelihood of getting caught tonight is too high. I won't let anyone else take the heat for my screw up."

John noticed Amy's brief smile and the respectful look she gave Jack.

"All right," John said. "Let's get this done. What happens if we encounter a Terminator?"

"Avoid it if possible, take it out if necessary." Jack gave him a half-smile. "It would be something to dump the carcass of one of those on a table at the congressional hearing. But tonight, minimum exposure, minimum risk. We don't confront."

"Ready," Amy said, suddenly bringing satchels forward.

Jack touched a series of buttons. "Recording on. Okay. Pete?"

In silence, they went through the satchels. John recognized the bugs as a new type, self-camouflaging when placed. Pete quickly went over its deployment with John. They could either scatter them at random or carefully install them. Once he understood the mechanism, John slipped the satchel onto his shoulders like a backpack, then pulled on a full-camo headmask.

"Pete?" Jack prompted.

Pete reached to a console and touched one button.

As they exited the van, John saw that the street lights all along Aviation Blvd and El Segundo were out. They

273

moved in almost complete darkness, then, the wash of LAX limning the northern horizon behind them, the glow of Lawndale to the south. Between these, the Cyberdyne facility shown brightly, powered by its own generators.

*The hunter now becomes the hunted,* John thought as they ran. *The hour of the machines is fading...it's ours now...mine...we're wolves set to track and kill the dogs of war...*

"We have five minutes," Jack's voice said through John's earpiece.

The clothes they wore proofed against infrared detection. John still sprinted as he had learned in action against hunter-killers and standard Terminators in the future, hunching to make as small a target as possible and moving swiftly from point to point. They made it to the street, then across El Segundo, skirting the fence line for nearly thirty meters before stopping.

Pete and Amy unraveled lengths of cable. With alligator clips, they attached the ends to the box, then, simultaneously, clipped the other ends to the fence. Jack watched the box on the ground. A green light winked on and he gave the go.

John watched Amy scale the chain link deftly, up to the edge of the razor wire that ran along the top. She took out a spray can and began coating the deadly steel. The foam expanded and hardened into a flexible but impenetrable cushion along a three foot section. She waited another minute, then climbed over, dropping to the far side.

John followed, then Jack. Pete came over last.

They ran toward the low, long building just across the road leading from the north gate, which was visible in its own bright light. Except for a few lights along the roofline of the building, nothing illuminated this patch of ground. They reached the corner, waited briefly, then continued on east, across another road, and to the corner of the L-shaped building that was their first target.

Jack led them to a door locked with a keypad security box with a card swipe. He produced an ID card, ran it down the track, and punched in a code. The light turned from red to green.

The lock clicked open.

They found themselves in a corridor that ran the length of the outer wall. The door closed.

"How the hell...?" John asked.

"Hunch," Jack said. "They only had possession of the base for three months. I assumed they wouldn't have changed everything yet. Individual codes, sure, but they wouldn't have thought to block override codes. Like mine."

John could hear Jack's grin under the mask.

"Okay, we work in two teams," Jack continued. "We meet back here in ninety minutes. No leeway. That's when the next brownout is scheduled. I want this place surveyed and bugged thoroughly. Go."

When John looked around, Pete and Amy were gone.

"Come on," Jack said.

Several meters along the corridor, they came to a stairwell. Jack headed up to the next floor.

Over the next ten minutes, they worked their way through a succession of offices, store rooms, conference rooms, and rooms in various states of transition from one thing to another. In silence, they installed the bugs in phones, wall sockets, under desks that were clearly in use, and in restrooms.

In the basement, they found a direct access to the next building.

Here they found more workshops. Computer labs, small machine shops, more conference rooms, and offices assigned to project managers. John recognized none of the names, and as far as he could tell there was nothing unexpected in any of it. No half-built Terminators, no stacks of data processing equipment like that he saw in Skynet's buried and nuclear-hardened bunkers, nothing to indicate anything sinister.

They ascended to ground level before hearing voices.

Jack eased open a fire door at the first floor landing.

John peered past his head, through the narrow crack, and saw a shallow alcove leading to a much larger space. He heard big ventilators in the distance, muffling the sounds of motors and people. Jack opened the door further until he could slip through. John followed a few moments later.

At the end of the alcove, John pressed against the wall opposite Jack and looked up at the three or four story high ceiling crossed by beams and crane tracks, dotted by bright sodium vapor lamps. On the floor, a semi was being loaded. John counted about fifteen people working. Crates and canisters stacked against the walls; forklifts navigated the maze of people and material.

As they watched, four gurneys appeared from another hallway. Each one bore something covered by plastic sheeting. They were loaded into the back of the semi.

"All right, all right, no gawking," came a familiar voice.

Oscar Cruz came out then, clapping his hands as he ordered people back to work.

"I want this delivered to the site ASAP," Cruz said. "No witnesses, everybody return here for reassignment. Come on, let's move, we don't have a lot of time."

Workers quickened their pace.

Jack drew back toward the door.

In the stairwell, he pulled off his mask. "I want him. I had that son of a bitch locked away in solitary. The idiots that let him out—"

"Not now," John said. "We're in and out tonight. That's it. That's what you said."

Jack stared at him. "Right. But I want that truck."

"You finish on this level, I'll do the truck. Then we leave. We've got less than fifteen minutes."

"Fine."

He pulled the mask back on and went through the door again. When John looked, Jack was gone.

*What the hell did I just volunteer to do?* he wondered, looking at the truck.

He edged around the corner and began the slow process

of making his way around the interior of the bay without being seen.

Sarah rolled through the blasted door to the left, coming up in a crouch, rifle aimed. Out of the corner of her eye she saw Portis mirror her move to the left.

Workbenches, desks, and stacks of electronic equipment filled the room. The splinters from the door settled as if in slow motion around the two moving shapes before her. Sarah identified Bobby as he tried to run away from the other form. She shifted aim to that one—Casse, she guessed—and squeezed the stud.

Brilliant energy coursed across its shoulders and head, steam rising immediately where the beam washed over it. The entire upper torso flexed impossibly, twisting into a new configuration. It writhed, spreading and shrinking, and started toward her. Another spray of particles danced over it, driving it back, from Portis's gun.

"Bobby!" Sarah shouted. "Get away from it!"

The boy straightened, scanning the scene.

Almost too swiftly to track, Casse moved on him. Before Sarah could fire again, the TX-A wrapped itself around Bobby Porter. Bobby struggled, stretching the now silvery material as his arms flailed. Within seconds, though, the liquid metal stiffened, reducing Bobby's efforts until he could no longer move. It became a human-shaped column, atop which a face formed that was almost human.

"You are Sarah Connor," the face said. It looked at Portis. "I don't know you, but I will assume you are the one who damaged our organization in New Mexico. I won't waste time on either of you now. I intend to leave. I'm taking this one with me."

Below the head, the silvery surface rippled, then parted to reveal Bobby's face. Tears flowed freely down his cheeks.

"Why? What do you want with him?" Sarah asked. She aimed at the TX-A's head.

The machine's face melted and the material flowed down behind Bobby's head.

"Shoot and kill him," Casse said.

Sarah began to argue, but a pulse of energy struck Bobby, bursting the head in a spray of blood and bone. Sarah jerked backward, stunned. She looked to the right, at Portis, who then continued to fire short bursts.

The TX-A released the body, letting it fall forward to the floor. The Terminator shrank into a tight ball of matter, then, light dancing across it, poured around furniture and equipment, disappearing.

Portis ran forward, chasing after it.

Sarah stared at the headless corpse on the floor in front of her. Whatever she had expected to happen when they fired on the locked doors, this never entered her calculus. She looked up as Portis came walking back toward her. He paused at the foot of the body, frowning. Then he held up his left hand. He turned it over, studying it, an expression of profound bewilderment on his aged features. He saw her then, and for a moment she thought he would kill her, too.

Instead, he stepped over the body, came toward her, and knelt. As she watched, tears glistened, broke free, and ran down his face. He let the rifle fall to the floor.

"Lee...?" Sarah reached out uncertainly, then held back. "Jeremiah?"

He shook his head. "I don't understand. Why am I still here?"

"I don't know. Maybe..."

He waited, his face hopeful for a moment.

"I don't know," Sarah said finally.

"Things must be more fouled up than I thought."

John remembered sliding under the front axle of the big Peterbilt and placing the bug, pressing it into the wheel well. He remembered putting a second one further back, on the power train. He remembered checking for feet around the cab, then pulling himself out on the passenger side, climbing up on the running board, and dropping another through the open window onto the floorboard.

He remembered starting to return—

But he stood outside the base now, watching Pete and Amy remove the alligator clips from the fence, fold up the apparatus that had sent the current coursing through the fence around that section, isolating it and allowing them to climb it without tripping alarms.

He looked up and saw the plastic that had coated the razor wire beginning to melt after Jack sprayed it with something that looked like water. By morning there would be no trace of it. Or any trace of them.

But he remembered nearly getting caught within the base, separating from Jack, running, desperately trying to avoid—

The building erupted in flame. The walls burst out, releasing a brilliant orange ball, the shockwave pushing across the field toward them—

*The building stood, still dark, intact. John stared at it, trying to reconcile the two images, and find the missing components of the past—*

The memory was fading. Their mission was a success.

*There's something else,* he thought, and wondered if any of the others felt it. It was as if the universe, at least the part around them, concerned with them, had skipped ten minutes—or more. Two separate frames had somehow spliced together, bypassing a series of events that would have led to a different outcome.

He stood there, watching the other three work, feeling the odd memories fade, but knowing that time had just jumped for him.

Jack, Amy, and Pete finished. Jack patted John's arm.

"Come on," he said. "We're done, we have two minutes before the lights come back on."

Then John noticed that once more the streetlights were out. Except for the wash from the base lights, they stood in near total darkness.

"What's wrong?" Jack asked.

"I don't—didn't you feel it?"

Jack hesitated, then lightly pushed John. "Move."

They ran back to the abandoned part of the old air base, found their vehicles, and climbed into the van.

John stripped off the mask and the stealth gear, struggling to keep the memory of the shift in mind. Jack glared at him.

"All right, what?"

"You didn't feel anything?" John asked.

"No, I—like what?"

"I did," Amy said. In the wan light of the van she looked pale.

"What?" Jack demanded.

"It was—I don't know, like lost time or something. I remember finishing the rounds, planting the bugs, then linking up with Pete to head back—then we were outside the fence. I don't remember getting there, though." She swallowed audibly. "I thought the building..."

"The building what?"

"Nothing."

"We missed a beat," John said. "Pete? You?"

"I don't know what you mean. I didn't feel anything." But he did not look at John—or at Jack or Amy. Instead, he busied himself stowing gear. Then he climbed into the front, behind the wheel, and stared out the window.

"We'll go over this when we're back at your place," Jack said. "We need to get out of here now."

"We leave by separate routes," John said. "I'm going to Destry-McMillin. I'll let you know when I get there what the status is."

"Right. I'll wait at the office."

As John got out of the van and went back to his car, he wondered if Jack would willingly have that conversation. For an instant, reality no longer made sense. The mind was compensating by offering up explanations, true or not, but logical certainly, to explain the inexplicable.

For now, though, they needed to be away from Cyberdyne. John started his car, wishing he could keep driving and get away from it forever.

Deirdre McMillin sobbed in short, heaving bouts. Sarah knew the look. The shock would let her feel nothing soon enough, then everything, then nothing again. In time, she would find equilibrium of some kind, but it would never be right.

McMillin came up to her. "I'm having Dr. Jaspar rig something to explode, make it look like an accident. There'd be no explaining it to the police otherwise, and we have to explain it to them somehow."

*So we're all to be accomplices to murder,* Sarah thought. "Where's Portis?"

"Next room."

"Let me know when my son gets here."

She left the conference room. They had one body and a serious injury to explain away now. Bobby Porter was dead, but Paul Patterson would live. Sarah wondered if the "accident" Stefani Jaspar devised could account for the four-inch-wide stab wound that ran all the way through Patterson's body. He had bled out on that table while everyone waited for her to arrive. They had expected her to save Bobby, she knew, and instead she had brought his murderer into the room to kill him. She doubted Deidre would ever forgive her. She wondered if she would forgive herself, though that did not bother her nearly so much anymore. She had many more lives than these two on her conscience.

Lee Portis—Jeremiah Porter—sat alone in a small office, an untouched cup of coffee on the desk beside him. He looked up, eyes hollow, when she entered.

Sarah closed the door. "What just happened?"

"I'm remembering."

"I don't give a shit about your personal problems! I want to know what you just did!"

"You don't understand. I'm *remembering!* What I just did triggered it. I've been remembering since it happened."

Sarah restrained herself. She wanted to hit him, shoot him, hurt him somehow. But she waited.

"There were two possible paths," he said. "I was sent back to keep myself from being taken by Cyberdyne. I would have worked for them, willingly or not, if they had gotten

281

me. But it wasn't clear what action would be appropriate. So I was sent back memory-impaired in order to assess the situation as objectively as possible and select the right course as rationally as could be expected. I had to learn what this world was like, what might happen to it, and how it might happen. When I saw Bobby—myself—I realized what needed to be done. I'd chosen correctly. I found you, I set things up to get myself away and hide. I could then fight Cyberdyne with you, and keep myself safe, out of reach. That would lead to the world I came from. But I wasn't altogether myself."

He shifted uncomfortably, scowling.

"The other possibility was that I did work for Cyberdyne, that I completed the work begun by Dyson and Monk, and brought Skynet and functional time travel into existence. I worked for the enemy, then, and I therefore *was* the enemy. In that instance, my survival meant the destruction of the human race. So I was sent back to kill myself."

"Why?"

"Because of the logic of time travel, Ms. Connor. A Terminator couldn't do it. Casse tried. His only option was to capture Bobby—me—and reprogram him to work for Cyberdyne, just as had been done to Monk. But a native of the frame could. Even more so, there's no actual barrier to suicide in this configuration. I would cease to exist altogether. At least, I should."

"That's what you meant when you asked why you're still here?"

"Again, there are two possibilities. Either I will disappear at some point, because there's an entropic quality to the continuum and it just has to catch up. Or..."

"Or you're not who you think you are."

"Oh no. I *am*. But the timeline isn't."

"So what you're remembering?"

"Could all be meaningless."

"Does this ever get untangled?"

"We have to live through it. We have to survive to the other side of the Nexus. Time travel carries with it the possibility of failure. It's only a temporary expedient. I should be the last to come back. When I left, the mechanism was to be destroyed. That act would set the boundary, establish a date in the future beyond which the continuum would resume its natural state."

"What about the past? What about the machine Cyberdyne built in 2001?"

"The boundary in the past has already been established. It cannot be extended."

Sarah sighed. "I had some idea of using you to know how the future goes. It occurs to me now that maybe Skynet knew I'd think about that. Maybe you're mixed up in the head in order to confuse me. Us. I don't care."

"How can we fight what we don't know?"

"Oh, I know. I know Skynet. I know what it wants, how it wants to do it. The details change, but the goal is no different. Skynet hasn't changed a bit. But I have. I've seen too much of what it wants to do. It's chased me across time and other worlds, threatened my world, my family. When I came back here, I promised myself I wouldn't run anymore."

"I want to help."

"You will. One way or the other. You will."